CONTENTS

Copyright

Dedication

Thank you to:

Title Page

1. Love isn't Complicated 1
2. A relaxing night out 16
3. Just following orders... 27
4. What happened last night? 37
5. Happily Ever After 44
6. Reverence 55
7. I feel a lot better 61
8. For King and Country 76
9. Measuring Up 85
10. Let's Take a Look at Your Resume... 103
11. Want to Talk About it? 119
12. It all started when I was born... 131
13. Onto Phase Two 142
14. Fresh Starts 151
15. First Day Jitters 158
16. Can't Get a Rhythm 172

17. Fist Fights 186
18. Coffee? 198
19. Pick up the Pace 208
20. Snap Decision 216
21. Friends in Low Places 226
22. Fuera de Control 238
23. Political Fallout 245
Wrong 255
About The Author 259

ISBN Ebook: 978-1-7351084-1-4
ISBN Paperback: 978-1-7351084-0-7
ISBN Hard Cover: 978-1-7351084-2-1

Cover design by: Art Painter
Library of Congress Control Number: 2018675309
Printed in the United States of America

For that chubby thirteen year old kid who started this whole thing. You finished it. Try not to let the second book take twelve years.

THANK YOU TO:

Kacie White, My loving wife.

Hunter Garrison, For editing my novel.

Seamus Stahl, For the cover art. Find him at:
https://twitter.com/producedbymoose
https://www.behance.net/northstahlcdce

Will and Megan Voss, For introducing me to my editor.

All my family and friends for your support!

UNAVOIDABLE EMINENCE

Jonas White

1. LOVE ISN'T COMPLICATED

"Zack, cut it out! I'm serious!" The beautiful woman in Zack's arms squealed as he tickled her ribs.

"Oh you're so serious, why you so serious?" Zack said, finding an opening to smooch her neck.

"AHHH!!" She squealed louder, her whole body cringing before finally pushing him away. "GOD!"

"Nope, it's just me, gorgeous," Zack said, giving her a big grin. She glared cutely in response.

"Zackary Taylor, I did not come over here before work just so you could terrorize me with your sense of humor!" She said. Zack scoffed back.

"Terrorize? Seriously? Well, Ms. Sarah Evans, why did you come over here so early?" He said, pulling her back to his chest.

"I was trying to wake you up so I could make you breakfast and be all cute, but YOU thought it would be fun to pull me into bed and tickle me!" Sarah said, puffing out a cheek.

"It's not my fault that I just want to eat you up." He kissed her cheek softly.

"Okay quit that, not in your bed," she said, pulling away and getting up out of bed. "Come on, you'll have to make do with cereal now mister, I don't want to be late."

"UUUGhhh... fine...." Zack groaned, rolling out of bed and flopping onto the floor.

"Oh, don't even right now..." Sarah rolled her eyes. "Come on, get dressed!"

Zack struggled to his feet while grabbing a shirt off the floor. He lazily changed out of his pajama bottoms into a pair of jeans. He walked down the steps pulling his shirt on as he met

Sarah in the kitchen.

"You're out of cereal?" Sarah said, looking in the different cabinets.

"I don't like cereal, it's too expensive, here." Zack reached up and grabbed two of his military power bars out of the cabinet by the fridge, and tossed one to Sarah.

"Oooh, do you have the peanut-butter ones?" She said, looking at the package for a second.

"Nope," he said, grabbing one of his special multivitamins.

"God, how do you not have any food in your house?" Sarah huffed, flopping her arms against her sides, making a clapping noise.

"Once again, still Zack here, God is way up stairs." Zack pointed up. Sarah scowled again. "And if I had know that someone was coming over to play housewife, I would have had a smorgasbord prepared."

"Maybe it wouldn't be playing if a certain SOMEONE would get me a ring," Sarah said, bobbing her head in that way that she did when she was agitated.

"Seriously? With a certain someone's mother threatening to castrate me? You have to finish that medical program first, remember?" Zack said, matching her aggravation.

"Doesn't mean we couldn't get engaged now; I'd like a little time to plan a wedding." She turned towards the table.

Zack looked at Sarah's back as she fiddled with the packaging of the power bar. She sighed lightly, her shoulders drooping. He walked over and crouched to gently wrap his arms around her waist.

"I didn't know this was bothering you...." He said. Sarah put down the bar and slowly began rubbing his forearm.

"It's not bothering me really, it's just... I don't know...." Sarah said, leaning back into him. "I'm just done with school; I want to start our lives together already. I'm sick of all this waiting...."

Zack kissed her neck softly. "I know... me too...." He held

her there for a moment as they slowly rocked in his little kitchen.

BRIIING BRIIING

"Whose that this early?" Sarah asked, her head popping up off his shoulder. "One of your side chicks coming over thinking I won't be here??"

Zack smiled at the ridiculousness of that statement. "Dang it, I told them not to be here until nine."

"Uah! You're such a jerk!" Sarah yelled, shoving him. "Go get the door!"

Zack snickered as he headed to the door. He opened it to see Kevin, the youth pastor on his porch.

"Hey, Kevin, what's up?" He said, leaning against the door frame.

"Hey, Zack, do you have those eggs for the bake sale girls?" Kevin asked.

"Oh yeah, I was gonna bring them by this afternoon," Zack said, raising an eyebrow.

"Ah the girls wanted to get started earlier so the sent me a'runnin'."

"That's fine, I got some in the fridge." Zack held open the door.

"Who's here?" Sarah said from the kitchen table.

"Kevin; he's picking up some eggs for the ladies doing the bake sale," Zack said, walking to the fridge.

"Hey, Kev! How's Marsha?" Sarah asked, as Kevin followed Zack in.

"Oh, hey, Sarah, she's good. Hip still bothers her once in a while," Kevin said, grabbing the foam cartons Zack was handing him.

"Here you go" Zack said, handing him three cartons in total.

"Thanks! I got to run, Marsha would be ticked if I stood around jawing all day," Kevin said, handing Zack a five dollar bill.

"Yep! See you Sunday!" Zack said, walking him to the door.

"Bye, Kev!" Sarah waved. "Hey, I've got to get going too, I don't want to be late. I'll see you later okay?" Sarah put a hand on Zack's chest and looked up at him. Zack instinctively leaned down and hugged her tight and gave her a long kiss.

"I got to go to worrrkkk...." She groaned, pulling away from him.

"That's no fun though...." Zack said.

"Get your chores done Farm-boy, I'll see you later." She said as she pulled on her shoes. "Love you!"

"Love you too Sweetheart!" He said as she headed out.

Zack ate his power-bar as he put on his boots and went to feed the chickens. He dug out cornmeal from an old metal trash can with the dented pot he kept inside it, nudging the clucking little punks as he filled the troughs. He opened the door to the outside pen and grabbed what eggs he saw, putting them in a worn carton.

After placing those in the fridge, Zack grabbed his jacket and workout bag. S.W.O.R.D. had gotten kind of particular on the GSA physical time sheets.

That, and it was still Daniel's first year commanding their unit since Lydia had left, so they had all been dotting I's and crossing T's since summer. Zack was set in his career, once Sarah was done with school they could get married right away.

And it's not like a military man in the GSA had time to waste anyway.

At least it's warm for early spring.... He thought. He sighed as he crossed the empty street. When he finally made it to the tiny gym in town, another member of the IN-14 GSA squad, John, was flopped on one of the benches by the door.

"Hey buddy!" John said, flipping through their local paper: *The Midwest Minute, Thursday, March 12, 2144.*

"Morning." Zack walked in and unzipped his bag. "Where's Rose and Daniel at?"

"Eh. They ain't coming. It's their anniversary so they... aren't here." John shut his paper, not quite awake. Zack looked at him for a second before zipping back his bag shut.

"Well, that's fricking awesome.... I could have walked Sarah to work."

"Bleh... you whipped boys and your girlfriends...." John was single, and a pain in the butt sometimes, but he was also Zack's best-friend.

"Yep... you want to go get some coffee?"

"I want some pancakes from Ray's." John stood up, grabbing his bag.

"You're such a fatty, John." Zack scoffed.

"Uh, child, excuse you. I am 6' 5 and a half, 250. Only part of me that is fat is this LONG-" John half yelled as Zack shut the door on him so he ran into it head first

"Maybe you should lead with that, you might not be single." Zack opened the door.

"I have never NOT led with it, boy, I thought you knew me."

"I know you're an idiot." Zack laughed. John flicked his bangs to the side like he thought he was sexy.

"Phhss... whatever."

They both laughed lightly as they walked. Sarah's mom worked at Ray's Bakery, they had a diner in the back part so after working out they sometimes went for breakfast.

Sarah's mom wasn't really a fan of Zack. She was a single mom who had to work as a waitress her whole life. She had gotten pregnant with Sarah while she was still in school and was dead set on Sarah getting a good education and a great job.

So her daughter falling for some poor farm-boy-soldier didn't exactly thrill her.

That's why it took them so long to get together. Zack and Sarah even went to her mom's church and took a purity oath that they would stay abstinent until they got married.

"One hundred percent pure, Mr. Taylor." Zack could still hear Ms. Evan's voice. That was the most awkward thing he had ever done.

John and Zack pushed through the doors in the back half

of the building and grabbed a booth. Zack met Ms. Evans's eyes and gave her a wave.

"Hey, Ms. Evans!" Zack said, sliding into the booth.

"Zack, what are you doing over here? Sarah said she was going over to make you breakfast before she went to the office," Ms. Evans said, walking over to the table.

"Heyyy, Stephanie...." John said, exaggerating the 'hey' in a flirtatious manner. Ms. Evans glared at him.

"What, is my daughter's cooking not good enough for you?" She folded her arms, glaring at Zack.

"I don't even get a hello?" John asked.

"No, she ended up not having enough time. We just ate power bars instead, and John was hungry," Zack said, wishing once that Sarah's mom would just assume the best of him.

"She left the house at 5:30. How did she not have enough time to make breakfast?" She asked, tilting her head to the side.

"Uhhh...." Zack blanked. God this woman was sharp as a tack.

"What were you doing to my daughter for an hour and a half?" She stared daggers into him.

"Nothing! Nothing happened! I just didn't want to get up this morning so we just ended up talking instead!" Zack said.

"Uh huh." Ms. Evans was not having it.

"Uh I'm just gonna go ahead and jump in here really quick." John raised his hand like a kid in grade school. "Ms. Evans, Zack really really cares about Sarah. He's like the best uh...." John moved his hand in a circle, trying to think of the words to use. "Like, all around person I've ever met. He's treating your daughter right, and being totally moral to her."

"Totally moral?" Zack asked, the words hitting his ear oddly.

"Yeah, the opposite of immoral," John said.

"I don't think you're using that right, but thanks," Zack said, glad his friend had his back. Ms. Evans paused for a bit then sighed and unfolded his arms.

"Alright what can I get you?" She said, pulling out a pad.

They sat there drinking coffee for a while. Zack didn't get any food, but John packed on two orders of pancakes. Making small talk, in their small town with small problems. When Ms. Evans came back a third time to refill coffee, Zack remembered what Sarah had said that morning.

"Hey, Ms. Evans?" Zack asked.

"What's up?" She said, not taking her eyes off the mug.

"How long do you think me and Sarah should wait before we think about getting married?" He said, flicking a sugar packet. Ms. Evans straightened and looked at him.

"Sarah has to finish school and have a good job. You didn't get her in trouble did you?" She said.

"No nothing like that, Sarah just mentioned it this morning. I hadn't really thought much about it, but she said she wanted to have time to plan a wedding," Zack said, putting in the sugar. "How long does it take to plan a wedding?"

"I thought you just had to fill out a paper at the courthouse?" John mopped up syrup with his thumb.

"No you don't just 'fill out a paper at the courthouse'," she said, flicking John in the ear. John yelped, grabbing his ear. Ms. Evans turned back to Zack. "Well let's see, you've got to do invitations, she'd have to get a dress, have a wedding shower.... Might take about a year to plan."

"Seriously? I didn't think it took that long."

"Mandy from our class got married in like two weeks!" John said, rubbing his ear.

"That's because she got knocked up by her cousin and had to get married before her bump started to show." Ms. Evans glared at John, swinging her hips angrily. "And that is not the case with my daughter."

"It's not," Zack said, confirming that for her. "But what do you think about us getting engaged now?"

Ms. Evans bit the inside of her lip a little bit as she eyed Zack. "I think that Sarah is always trying to rush everything," she said with a sigh. "I wish I could get it through to that girl that she's got her whole life to be married and have a family; there's no reason to go rushing in to everything." She turned and put the pot back on the warmer and grabbed a washcloth for one of the tables.

"How old were you when you got married, Stephanie?" John asked.

"Sixteen. And it left me totally unprepared for life." Ms. Evan's began washing a table.

"If you could go back now and do things differently, would you?" He asked, finishing the last of his syrup. That left Ms. Evans quiet for a bit.

"You can't go back so that's a pointless question," she replied.

"You know I always would complain to my mom when we got math homework. I used to always say that I would never have to sit at a table and do twenty math problems long hand and that it was totally pointless." He paused to sip his coffee. "She told me that the only value that anything in this world has, is the value that you assign it. If you don't value education, then school is pointless. If you don't value yourself, then making yourself better is pointless."

"Uh huh," Ms. Evans said, not really interested in what John was saying. "What's your point?"

"My point is that the questions and tasks we find pointless or meaningless often shape us the most. Life isn't about choices made, it's about doing all we can with all we got," John said, feeling very smug with his psych evaluation.

"Wow, that is so smart that it goes right back to being stupid." Ms. Evans laughed at him a little.

"Do you treat all your customers this way? Or is it something about my good looks that puts you on the defensive?" John asked with a glare. Ms. Evans bopped him on the head with the notepad she had, and shook her head.

"Do you even have money for a ring?" She turned to Zack.

"How much does a ring go for?" Zack, again, hadn't even thought about that before.

"Well if it's a ring for my daughter it should be the same

amount that you love her," she said, leaning on the table.

"So, uh, three hundred ?"

"Make it four."

"Okay. Four hundred it is," he said thinking about what he had saved. "Where can you get an engagement ring around here though?"

"There's that jewelry store over in Hanover. They'd probably have some," John said.

"You want to head over there?" Zack asked.

"Sure, I've got nothing to do." John grabbed his wallet. "I guess I'll get your coffee this time."

"Well first time for everything I guess," Zack said.

They headed back to Zack's house to grab his Military Response Vehicle since Hanover was a forty minute drive.

"Frickin' A', you need the shocks replaced on this piece of crap," John said as they passed a few of the rusted and broken down vehicles on the almost completely rubble, cracked highway.

"Be nice to my old truck. Betsy's only twenty-four!" Zack said, rubbing his permanently dusty dash.

"Yeah that's scraping age!"

"Lydia would kill me. She kept this thing nice. They didn't want to give us more than one vehicle anyway."

"I'm pretty sure this is less of a hand-me-down, and more that S.W.O.R.D. didn't want her to bring this thing back to Portland!" John shook his head.

"Well I like it. It has character."

"Suuurre... you think they're ever gonna get out here and scrap all these cars?" John asked as Zack weaved through the broken down pieces of rust.

"Eventually. They'll have to bring a bunch of blow torches to cut them all apart though; I doubt you can even move them anymore." Zack slowed down to maneuver some larger potholes.

"You remember when we went to Joliet and they had all their roads repaved and we saw that guy with the fancy sports car?" John grabbed the handle of the truck.

"Yeah, I don't know if it's ever gonna get that nice." Zack laughed.

"Well, you remember what Mrs. Mackler used to tell us?" John asked, grinning with his tongue in his lip. "She said that everywhere used to be that nice before we had the nuclear fallout. All these roads were paved, all these cars used to run, and everyone had two or three of them 'cause they could make that many."

"Yeah and people used to whine about working forty hours a week and coming home to clean water, having all the power they wanted, and they could heat and cool their houses with no trouble. And food! All the food they wanted wherever they wanted it...."

Zack shook his head, thinking of how crazy it was. Sure, he did fine on Military rations and stuff he canned, but a lot of people struggled in the winter.

"You could get a hamburger for a dollar...." John said.

"Most people could get up to three or four hundred pounds...." Zack said.

"Then pay a doctor to cut the fat off them...."

"And have plastic put in instead!" Zack finally laughed, shaking his head at the audacity of the kind of life that people had before everything when to hell. John laughed as well, though soon he sighed....

"...And a bunch of people didn't get genetic mutations, that gave them Leukemia at forty...." John said, reserved.

"And they weren't put in the military at thirteen..." Zack said, picking up on the change in mood.

"And there weren't lynchings for treason... or food riots down south," John said.

"Pointless questions, huh?" Zack sighed.

"Pointless questions." John nodded. "You realize that best case scenario, we're almost middle aged?"

"I try not to think about it too much," Zack said, watching the road.

"Well you're getting married and Rose and Daniel are

together forever so I need to hurry up and find a wife...." John said, kicking the dash lightly.

"Oh God," Zack said.

"What?" John looked around trying to find the problem.

"I totally forgot about Daniel and Rose," Zack said, running his hand through his hair. "Fuhhhh... Rose is gonna be pissed."

"Oh yeah, they've been together longer than you and Sarah, huh? Daniel's gonna be pissed too because now Rose is gonna be all: 'Sarah has a ring. Why don't I have a ring!'"

"Ugghhhh...." Zack groaned. John switched to his Daniel voice.

"'Zack, why do you have to always screw me like this? Now I'm never gonna hear the end of it. How much did you spend on the ring, I've got to double you or 'I'm a bad boyfriend!'" John said.

"Please stop...." Zack shook his head.

"Ahh it's another beautiful day in the King's Military!" John laughed, quoting their old training videos.

"Long live the Soldiers Watching Over the Royal Defense!" Zack said in a proud military voice.

"Long live S.W.O.R.D.!" John said.

* * *

It took them a bit longer to get to the jewelry shop in Hanover because of the rough terrain. They had started to go through the selection with one of the snooty women who worked there, trying to figure out what ring size Sarah would be, what kind of metal to get, what kind of stones to use for a good twenty minutes. At that point Zack and John realized they had no idea what they were looking for.

"Frickin' A' do they have enough options or what?" John

asked after the lady went to the back to check what else they had.

"I have no clue what I'm supposed to get. I thought they could do finger size like, off height and weight or something?" Zack grabbed his head with both hands.

"What? That's dumb," John said.

"John? Zack?" A female voice popped up from the door. Zack turned around to see Rose standing in the doorway with Daniel.

"Dang it...." Zack whispered. "Rose? Hey!" He changed tone, faking enthusiasm.

"Heyyy...." John waved.

"What are you guys doing here?" Daniel asked as they walked over.

"Not much, just hanging out. How about you?" Zack said.

"You're hanging out at a jewelry store?" Rose tilted her head in an 'I can't believe you just said something so stupid' kind of way.

"Seriously dude? That's the best you could do?" John asked, raising an eyebrow.

Zack was going to say something else when the store lady came back....

"Alright, I can't really tell without knowing her size but we have these in white gold. Do you know what kind of metal she would prefer?"

Zack wasn't sure what his expression was when the lady finally looked up at him. After a quick survey of the situation however, the lady seemed to understand she had walked over at the worst possible time.

"YOU'RE GETTING ENGAGED?!?" Rose asked. The few people in the store all turned to stare at them. Zack rubbed his forehead and looked at the ground.

"Yes!" John said, swooping in to cover him. "I didn't want you to find out like this, but I ended up hooking up with a girl from Anderson and now she's pregnant. So I have to do the responsible thing and get married."

"What?" Rose asked, stunned. Daniel started to giggle as

John moved in and took her hand in his.

"Listen, I know this is a shock, but things would never have worked out between us. You should do your best to forget me and move on." Daniel busted out with laughter.

"Would you shut the hell up!?" Rose shoved him away, fed up with his bullcrap. "Zack, are you getting an engagement ring?"

"Uh...." Zack thought about lying for a second, but one look at Rose's face told him that she was generally upset. "Yeah. I'm trying to pick one out."

"For Sarah?" Rose asked.

"I'm sorry, do I just radiate this feeling that I have all sorts of side girls around?" Zack was becoming concerned about his reputation since Sarah had asked something similar this morning.

"Okay! Okay! Dumb question," Rose said, getting defensive.

"So, you're seriously asking her to marry you?" Daniel asked, calming his laughter.

"Yeah," Zack said nonchalantly.

"Why didn't you tell us you were thinking about getting married?!?" Rose asked.

"Well, I wasn't really thinking about it before today!" He said, raising his voice to match her hysteria.

"So you just got the feeling this morning and you go to pick out a ring?" Rose folded her arms.

"Yes! Sarah came over this morning and mentioned that she wanted to be engaged so she would have time to plan the wedding. Then me and John went to the diner and I talked to her mom about it. Then we came here to get a ring!" Zack said. Rose was quiet for a second, staring at him.

"So she MENTIONS it once and you just go do it?" Rose asked in awe, tilting her head incredulously .

"Yeah...?"

"Hmpf. Must be nice," Rose said, shifting her glare to Daniel.

"Aaand there it is...." Daniel rolled his eyes. John tapped Zack with the back of his hand.

"Hey, Zack, you might want to pick up that phone," John said.

"What ph-"

"Because I, FRICKIN called it," John said, smiling while doing a little jump-shot motion, and making Zack laugh.

"Called what?" Rose asked, turning back to them.

"Nothing, it's nothing." John giggled.

"You think you are so darn funny don't you?" Rose asked, hands on her hips, realizing she was getting made fun of.

"Woman, I am hilarious!" John said.

"Okay, let's chill!" Zack said, stepping in. "By the way, Rose, do you know what Sarah's ring size is?"

"Nine and a half," she said, switching attitudes. Everyone was quiet for a moment, surprised by how quick she answered that. "What?"

"You seem to be very sure of that." Daniel raised an eyebrow. "How do you know what her ring size is?"

"What? We just talked about it a while back," she said, brushing it off.

"And you memorized it?" He asked.

"Oh, hello again Ms. Tenabalm!" The store manager came up to Rose. "Is this the lucky guy?" Everyone eyed Rose.

"Hi.... Yeah this is Daniel...." Rose said slowly.

"Awesome! You did get him in here finally!" The manager laughed. "And are you guys the support group?"

"Yeah...." Zack said, figuring out what had been going on. "Say, by chance did Rose come in with a girl about yea tall? Really tan, brunette?"

"Yes, uh, Samantha...?"

"Sarah. Right. I'll take whatever ring she picked out last time they were here."

"Oh, I can't quite remember which one she liked best that was three days ago." The manager rubbed her temple. "Are you Sarah's boyfriend?"

"Three days ago?" Daniel asked, staring down Rose.

"Yeah, can you just show me the ones she looked at then?" Zack asked.

"Sure! I'll go get that set!" She said with fake manager happiness. She walked off while everyone turned to look at Rose.

"We were out shopping and we just ended up looking for a little bit," Rose said, flicking her hand around.

"Uh huh. I'm guessing you talked Sarah into this?" Daniel was still skeptical.

"I didn't talk her into anything! I just thought maybe YOU would think about proposing, and we got to talking, and got to looking at rings," Rose said.

"Well you never said you wanted to get married!" Daniel said, getting louder.

"Why do I HAVE to say it? Don't YOU want to marry ME?"

"See what you did?" John asked, looking at Zack.

"ME?!?" Zack asked loudly.

"Uh... I believe this was the case she was looking at...." The manager cut in quietly.

2. A RELAXING NIGHT OUT

Zack pushed the door open to Dr. Wilkins' office in town. He looked for a receptionist but the counter was empty like the rest of the office. He ended up being distracted by the gigantic fish tank in the corner with three small fish in it.

You always see the stupidest stuff in a doctors office.... Zack thought. Why would you need a fish tank this big for three fish?

"Oh hello!" A voice said, bringing Zack out of his thoughts.

"Hello!" Zack said to the older woman smiling at him.

"Can I help you?" She asked.

"Uh, yeah, is Sarah still here?"

"Yes she is. Did you need something?"

"Ah- I was just gonna see her real quick, ask her out to dinner," he said.

"Hang on I'll see if she's free. You're Zack right?"

"Yes Ma'am," he said with a smile.

"I thought so, she talks about you a lot." The receptionist returned his smile.

"Ha, only good things I hope!" Zack said, continuing his 'I don't know you very well, but I'll joke with you to keep this from being uncomfortable' smile.

"Oh always!" She said, heading back to a different part of the building.

Zack rocked on his heels as he continued to pace around the waiting room. He got to the wall that held pictures and degrees that caught his attention again.

"'On this date, Monday, June second, in the twelfth year of our glorious Nation, Timothy Wilkins has met or surpassed all requirements to practice medicine,'" Zack mumbled to himself.

"What is that, like twenty years ago?"

"Zack? Come back here for a sec." Zack walked over to a little half door and leaned over to see Dr. Wilkins half way in the hall calling for him.

"Come on, come on!" He waved at Zack hurriedly. Zack opened the little half door and walked back to the room Wilkins had disappeared into.

"What's up?" He said as he walked in. Zack saw Sarah, and a woman he had never seen before, standing to one side of the room. There was a white sheet covering what looked like half a body on the table.

"Over here, can you see if you can crack this guy's sternum for me?" Wilkins said, looking at him from the other side of the table.

"Uh.... What?" Zack said, tilting his head to the side.

"His sternum, this part." Dr. Wilkins pointed out the sternum.

"No, I got that," Zack said as he walked over to the table. "Why do you need me to break his sternum?"

"Ehh, it's weird, his body keeps gunking up my saws. There's some kind of thickening agent or something in his bone marrow," he said. "He's a Blood too, so I can't really break it myself without a sledge hammer."

"Ah. Hey, I'm Zack," Zack said, extending his hand to the lady he didn't recognize. She wore black business attire and her short blonde hair was pulled back into a bun.

"Samatha Kruger, S.W.O.R.D. Investigative arm!" The unknown woman said. "I'm guessing you're a Blood as well?"

"Yeah, that obvious? Operative Zackary Taylor, S.W.O.R.D.'s GSA division IN-14. Been in the GSA for four years now," Zack said. 'Blood' was a relaxed term for a GSA soldier.

"Yeah, being that tall and... built sort of gives it away." Samatha giggled.

Sarah's head snapped sideways.

"What's IN-14 mean?" Samatha asked.

"It's my unit's call sign or designation. We're the

fourteenth GSA unit located in the Indiana territory," Zack said before turning back to Dr. Wilkins. "Hey, this isn't somebody I know, right?"

"...I don't know actually. Looks like another poor soul looking for a cure to Adam's Polycythemia Leukemia. His lower half had already liquified by the time they found him," Dr. Wilkins said.

"We're working on an I.D. GSA operatives going AWOL after being diagnosed isn't that rare, though...." Sarah said, walking up to the table. "...Are you gonna be okay?"

Zack sighed. "Yeah I've seen this stuff before...."

"Try just reaching up in his body to pop the ribs away through the sternum," Dr. Wilkins said as he handed Zack some gloves.

"What if I break the ribs?" Zack said, putting on the gloves.

"Don't worry about it; I just want to see how his heart and lungs look," Wilkins said.

"Okay." Zack reached into the chest cavity, the abdomen having already been removed. Zack started to sweat as his blood rushed through his veins and he tried to get a good grip on the soldier's sternum. Leaning further over the table, he held a rib in each hand and tugged apart the man's chest cavity with a grunt.

CRACK

POP

CRUL-CHH

It took him three big tugs to finally pull the ribs apart and pop the sternum off.

"That good?" Zack asked, handing the doctor the bone.

"Yeah hold that up a second." Dr. Wilkins used some tool to measure the thickness of the bone. "Sternum is about three centimeters larger than average."

Dr. Wilkins produced a metal bowl and Zack dropped the piece in while Sarah wrote down the observations on a clipboard.

"He's definitely larger than your typical forty year old

white male," Sarah said, looking through her paperwork.

"See, this is the weird part. See how his muscle tissue is on his ribs here?" Wilkins started explaining stuff to Sarah.

Zack washed his arms and got out of their way.

"So... would you be bothered if I asked you about all this stuff?" Ms. Kruger walked over to Zack.

"What stuff?" Zack asked.

"About, like, GSA and that Adam's stuff," Ms. Kruger said. "Dr. Wilkins was trying to explain it to me but it was too science-y."

"No prob." Zack laughed. "Basically, I have Genetic Systemic Augmentations, or GSA for short. 'Blood' is like a nickname term or something. Adam's Polycythemia Leukemia is a disease Bloods gets around forty. It only happens to GSAs though."

"So what all are the symptoms of people with GSA? I've heard all kinds of rumors, so I'm not sure what is what. You guys are all in S.W.O.R.D. right?" Ms. Kruger asked.

Sarah glanced over at Zack and Ms. Kruger but kept working.

"Yeah, everyone who gets diagnosed is conscripted. The way it got explained to me was it was kinda like gigantism, but not quite. The 'Systemic Augmentation' part basically means that every system of the body is pumped up. So, like, your skin is a whole system, I've got more skin cells and thicker, stronger skin. I'm more muscular, my bones are thicker and stronger, etc etc," Zack said.

"So that's for, like, everything? Are you super smart because of extra brain cells and stuff too?" Ms. Kruger laughed.

Sarah shot a look over again.

"Nah, nothing like that." Zack laughed as well. "But I guess to compensate for things like skin thickness and stuff I have a larger nervous system to compensate so, you know, I wouldn't be able to feel things as easily. That, and the other senses take up extra brain power. Like, I guess we in the GSA have better depth perception in our vision and hearing than regular people."

"Mmmm, so it's like subconscious stuff then."

"Yeah basically." Zack nodded.

"So what happens with APL then? I got tasked with bringing this guy over here and he's half missing. I thought he was blown up or something, but they said it was APL?" Ms. Kruger asked.

"Yeah, so, Adam's Polycythemia Leukemia is a disease where cells get confused and start forgetting how to copy themselves right." Zack bit his lip. APL was not a topic most Bloods cared to talk about. "Basically, instead of a muscle cell making a new muscle cell, it makes a blood cell instead and you just... get to a point where there's not enough cells actually holding you together."

"Oh God, so his bottom half...." Ms. Kruger shuddered.

"Probably just melted away, yeah. It can happen to different parts depending on your luck. Sometimes it's brain cells and you get a couple weeks, sometimes it's something else and you hold on for a while." Zack shrugged. "Happens to everybody with GSA though, so it's sort of an eventual side effect."

"How long... er...." Ms. Kruger hesitated.

"Typically hits around forty; the oldest person I ever saw still alive was forty-nine," Zack said.

"That's rough...."

Sarah finished writing something down and walked over.

"Hey," she said to Zack. "Did you need to talk to me? We can get out of here for a second."

Zack followed Sarah into the hallway.

"That S.W.O.R.D. lady has got me on edge," Sarah whispered and then sighed. "You seemed to be getting along great, though. Chatting up a storm."

"...Are you jealous?"

"Nope."

Right... Zack thought.

"What are you nervous about?" Zack asked.

"Because she's like standing right over us, and has asked me to copy all the notes I take and Dr. Wilkins is being super anal about the notes being clear now. You know the whole system thing. Is she, like, important?" Sarah said, looking around the corner.

"Investigators are kinda..." Zack made a flipping motion with his hand, "if she asks you any personal questions be vague. It's probably all just routine stuff though."

"Okay...." Sarah looked concerned. "Hey, what, uh, group are you in?"

"Group? I'm in the GSA branch of S.W.O.R.D....."

"Right! Sorry! Stupid question!" Sarah shook her head. "It's been a day. Why are you here, by the way? You don't usually...." She trailed off, looking at him.

"What?" He asked, tilting his head.

"Your eyes are really bloodshot still," she said, touching his face.

"Yeah it goes away after a bit," he said, rubbing his slightly puffy eyes. "When the adrenalin hits me to break stuff it happens."

The adrenal system was a system like the rest in Zack's body. Larger and more active than the average person. For some reason, an elevated adrenalin state led to blood filling the whites of his eyes. One of the reasons the GSA were called 'Bloods' he guessed.

"Anyway, I was going to ask you if you wanted to get dinner tonight. If the mood isn't totally dead."

"Tonight? What's the occasion?" She asked.

"I don't know." Zack realized he had no reason to ask her out tonight. "I want to eat dinner with you since we missed breakfast I guess?"

"Geez, you're that bummed out I didn't cook this morning, huh?"

"Well yes, I'm devastated. But, I'll take you out somewhere nice tonight," Zack said, pulling her close.

"Somewhere nice? Quit, I'm at work...." Sarah said, pushing him a little, trying to hide a smile. While she protested Zack snuck in a kiss on her cheek.

"Yeah so wear something nice, like a dress," Zack said.

"You. Are. Rotten," Sarah said with a glare. "Alright, what time?"

"Seven."

"It'll be dark by then!"

"God, six then, Ms. Picky!"

"I hate you." Sarah shook her head, tongue pressed inside her lip.

"Love you too, beautiful." Zack gave her a kiss on the forehead and headed to the door. "Have a great rest of the day!"

"Love you too.... You're still rotten!" She disappeared into the hall. Zack headed back outside where the rest of IN-14 was waiting.

"What did she say?" Rose popped up off the hood of the truck.

"We're gonna go to dinner at six," Zack said.

"What, did you think he was gonna ask her in there?" John gave Rose a dirty look.

"No you idiot, I was asking if she could make it to dinner," she said, lightly glaring at John. Daniel started to chuckle.

"'My dearest Sarah, would you do me the great honor of marrying me right here next to the stool samples!'" Daniel said, making John and Zack laugh too. Rose tried to keep the smile off her lips.

"Keep it up, jerks." Rose folded her arms.

"Oh don't be that way babe." Daniel hugged Rose, giving her a kiss on the head. "I know you are just excited to see your favorite couple get engaged."

"Favorite couple?" Zack repeated, raising an eyebrow.

"Oh yeah, Rose ships you and Sarah hardcore," John said as they all got in the truck.

"Ships?" Zack repeated once again as he started the engine.

"Yeah," John said.

"'The hell are you talking about boats for?" Zack asked. Everyone started laughing.

"Boats! HAHA!" John was losing it.

Zack didn't get the joke but he figured he'd push it a little farther anyway.

"We are nowhere near a lake, retard! I don't think Rose even has a boat!" Zack half-yelled.

John and Daniel started howling while Rose shook.

"It's not a boat!" Rose said, giggling. "It's like, I like the idea of you and Sarah as a couple."

"Then what does 'ship' stand for?" Zack wasn't sure of the title.

"Like...." Rose tripped up for a second. "I don't know...."

"It's short for relationships, isn't it?" Daniel happily sighed.

"Oh I see, you 'relationship' us, that makes sense," Zack said, getting onto the road. There was more laughter.

"'You relationship us', oh my God I'm loving today," John said through the giggles.

"You guys are such children...." Rose giggled, shaking her head.

"Why do you like me and Sarah as a couple?" Zack asked, genuinely curious.

"'Cause it's the cutest story in the world!!!" Rose yelled excitedly.

"In what way?" Zack asked.

"Oh boy here we go...." Daniel smiled with an eye roll.

"Like how the first time you met you were kids and she was getting bullied and you rushed in and saved herrrr...." She said, dragging out the last word as if she was starting a list.

"Knight in shining armor move." Daniel teased.

"Yeah, you messed up Will Thompson." John nodded.

"Well he deserved it. He was being a punk," Zack said, gripping the steering wheel harder. He still hated the kid.

"And then when you guys first started to talk and her mom didn't like you so you had to work and work to change her mindddd...." Rose dragged again.

"I don't think Ms. Evans likes any man," Daniel said from

the backseat.

"Nahh that's just Stephanie's front, you got to get deeper inside to really see how she is," John said.

"Yeah, I bet you want to see that," Daniel said.

"Ew! Urroa...." Rose imitated throwing up. "Can you two stop being gross?!? I'm talking about cute stuff here!"

"Sorry," they said, laughing.

"Anyway, there's all that and then how you said you were gonna wait for her until she was all done with school and was ready to go to the next level," Rose said, not dragging the last word this time, but there was a smile in her voice. "I've always really respected that you're doing that for her. It's so sweet...."

"Awhhh... Zack's such a sweetie-pie!" John teased.

Zack felt his face burn a little bit. Before he could say anything though...

CRACK!

"OW! ROSE!" John jumped in his seat, holding his head.

"DON'T YOU DARE MAKE FUN OF HIM, JOHN HENAGAR, I'LL GIVE YOU A CONCUSSION!" Rose yelled.

"Okay, Okay! I'm sorry!!" John's voice quivered.

"You know you could learn a thing or two about how you're supposed to treat women from Zack! With respect and dignity!"

"And you definitely don't poke fun at Rose's ship," Daniel said with a laugh.

"It's okay, Rose," Zack said, laughing as well.

"Man, I'm seeing stars." John rubbed his head.

"Oh, I didn't hit you that hard," Rose said.

"Hey that makes me wonder though, Rose." Zack looked at Rose in the rearview mirror.

"What?" Rose met his eyes.

"Well with you saying that, about me and Sarah holding off...." Zack paused for a second as he turned a corner. "Do you wish that you and Daniel had held off on... everything?"

Rose's expression flushed and her eyes got a little wider. "Who said we weren't waiting??"

"Daniel" John said quickly.

"DANIEL!" Rose shouted.

"NO, OKAY, BULLCRAP! I AIN'T SAID NOTHING!" Daniel shouted back.

"You didn't as much say it as bragged about it," Zack said, picking up on John's joke.

"BRAGGED ABOUT WHAT?!?" Rose started to get hysterical.

"NOTHING! THEY'RE LYING!"

"I got to say, Rose, I never figured you to be the type that was so...." John started.

"...Open to experimenting, would probably be the best way to say it." Zack finished, trying so hard not to laugh. John started to giggle, though, and they couldn't keep it up.

"You guys are jerks!" Rose said, calming down a little bit and realizing it was all a joke. "You really didn't say anything, did you?" She said, turning to Daniel.

"NO! I would never do that to you," Daniel said, exhausted.

"For real he's never said anything," Zack said.

"No, he never said anything," John said.

"Okay...." Rose said. "Why do you think we did?"

"Eh, just the way you talk about it. Like, remorseful...." Zack said.

"My grandpa is the pastor of our church. Dad is super religious. A good christian girl wouldn't do that stuff," Rose said.

"I know your dad is all weird, but isn't your mom a bit more worldly?" John asked.

"Dad is not *weird*, if you ever gave church a chance-"

"Hard pass. You guys can be baptist and go get screamed at about fire and brimstone all you want. I'm not doing it," John said.

"...But yeah, mom is more worldly as you put it," Rose said.

John was the only one who was not a member of Rose's grandfather's church. Zack didn't push him. Honestly, if it wasn't for Sarah and her mom, Zack probably wouldn't go either. Not to say he didn't believe in God, just that being Baptist was...

intense.

“At least when we are near town we don’t have to swerve all over to miss broken down cars,” Zack said, changing the subject.

“Yeah, you think the scrap yard guys would get all those cut up,” Daniel said. “You can run us to my house after you drop off John.”

“Sounds good,” Zack said as he pulled down John’s road. Zack stopped in front of John’s duplex.

“Welp, let me know when she says yes. I'll buy you a drink at the bar,” John said, hopping out.

“Yeah! Call us up so we can all celebrate!” Rose said, slapping his arm.

“Sure. You guys won't be busy?” Zack said.

“...Getting busy?” John continued jokingly.

Rose glared at John. “Can you not...?”

“Okay, I'll call Rose's house later?” Zack asked.

“We will be there!” Rose nodded.

“I'll just meet you at the bar. Sound good?” John said.

“Yeah brosef, first rounds on you,” Daniel said.

“Sweet, maybe I'll get married tonight. Just to spite you love birds.” John flipped everyone off.

“You won't!” Daniel called after him.

“Bet,” Zack called out one of John's catch phrases.

“You boys are all dumber than a box of rocks.” Rose sighed.

3. JUST FOLLOWING ORDERS...

Zack picked up the little black box off the counter. Opening it, a shiny gold ring with a single stone twinkled in the light of his kitchen. He snapped the box shut and tucked it into his jacket.

Zack walked out his front door, locking it behind him. It was only a short, silent drive to get to Sarah's duplex, but it felt longer than usual, he tried to think about how to pop the question. He pulled into a spot close to her door and bounded up the stairs to the second story. He knocked on the door then backed up to straighten up his tie.

"Hey honey!" Sarah said, opening the door. "Ooh, a tie and everything. What, are we going to church?"

"Well I get to take the most beautiful girl in world to dinner, so I thought I should look the part." Zack smiled at her.

"Oh really? You've seen every woman in the world? I didn't think you had traveled that much." Sarah leaned on the door frame with a smile of her own.

"Well let's see I've been to this town..." Zack said, thinking.

"Uh huh."

"And I've been to the next town over..."

"Mmhmm."

"Yeah, that's pretty much the whole world right?" Zack said. Sarah rolled her eyes.

"Yeah, not even close." She shook her head. Zack reached around her waist, pulling her close slowly so he had enough time to think up a charming comeback.

"Well I've looked at you, and you are my whole world, so...." Zack said.

"Ha!" Sarah opened her mouth in surprise the way she did whenever she was caught off guard by one of his flirty comments. "You. Are. Rotten." She pulled him in by his tie for a kiss.

"You love it," he said, with his forehead against hers, swaying in the doorway.

"My, my, where did you learn to seduce girls like that, Mr. Taylor?" Ms. Evans said, popping out from the kitchen.

"Uhh... ha ha...." Zack stuttered nervously.

"Mom, be nice," Sarah said, grabbing her coat. "I shouldn't be out too late, love you!!"

"Love you too. Be good to my daughter, Taylor," Ms. Evans called after them.

In an effort not to be out too late, Zack decided to stay closer to home, which left only one restaurant in town that was even remotely fancy. Marcelino's was a nice little Italian place, made their own pasta, dim candle light and romantic.

...That's a nice enough place to propose, right? Oh god... please say yes.... Zack's feet went cold.

"Aren't you being quite the gentlemen tonight?" Sarah said, as he pushed her chair in.

"Only the best for you sweetheart," he said, with a kiss on the top of her head.

"Okay, spill," Sarah said. "What's going on? You're acting all lovey-dovey."

"Huh? I don't know what you're talking about."

"Mmhmm...." Sarah said, eyeing him. Zack looked back at her pretty smile. She looked beautiful the way she leaned on her hand trying to figure him out.

God, I love you....

"Okay, you got me," he said, with a smile.

"Oh?" She said, raising an eyebrow. Zack got out of his chair, and knelt by her, pulling out the ring. A few older folks quit eating to watch the cute scene. Whispers and giggles seemed to ignite the restaurant.

Sarah's eyes widened. "Oh!"

"Sarah Evans..." Zack opened the small box. "Will you marry me?"

"Oh...." Sarah said, as she looked awe struck at the box. She ran her eyes over the ring for a long time. Then picked it out of the box and analyzed it.

Zack laughed nervously. "Uh... hon you haven't said anything yet."

Sarah stared at the ring for a long time. Her surprise faded, and slowly, her face changed. She put the ring back in the box and walked out of the restaurant. The whole restaurant went dead silent.

"Um... should I...." A waitress behind him started as Zack's arms fell down, and he watched Sarah leave.

"Sarah?" Zack said, realizing what had just happened. "Sarah! Wait!"

Zack ran after her, catching up to her just outside the restaurant. "Sarah, what's wrong!?"

"I don't want to talk about it," Sarah said, not looking at him.

"What?" Zack said in disbelief. "What do you mean you don't want to talk about it!? This morning you were upset that we weren't engaged yet! So I propose and you just leave?!"

"Exactly!" Sarah yelled, turning on him. "I say I want to be engaged and THAT NIGHT you propose?!"

"What?" He said, confused.

"And on top of everything it is the *EXACT* ring I picked out!" Sarah threw her hands in the air. "How did you even do that?!?"

"What are you talking about?! I thought you wanted to marry me!"

"I DO!!" Sarah yelled, stomping her foot. "But that doesn't mean I want you to marry me only because I'm telling you to marry me!!"

"Wh- That's not the only reason! I want you to marry me!"

"Oh, shut up! You never even thought about marrying me before this morning, did you!"

"Oh my God, I thought, you know, big picture wise about it."

"Big picture wise. Meaning like eventually it'll just happen. Just like everything happens with you!" Sarah walked away.

"*MEANING* I know I want to spend the rest of my life with you! Look, I went to the jewelry store with John and then Rose and Daniel showed up and I found the ring you were looking at and it all just fell together," Zack explained, following her closely.

"So what, your friends pressured you into buying it? God forbid you taking anytime making the decision for yourself! That might mean that Rose would have to wait even longer for Daniel to propose!"

"WOULD YOU STOP IT?!" Zack grabbed Sarah by the arm and turned her around. She was crying now. She grabbed above Zack's hand with her free arm, and wouldn't look at him.

"Let go of me!" She hissed through the tears. Zack held her for a minute before releasing her. She stormed off again.

"Where are you going?" He called after her.

"To the office!" She shouted over her shoulder.

Zack stood there watching her leave. He sighed angrily and kicked the ground. He walked back to where his truck was, and drove to the bar that they were supposed to celebrate at. He walked into the rather busy bar to see John already there watching TV with a beer and an order of fried morels. Zack sat down next to him.

"Hey buddy! Wait isn't your..." John looked at his watch, then at Zack's face. "Oh crap, what happened?"

* * *

After about an hour, and many, many drinks, Zack was feeling the appropriate amount of inebriated to whine about his girlfriend.

"You know what? Screw that crap about me being

pressured into proposing! I am a MAN, and I make my own GOT-DAng desci-shh... choices!" Zack said, giving up on the pronunciation of 'decisions'.

"Yes, you, do! Yes, you, do!" John said, slapping Zack's back. "You see? This right here is the stuff: They ask you to do something, and you do it, and they are pissed that you did it because they ask."

"YES! YES!" Zack nodded in agreement.

"My mom is the same way. It's like 'Woman I ain't a damn mind reader! You want me to do stuff, ask me to do stuff!' But no that's too much to ask. If women don't have a reason not to be happy they're mis-marbles."

"What?"

"They're mis-marbles." John repeated hearing it this time. "Mis-marbles... Fudge nuggets!"

"Dude it's fricking 'mis-marbles'." Zack clarified.

"THAT'S EXACTLY WHAT I SAID DILLWEED!" John shouted. They both broke into laughter.

"Jeez you guys couldn't wait for us?!" Rose said, coming up behind them. "Sarah didn't want to come celebrate?"

"Nothing to celebrate," Zack grumbled, leaning heavily on the bar.

"What?" Daniel said, coming to Zack's free side. "What happened?"

"She fricking said no!" Zack threw his head around aggravated. Everyone was quiet for a second.

"WHAT DO YOU MEAN SHE SAID NO?!" Rose yelled, spinning Zack around on the bar stool. Zack almost fell off the stool as he wobbled back and forth.

"I- Whoa, crap- She didn't, like, say it, but she walked out on me!" Zack said, grabbing his head. "She said I only asked her because she brought it up this morning, and I don't really want to marry her or something...."

"What? That's not true!" Daniel shook his head.

"Ooooh...." Rose cooed. "I get it."

The men all looked at Rose as she shook her head.

"How do you 'get it'?" Zack asked.

"She's super nervous about getting married and the future. When she said she wanted to get married, she was asking you what it was that you wanted in the future. She wanted you to take your time and worry about your future with her. When you do it as soon as she asks it's like you didn't put any thought into it at all, you're just doing what she tells you to do," Rose explained. "No girl wants that."

"I feel like you have gotten mad at me several times for not doing something you told me to do." Daniel folded his arms.

"That's different."

"In what way is that different? You got pissed today because I *didn't* do what he did." Daniel pointed at Zack.

"I did not get pissed! What I'm saying is that by doing it so quick, Sarah feels like the only reason he asked her to marry him is to appease her. Boys always have to make us feel like the bad guy for wanting things!" Rose put her hands on her hips.

"Well you know, if WOMEN would ever just come right out and say what they want nicely instead of making US do this little guessing game this wouldn't happen," Daniel said.

"Ha. I just said that." John laughed pointing at Daniel.

"Cram it, Henagar." Rose spat. "Well MAYBE if boys weren't huge jerks, WHO BLATANTLY IGNORE THE MOST OBVIOUS HINTS, we wouldn't have to put up billboards to let you know to be nice to us!"

"I am so nice!" Daniel protested.

"Whatever. So where is Sarah now? Did she tell you where she was going?" Rose asked, turning back to Zack.

"Uh, yeah I asked as she was going while she was storming away and she said she was going to the office."

"How long ago was this?"

"Uh, maybe an hour or two ago?"

"Okay, well you should probably go talk to her now," Rose said.

"What? Why would I do that?" Zack asked.

"Because dummy, when a girl storms off and DOESN'T tell

you where she's going, she's really upset and doesn't want to see you at all. When she storms off and TELLS you where she's going, that means she's really upset right now so meet her there in a couple hours."

"What? How the hell was I supposed to figure that out?" Zack squinted at Rose.

"Oh my God... Just do it okay?" Rose said, rubbing her eyes.

"Alright, alright." Zack stood up and started walking towards the door.

"Wait, hold up, are you okay to drive?" John called out. Zack thought about it for a second. He turned around and started to hand his keys to John... then turned again and handed his keys to Daniel instead.

"I'm not driving you!" Daniel said.

"No, no, I'm gonna walk, God!" Zack said, flipping his arms out. "Just take the fricking truck home for me."

"Go get her, Romeo!" John said, giving him a thumbs up. "And may I just say, the lengths you and Daniel go to to keep your women happy astounds me!"

"Oh shut up, Henagar, this is why you don't have a girlfriend," Rose spat.

"Really? And here I thought it was his face," Daniel chimed in.

Zack walked out of the bar and started walking towards the office. He wasn't falling over drunk, but he could tell if he didn't put some effort into walking he might trip.

Small towns have the luxury of everything being within a close walking distance, even if the doctor's office was on the other side of town. It only took him maybe 20 minutes of walking to get within view of the building lit up by the street lights. Luckily he wasn't as drunk as he thought. If he was drunk, he would definitely trip on the cracked and jagged sidewalk.

Oddly enough he saw Dr. Wilkins outside with Sarah. When she noticed Zack, she ran at full speed at him

"Whoa what's...?" Zack started, before getting rammed by

Sarah. She started to sob into his chest.

"Hey, whats- what's going on?" Zack asked, now .

"Oh, Zack, thank Christ it's you." Sarah was shaking. "I don't know what to do...."

Tears and sobs followed as she fell apart on the last word. Zack hugged her tightly as she tried to calm down.

"Sarah, what's going on?"

"I-I don't know, I... I came in and everything was fine! Dr. Wilkins was in late doing this blood analysis so I helped out, and he said he got it back to a thin blood like viscosity, so we were gonna try to patch up the cadaver and run the blood through with a pump to see how it deteriorated and-and...!"

"Sarah! What. Happened. Why are you panicking?"

"IT WOKE UP OR SOMETHING! I DON'T KNOW!"

"What?" Zack asked.

"IT WOKE UP AND FREAKED OUT AND WE RAN AWAY BUT DR. WILKINS' LEG IS HURT AND HE'S IN SHOCK AND I DON'T KNOW! I DON'T KNOW, OKAY?!? I DON'T GET IT, I DON'T UNDERSTAND, I DON'T KNOW!"

Zack pulled her close again and held her as she panicked for a moment. In the distance Dr. Wilkins was laying down on his back, arms in the air as if he was trying to run his hand through the night sky like it was water. One panicking, one in shock, with a possible threat, and Zack was buzzed at least.

This isn't good.

Zack grabbed Sarah by the arms and looked into her eyes.

"Listen to me okay? Rose, John, and Daniel are all at Kevin's bar. Get there and tell them what's going on. I'll stay here with Wilkins okay?"

"Okay." Sarah rubbed her eyes dry. "I don't know what happened! Is S.W.O.R.D. gonna get mad? We didn't do anything!"

"Sarah, everything is going to be okay. I promise. Go get Daniel and the rest."

"Okay...."

Sarah started to run to the bar as Zack made his way over to the office. He stopped in front of Wilkins.

"Hey, are you alright?" Zack asked. Wilkins laid on his back, leg wrapped in a now bloody coat, his hands folded together. He didn't even look at Zack.

"I don't feel... present," Wilkins said to the sky. "I don't feel like I'm in my body. Things aren't making sense right now."

"Ouuukay..." Zack said.

"I think someone might want to stop it soon. If it destroys our equipment much more we aren't going to be able to reopen. I think S.W.O.R.D. will be very angry with us as well."

"Wait, why couldn't you reopen?" Zack rubbed his face.

"Well I wouldn't have the money, and if this is a big deal and turns into a major investigation I probably won't be able to apply for funding to cover the damages."

"What? Sarah only has a year left of studying under you. What happens if you have to close?"

"I'm not sure. She'd either have to wait at least a year, or go somewhere else. Assuming they would take her."

Zack squatted down, holding his head in his hands for a second. Sarah didn't even want to wait one more year to get married. What if she got burnt out and quit? What if no one else would take her on? What if she had to move away for a while? It was hard enough not seeing her for weeks when he got called away for S.W.O.R.D. crap.

I don't want her to have to wait another year... I don't want her to leave.... I don't want her to fail!

"DAMN IT!"

Zack flew up to the front and shouldered his way through the door, blood flooding into his eyes and tinting his vision as he made it to the hallway. Half of a man turned himself around with his arms to look at Zack. Zack saw immediately that the chest and stomach was wrapped heavily in dingy bandages. Inky, soulless eyes that mirrored Zack's blood-filled eyes stared into him like an abyss.

"Hey!" Zack yelled, trying to lure the half-man away. It pushed itself up on its palms and started to hop towards Zack rather fast. Still feeling the alcohol in his system, added with the fact that he was in his adrenal state, he had to fight for focus. When the torso of a man leapt for his throat, Zack just missed his window to counter.

Now feeling his liquor and off balance, Zack smacked the back of his head into the wall. Zack's eyes went foggy before losing his vision entirely for a second. He slammed the half-man into the opposite wall in the tight hallway.

Two of the half-man's fingers dug into Zack's mouth as he pushed the creature into a clinch against the wall. However, now having a point to push off from the creature was able to throw Zack back into the opposite wall, jamming it's fingers down Zack's throat. Zack's head hit the wall again, but the way he fell made him bite down on the fingers that were jammed down his throat. The force and the motion caused him to swallow, and a panic overcame him as he felt two human fingers scrape down his throat.

His vision returning, Zack grabbed the half-man's wrist and ran through the doorway. Ink-black blood sprayed into one of Zack's eyes from the stubs where the creature's fingers used to be. Pulling the wrist up over his head, Zack smashed the half-man into the floor. He slammed down again and again, feeling the forearms snap like twigs under the force of his hammering. He felt the wrist bones turning into powder under the force of his grip. Soon the entire mass felt limp, not able to withstand the force Zack was channeling into it. He felt a mist start to soak his skin as he bashed what was once the body of a man into a sloppy, blackened paste.

Finally releasing his grip as he fell to the ground, Zack tried to catch his breath. The room spinning all around him, Zack's vision becoming fuzzy once again. An intense nausea settled in his stomach. He couldn't catch his breath as his body heaved trying to vomit the disgusting results of his accidental cannibalism. The red tint to his vision began to fade and dark circles replaced it as he lost consciousness.

4. WHAT HAPPENED LAST NIGHT?

Zack woke up in a haze, his pillow hot and coarse on his ear. Zack could see a blurry version of Rose standing over him.

"He's awake," Rose called over her shoulder. "Thank God."

"Hey bud, how you feeling?" John's hand gently rested on Zack's shoulder.

Zack tried to blink the fog out of his eyes, only to have a stabbing pain replace it. He had been hungover before, but this was worse. While he let the pain subside, he remembered the events from last night. John and Rose must have found him unconscious.

"Like I'm getting skull-drilled through my eyes," Zack grumbled.

"You got a bunch of nasty stuff in your eyes. We tried to flush it all out with water, but Sarah said your eyes are gonna be really dry," Rose said.

"Yeah, she went to get eye drops and some other stuff from the office," John said. Zack started to feel pressure at the top of his stomach.

"I'm gonna throw up," Zack said, crawling out of the bed and dropping onto the floor.

"Hang on! Hang on!" Rose said, sliding a small trash can underneath him.

Zack heaved once, getting it caught in his chest and having to swallow it. He was only allowed a few breaths before violently throwing up. He leaned back against the bed and John handed him a glass of water.

"Man, that don't look good," John said, looking into the bucket of blackish bile. Zack chugged some of the water, trying to cool the burning in his chest.

"I swallowed his fingers." Zack coughed.

"What?" Rose asked.

"It shoved two of it's fingers down my throat and I hit my head and I bit down and swallowed two fingers," Zack said.
Rose and John both gagged.

"That's so nasty," Rose said.

"That's messed up...." John said.

"I know. My head hurts," Zack said, moving back to the bed.

"Hey, you're possibly concussed, I don't think you are supposed to go to sleep right now," Rose said.

"He was just asleep a minute ago," John pointed out.

"Well, I don't know...." Rose said, trailing off.

"Do you guys remember the first time we went to Portland for S.W.O.R.D.?" Zack stared at the ceiling.

"Yeah, which part?" John asked.

"When Lydia took us to hospital. We saw the GSA dying from APL," Zack said.
John and Rose winced.

"Ugh. I don't want to think about it," Rose said, shaking her head.

"It's important. It's gonna be disgusting hearing it, but it's important," Zack said, feeling sick himself. "There was the old guy whose eyes had melted out of his head? It was sort of like that... this guys' fingers exploded in my throat like a balloon."

"Holy cow, I might puke..." John and Rose gagged.

"What was left of him wasn't swollen when we got there though... was he that old?" She asked.

"Even if he was old enough to be swollen up, his fingers wouldn't dissolve right?" John asked.

"Frick if I know, I thought he was supposed to be dead!" Zack rubbed his face. "What happened after I passed out?"

"Well after you killed the guy, again apparently, Sarah ran

in the bar, told us what happened, and we rushed over. You were unconscious and the doctor's office was pretty destroyed so we brought you here and got you cleaned up. Daniel called S.W.O.R.D. and filed a report, so they are supposed to be sending someone for investigation," Rose explained. "Oh, and Wilkins is at the office still collecting samples."

"Yeah he's still kind of out of it." John nodded. "Still man, freaking zombies? That's crazy."

"You watch too many movies." Rose rolled her eyes.

"That's what he said it was! I'm so pumped for the apocalypse!" John said, fist pumping.

"Don't you mean the second apocalypse? The first one was a long time ago."

"I thought that was a holocaust?"

"A nuclear holocaust IS an apocalypse." Rose sighed.

"What actually happened with that guy? Did Wilkins figure anything out?" Zack asked.

"Nope. He's still in shock. Sarah's real torn up too. All we got is they tried running that black crap though him oxidized for some reason and *BOOM!* Feral half-man."

"Is that how zombies are made?" Zack asked.

"Everything makes zombies bro. Satellites falling to earth, mushrooms, disease, cures for cancer...."

"Please don't encourage him...." Rose said, exhausted.

"GUYS!" Daniel's voice echoed through the house, the door slamming behind him. Zack sat up as Daniel appeared in the doorway. "The doctor's office is up in flames!"

"What?" Rose stood up.

"It's on fire! We can't find Wilkins either!" Daniel half-yelled.

Zack got up as the group started to run out the door, his head pounding. They hopped into the truck and peeled out towards town.

"Where is Sarah?" Zack asked.

"She's near the office, she was calling for help." Daniel sped around a hook.

Zack looked at the sky, seeing a smoke column getting thicker. His head was still pounding. Daniel squealed the truck to a rough stop and jumped out leaving it running. Zack jumped out on the other side to see a group of men struggling with the hoses.

"SARAH!" He cried out, trying to look around. His vision darkened at the edges, the motion and light making him sick. He ended up only tripping on his own feet.

"Zack!" Sarah ran over, grabbing his shoulders to steady him. "Deep breaths! In through the nose, out through the mouth! What are you doing out here?!"

"What- ugh..." Zack fought off another round of nausea. "What happened?"

"I don't know, the whole office was in flames when we got here!" Sarah said, panicked.

"Crap, hey, you alright man?" John said, running over putting a had on his shoulder.

"I'm fine, I just got out too quick," Zack said, rocking on his knees.

"We need to get you home, you're not well." Sarah helped steady him on his feet.

"Yeah, let's go man," John said, steadying him from the other side.

"What about the office?" Zack asked.

"It's already gone man...." John said, guiding him back to the truck. Zack looked back at the office as the flames billowed into the sky. Daniel and Rose were helping the volunteers roll out a hose.

John drove them back to Zack's house and Sarah helped him into bed. She took his temperature, and gave him more water.

"How are you feeling? Any confusion, headaches, dizziness?" Sarah asked, rubbing his hair.

"Yeah, a little bit," Zack said, leaning his head into her hand.

"You sure you just don't want me to baby you?" She said,

smiling at him.

"Heh, that too. But I feel pretty garbage actually."

"How's he feeling?" John asked, walking into Zack's room.

"Pretty garbage," Sarah answered for him.

"Yeah I bet...." John said, sitting down in a folding chair.

"You know how scared John was when he got to the office?" Sarah asked. "I thought for sure he was gonna cry."

"Yeah, well, that's my bro right there," John said.

"Thanks bro," Zack said.

"You two are adorable." Sarah shook her head smiling. "You make a great couple."

John was quiet for a bit, bouncing his knee. He seemed to be a little antsy, not exactly scowling, but not looking like he was in a joking mood either.

"Crap I forgot the chickens since you're all concussed and stuff," John said, getting up from his chair. He took a step to the door, then rocked on his feet. He dug a small box out of his jacket pocket.

"Hey, uh, last night you left your jacket at the bar. I put it up already, but this was in the pocket, I figured you would want to know where it was."

John slipped the black fuzzy box underneath his hand. He walked out the door and shut it behind him. Zack flipped it open with one hand, and sure enough the ring was still inside. Zack shut the box and set it next to his hip and shut his eyes, preparing for sleep.

"Do you want to talk about it?" Sarah asked quietly. Zack looked at her to see that she was playing with a tiny piece of the bed sheet. "If you don't feel well we can talk about it later, I'm sorry."

Zack sighed. "...What did I do wrong?"

"You didn-..." Sarah sighed as well, her hands lifting only to drop heavy on the mattress. "You didn't do anything wrong it's not like-"

Sarah frustratingly couldn't find the words to describe what she thought.

"Well then, why didn't you say yes?"

"Because...." Sarah said. "You know, we take everything at my pace. With the wedding and the engagement and... other stuff...." Sarah fidgeted. "I just, I want this to be something that you want, because you want it not because I want it."

"Would you rather I say I didn't want to get married, and demand 'other stuff' from you? Or are you thinking I only want to marry you for *those* reasons?" Zack asked, confused.

"No that's not- ehh~ it's neither...." She said, standing up, pacing around the bedroom. "What would you say if I told you that I wanted to move to Portland?"

"Are you thinking about moving to Portland?" Zack asked, sitting up to the edge of the bed.

Sarah looked down and shrugged her shoulders. "...Maybe."

"Then I would go with you, if I can. I could ask for a transfer."

"I know you would. And that's why I can't say yes." She scoffed, looking at the walls now.

"What? Why?" Zack asked, becoming frustrated.

"BECAUSE IT'S NEVER ABOUT YOU!!" Sarah shouted at him. "IT'S ALWAYS ME!! ALWAYS!!"

Sarah shook and tried to breathe for a moment. Zack didn't say anything, he could feel there was more for her to let out.

"Everyday it's always been like that, you know? It's like you don't make any choice ever because you think there's never a choice to make. 'I'm in S.W.O.R.D. and I have GSA so everything is decided for me.' You are such a- such a... soldier! And here we are, about to make one of the biggest choices of our lives, and you're putting it entirely on me! Zack, I want to try different things, I want to go different places, I want to save lives, I want to live and have all sorts of different experiences, I want to do things that maybe I'm nervous to try and find out that some part of me really likes it! And I want you, but, Zack! ...The only thing you seem to want is me... and it's just too much pressure!" Sarah stood there looking at him with tears of frustration in her eyes.

"I'm sorry if I hurt you, but I can't be the only thing in your life that matters for you. I can't LIVE for you," she said, chopping her hand around. "I don't want you to be an extension of me, I want you to be you. Until you know who that is... I can't marry you...."

"So that's it then...." Zack looked at his wooden floor, then laid back on the bed, not even able to get mad. Sarah came over and got on her knees next to the bed.

"I love you, Zack. I want to marry you. But I want us both to be able to have happiness in other things too! I don't want us to be married and ten years down the road and then we start to find out we are the people we wanted each other to be," Sarah tried to explain almost in a whisper. "You can see that right?"

THUMP THUMP THUMP

"Hey, we got problems," John said, house phone in hand.

"What's wrong?" Zack looked over at him; he looked worried.

"S.W.O.R.D. is on their way down here." John sighed. "They ain't happy...."

5. HAPPILY EVER AFTER

Zack walked up the concrete steps of the old brick library, which was probably the best looking pre-fallout building left in town. The bottom half was a community center where S.W.O.R.D. had set up their base of operations. It was the busiest Zack had ever seen it; there were several people in uniforms in the entryway, along with Rose and Daniel.

"There's more of them then I thought there would be," Zack said.

"Apparently this isn't the first time something like this has happened. S.W.O.R.D.'s getting pissed," Rose said.

"They've been mostly quiet so far," Daniel added. "I think that stresses me out more though."

"Yeah...." Rose said.

Zack turned to see John coming up with a carrier of coffee.

"Morning, who wants coffee?" John said, handing out coffee.

"Me, please. I didn't sleep at all last night," Rose answered.

"Yeah, me either..." John said. "You feeling okay man?"

"I'm feeling better. My throat is a little sore," Zack answered.

"Well, I'd make a joke here, but you gotta take it easy for a while...." John smirked.

"Hah, I think that HELPS with a sore throat," Daniel corrected, getting the joke John had in mind.

Rose gave him a dirty look.

"Yeah, yeah. How bad you guys think it'll be this time?" Zack asked.

"Eh, it can't be worse than the fall out after the farming

riots." John shrugged.

"Ugh, I don't want to remember that...." Rose reached out to hold Daniel's hand.

"Me either, babe...." Daniel kissed her head.

"Zackary Taylor? We're ready for your blood work." An older nurse said.

Zack followed the nurse to a room downstairs and they turned into a small room fashioned out of one of the rooms they gave state exams out of. Rather than the typical row of desks facing the wall there was an examination table and other medical equipment. When Sarah finished her time under Wilkins, she'd take a test here.

Or would have anyway.

They drew some of Zack's blood, then left him sitting there maybe half an hour until a S.W.O.R.D. doctor came in to give him an exam. Then he was left waiting again. Zack stared out the tiny window at the very top of the wall.

This was a test he couldn't do anything about, but he was trying not to panic about the results. Sarah would be freaking out about her test results, she didn't handle tests well.

...There was a silver lining, I guess.

"Operative Taylor? They're ready for you in B104." The old nurse said, peeking into the room.

"Thanks."

Zack walked down the short hallway, passing John and a S.W.O.R.D. official leaving. John was chewing his cheek, something he only did when he was upset, and he didn't seem to notice Zack at all.

"Well that can't be good...." Zack mumbled to himself as he walked down the hallway. He walked into the conference room.

At the table there was a man he hadn't seen before along with....

"Well I'll be damned," Zack said, taking his seat, not being able to hide a smile seeing his old Commanding Officer again. "If it isn't Lady Leather herself."

"Good to see that junk you got all over you didn't end up killing you," Lydia said with a smile back. "You feeling okay kiddo?"

"Well, I'm still alive and kicking. For now at least. What about you? How's the desk job?" Zack asked. Lydia didn't really do much field work anymore.

"Literally killing me." She groaned. "I think I've killed more trees than people at this point."

"Speaking of death, from what we've seen from your blood work, you'll be alive and kicking for some time yet, Mr. Taylor." Said the man, as he flipped through a few papers.

"Huh." Zack said surprised. "Is that right?"

"Looks that way." The man said, still looking at his paperwork. "Most people exposed to the same poison as you have needed to be hospitalized." He finally put down his papers and looked at Zack.

"Oh, right, I'm Dr. Higgins. I've been researching these incidences from a medical standpoint. I'm also the leading officer for this investigation," Higgins added.

"Ahh. So your the one doing all the evaluations." Zack nodded.

"Correct. Commander West, of course, was your instructor so she's been helping me with that," Higgins said.

"I needed a little country air anyway. Portland was wearing me out." Lydia stretched her neck.

"Since we have established that your physical health is all in check, the next step would be your mental health," Higgins said, closing his manilla envelope. "That's where your old CO comes in handy once again."

"That's right, we're going on a mission together," Lydia said. "Nothing major, just checking the area, see if we can't find a trail on Wilkins."

"Just like old times," Zack said.

"Well, I'll let you two get to it." Higgins got up from the table. "I promised to let Commander West handle your evaluation since I have other matters at hand."

Zack and Lydia followed suit. Lydia had a newer truck that S.W.O.R.D. had brought with them. Zack didn't see John or the others as they headed to the truck.

"Where did everyone else go?" He asked, hopping in the truck.

"Pfft. Probably all filling out paperwork. S.W.O.R.D. has a real hard on for documentation."

What paperwork would they have to fill out? Zack wondered. *You know what, don't care that much.*

"Hey." Lydia broke into Zack's thoughts as she got onto the road. "After this all blows over, we should all go out for pizza, my treat."

"What, did you finally get a raise?" Zack laughed.

"Ha. Ha. Even I miss my kids once in a while." Lydia rolled her eyes.

"But did you get a raise?"

"That's not important."

"Rose wants garlic knots."

"Rose has her own money."

"We missed you too, Commander Cheapskate."

"You know what? If you're all gonna be little smart mouths about it, you guys can treat me." Lydia pursed her lips.

"I'm just playing." Zack laughed. "So how is the big city? Portland is as big as it gets, isn't it?"

"Heh, it's at least three times bigger than Joliet, where you guys had evaluations, kid." Lydia nodded. "Though the city planner acts like it's nothing compared to the old cities like how L.A. or Chicago were before the fallout. I had to sit through this long stupid powerpoint about expansion funding a couple weeks ago."

"Why did you have to do that?"

"Because the drinks were free."

"Well good to see things never change." Zack laughed.

Lydia drove them to the next town over. Meeting with the local sheriff's department didn't lead much of anywhere. Asking some of the businesses in the area didn't unveil anything new either.

And when they finally got around to asking about Wilkins at a local tavern....

“Do you guys want another one?” The waitress asked, taking the empty pitcher.

“Hell yeah we do!” Lydia hollered.

“Hell no we don't!” Zack said, feeling a little sick. He couldn’t drink this soon after a hangover, he didn’t even finish one.

“C'mon! I thought you were supposed to be a big man now! You can't keep up with a lady a hundred-some pounds lighter than you?!” Lydia hollered.

“It's eighty pounds at the most. And while I might have some weight on you, I don't have the 40 years of liver pickling that you do,” Zack shot back at her.

“I'll have you know that I am only 36 you little punk!” Lydia exclaimed as she pulled out a cigarette. “You want one?”

“Nah, I quit. Sarah didn't like it.” Zack waved his hand. “You should quit too, you know? Those things give you cancer.”

“Okay, first off, everything will give you cancer. The food we grow can give you cancer. The water we drink will give you cancer. Took a wrong turn trying to get back to Joliet but instead end up a little too close to the giant crater that used to be Chicago? Better luck next time Jack, it's insta-cancer,” Lydia went off lighting up a cigarette, clearly sick of the 'you should quit' speech.

“Alright, alright....” Zack laughed, giving it up.

“I thought for sure you'd be a smoker for life when I caught you and John smoking behind the bar all those years ago.” Lydia said, shaking her head. Zack chuckled.

“I remember you gave us the crappiest 'Don't smoke' speech ever!” Zack said, thinking back to that day.

“It's not my fault you were such a little smart aleck.... I couldn't think of a good argument.” Lydia glared at him.

“I remember that you only caught us because you were going back there to smoke too.” Zack chuckled. “Rose gave us a better chewing out than you did."

"Rose always was a mother hen," Lydia said, smiling. They sat there a moment, happily reflecting on the past.

"How has everybody been doing with practice and everything?" Lydia asked, blowing out smoke.

"Not too bad, though without you there to watch us Daniel and Rose have gotten a little lazy," Zack said.

"Well they're young and in love," Lydia said. "Speaking of which, how about you and Sarah?

Zack spun the empty glass in front of him. "We are having a bit of a rough patch actually...."

Lydia let that sit in the air for a moment while she smoked.

"A rough patch?" She asked.

"Yeah, it's-" Zack sighed for a moment. "She started asking me about marriage the other day, and I love her so THAT day I proposed, cause I don't know how these things work. She ended up getting real mad and saying no. Then all this crap with Wilkins happened and we had another kind of fight about it."

"What did she say?" Lydia nodded along with the story.

"She said: 'I can't live for you' and said stuff about me not really having anything I want other than her and that's too much pressure...." Zack explained, flicking the glass.

"Well... what do you want, Zack?" Lydia asked.

"I- you know what it is?" Zack said, coming to a realization. "I just want to be happy, you know? I'm a soldier, born with GSA, forced into S.W.O.R.D., there's no way for me to change that. I'm stuck with that, I'm not gonna get to have a fulfilling career, so all I want is to be happy, that's really all I want. A little house, a loving wife and partner, good friends and a peaceful, happy life.... Do I have to have anything else? Am I a jerk for not having some goal?"

"Kid, sometimes I worry I made you exactly like me...." Lydia finished her drink, a melancholic look in her eyes. "And I have no idea."

"Anyway, S.W.O.R.D.'s gonna be pissed if we come back

drunk," he said, rubbing his face. "Actually, did we even do anything for you to evaluate me for?"

"Eh, you're fine." Lydia flipped her wrist.

"How did you get promoted again?" Zack asked.

"I asked enough times." Lydia stood up to stretch. "Oh God... I don't want to go back...."

"Is your job really that bad?" Zack got up as well, and threw some cash on the table.

"Zack, you have no idea how hard my job gets some days," she said with a heavy sigh.

"Do you need me to drive?" He asked, noticing the heavy way she stepped.

"Oh yeah, God forbid I drive this truck the eight miles back home in this 5 o'clock traffic!" She said, rolling her eyes before turning her head to him. "I mean hell, we could pass TWO tractors!"

"And Rose asks me why I'm always a smart aleck...." Zack said giving her a tired 'you're so funny' glare.

"Well you did learn from the best," she said, hopping in the truck.

Except for the occasional swear every time Lydia hit a pothole and almost sent them into a field, it was a typical drive home. Lydia took a side road that wasn't exactly a short cut, supposedly to get to the library faster.

"How long did you live around here? We added five minutes just to get in the back way to the library," Zack pointed out.

"Well, Jesus, cut me some slack, it's been a while." Lydia sat in the truck and drummed on the wheel for a second. "Hey, Zack?"

"Yeah?"

"I love you kiddo."

"Wow, I didn't think you were that wasted." Zack shook his head.

"Screw you, I'm serious."

"Alright, alright..." Zack put his hands up. "Love you too,

Commander."

Zack hopped out of the truck and started up the steps of the library. He pulled on the door only to realize it was now locked, and the lights were off.

"Hey, were we supposed to meet back here? It's locked, and the lights are off," Zack asked Lydia, who was at the bottom of the steps.

"It shouldn't be...." Lydia stopped at the start of the steps.

Zack heard someone's yelling gently dying on the wind. He turned around. It sounded like it came from the center of town.

"Did you hear that?" Zack asked.

"Eh, it's probably nothing, some townies probably getting in a fight," Lydia quickly explained. Zack hopped from the top of the stairs, getting around the library so he could see. A crowd was gathered in the distance, but he couldn't tell why.

"Hey, there is a big crowd...." Zack started to feel uneasy. He turned back to look at Lydia again. She didn't say anything this time, but her expression was not reassuring.

Unsure of what was happening, unclear about Lydia's expression, and suddenly suspicious about being taken away on a slapdash mission, turned Zack's uneasiness into terror. He ran towards the crowd.

"Zack!" Lydia called as the wind roared by his ears. "God da-, ZACK!"

It only took him a couple of seconds to get close enough to reveal what the crowd was staring at. The tightness in his chest made it feel as if his lungs were being shoved into his stomach. Right in the center of the street was a gallows pole.

"Zack!!" Lydia yelled, trying to catch him. She was still behind him, but her yelling got Daniel and Rose's attention who quickly cut Zack off.

"Zack! What are you doing back?" Rose said, stopping in front of him, as Daniel came to his side.

"Rose wh-, wait where's John?" Zack's voice broke as he struggled to hold on to a single thought.

"I'm right here! I thought you were supposed to be on assignment," John answered, also jogging over.

"Okay, you guys, Lydia, where's Sarah?" Zack started a head count.

"God dang it, Zack!" Lydia came up behind him, bending over to catch her breath.

"Sarah's back at my house with mom! We didn't want them all seeing this, but, you know, we are on duty, and stuff!" Rose gave a smile, waving her hand. Zack felt like he could breathe again.

"Okay, hoooo...." Zack bent over as well. "Thank God!"

"Here, let's get out of this crowd and we'll explain," John said, motioning the way he came.

"That's a good idea. You can barely hear anything in here," Daniel said, placing a hand on Zack's shoulder.

"May I have everyone's attention please," a voice from the podium announced. Zack looked up to see Dr. Higgins standing next to the gallows. "We are ready to proceed."

"God damn you, Higgins," Lydia mumbled.

"Zack, come on, I don't want to see this," John said, placing a hand on the inside of his friend's elbow.

"Wait, who's getting hanged?" Zack said, looking towards the podium. Daniel quickly stepped into his view.

"It's nobody; one of the old drunks got caught stealing from S.W.O.R.D.," he said, putting his hands on Zack's shoulders, turning him gently. Rose also placed a hand on his stomach.

"Let's go, these things always make me sick," Rose said, pushing on him as well.

"What are you guys pushing me for?" Zack said, brushing his friends' hands off of him.

"For the crime of treason against the king..."

Zack looked over the crowd to see several familiar looking women being dragged onto the stage.

A girl with dark brown hair and tears running down her cheeks was among them.

No....

"Sarah...." Zack's body locked up, his heart pounding out of his chest.

"...All employees of Dr. Wilkins' office are sentenced to death by hanging."

"NO!"

Zack tried to rush the gallows, but John and Daniel held his arms tightly.

"LET GO OF ME!"

Blood tinted his vision red as his heart-rate soared. Every muscle in his body burned as he drug his friends toward the gallows.

A commotion began near the gallows as well. Zack was able to see some people pushing up against the soldiers, families of the soon-to-be-executed. Higgins gave some kind of order, and the soldiers shoved the crowd back before opening fire.

Screams erupted as people either fled or fell. Zack was able to see Ms. Evans as the people she had been pushing the soldiers with fell around her. Already shot in the gut, she was only able to give one final longing look to her daughter, before another spray of bullets riddled her front half. At such close range, rifle rounds tore chunks of her apart, rendering her body unrecognizable in less than a second. Only a pulpy mass hit the ground. Zack slipped, losing strength as he witnessed the massacre.

"GOD DAMN YOU, HIGGINS!" Lydia screamed through the chaos as she ran up to the gallows herself.

"Oh God, Zack, don't look...!" Rose came up to block his view.

The last thing he saw was Sarah weeping before they roughly jammed a black bag over her face. Rose wrapped herself around Zack's face as he screamed into her, unable to even stand up with Daniel and John clinging to him.

The commotion died enough around him to hear the sickening sound of wood on hinges dropping, and ropes going taut.

He screamed. He kicked, and shook as hard as he could. He still had time.

Then a minute passed.

Then five.

Then ten.

His muscles begged him to stop, but he couldn't, wouldn't. There were no words, not in his head or the air or his screams. It was at least half an hour before he finally broke free from John and Daniel. Rose hugged his face as tight as she could but he shoved her away too.

Almost everyone was gone. Zack staggered towards the gallows, his body at its limits. He climbed the steps as two soldiers hesitantly moved to intercept him. Lydia shouted something, and they got out of his way.

Zack got to where Sarah was swinging before he collapsed. She swung lifelessly in the middle of the rest of her coworkers. As gently as he could, he lifted her up in his arms. Wrapping the rope she was attached to around his arm, he began to tug it with all his might.

Someone tried saying something as he pulled, but he couldn't hear them. The only sound he heard was the cracking of the wooden gallows. The cracking grew louder and louder, until Zack snapped the gallows in half. The beams holding up the bodies collapsed in a violent crash.

Zack freed Sarah's neck from the noose. Everyone gave him a wide berth as he carried her body away.

6. REVERENCE

"Zack."

Zack woke to a gentle shaking. For the second time this week, he saw Rose was kneeling over him.

"Are you okay?" She asked, her hand still on his shoulder. He flipped onto his back, the sun just starting to peek through the shade of the windbreak in the field near his home.

"Here." Lydia stood above him, handing him a bottle of water. He took it as he slid up to lean on the tree he was under. "John took the shovel that was out here back to the house."

Zack nodded.

"...There is uh... evaluation thing coming up. In about two weeks," Daniel started.

"Next Monday, not this one coming up," Lydia continued.

"They want us on the train by Friday. There's one leaving Wednesday too, whatever works best...." Daniel finished.

Zack nodded. Drank his water.

"Mr. Pence called us, said you were out here digging when he got home. He promised he wouldn't disturb the grave. He thought it might make Sarah happy to know that-"

"Don't," Zack cut off Daniel.

"...I'm sorry."

The early morning air left everything glistening with dew. There must have been some fog earlier.

John finally made it back to the rest of the group.

"Please say something...." Rose finally squeaked.

Zack got up and started walking to his house.

"There was nothing you could have done, Zack. You would have gotten yourself killed," Lydia said.

Zack kept walking.

"Hey!"

Zack kept walking. Lydia caught up and got in front of him.

"Would you *listen* to me?!"

Zack stopped for a moment.

"I..." Lydia huffed for a moment.

Then she couldn't look him in the eye.

"...I'm sorry."

Zack stepped around her, and headed to his house.

He showered, as hot as he could stand it. He put on fresh underwear, shorts, and crawled into bed. He trapped himself in the mix memories and nightmares sleep allowed.

Suddenly, there was a boy. It was dark. He's sore, calloused. Chores were done, he's exhausted, but he waited on the porch. Mom had been gone a long time. It was getting darker.

Don't make me go inside. *The house grew bigger.*

Mom's not coming back... Don't make me go inside... Mom, there's a monster inside. *The house grew bigger.* Mom, please come back, I'm sorry!

DON'T MAKE ME GO INSIDE!

Zack's eyes ripped open, his heart racing. He sat up looking around the room. There was food sitting over by the door to the bedroom, and it was still daylight outside.

Zack took a deep breath, and tried to settle down. The clock by his bed said six thirty-seven. He lay back on the damp sheets and stared at the ceiling. He could hear murmurs and movement below him in the living room.

For the next few hours, he watched the light slowly fade out of the room until sleep overtook him again.

Boy's body didn't fit. Masses screamed, starving.

He started to fall into them. They pulled him apart as he fell. It didn't hurt though; his body didn't fit anyway.

He fell faster and faster, they ripped off more and more! The teeth ripped away his face, nails peeled off his arms and legs in strings. Sarah's strangled purple face engulfed his vision, screaming in agony.

Zack awoke, swinging his arms violently. He slammed back into the bed screeching into his pillow. Sleep no longer existed.

* * *

Zack got about halfway down the stairs to see everyone besides Daniel was in his living room. The TV was playing gently as he descended. When he hit one of the creakier steps Rose's head whipped around and she quickly got out of the rocking chair he had.

"Hey," she said, wringing her hands in front of her. "You're up."

Zack looked down to see John asleep in a sleeping bag on the floor and Lydia was passed out with a T-shirt over her eyes on his couch.

"Daniel went home to shower, he'll be back soon," Rose said as Zack walked past her. Rose followed him into the kitchen.

"Are you hungry?" Rose asked. "I could make breakfast, whatever you want."

Zack grabbed a cup and filled it with water.

"I- well we, but, um..." she shook her hands. "Heard you... a couple times."

Zack set the cup in the sink after drinking the water. He leaned on it for support.

"If you want to talk about anything, I'll listen! Whatever you want! Anything you want! It's totally fine and...!"

Zack started back towards the living room.

"Zack, PLEASE!" Rose grabbed his hand, spinning him around and forcing him to look at her. She held his hand between both of hers, close to her lips bridging their eyes.

"Please say something. Yell at me. Cry. Make any noise at

all...." Rose's eyes filled with tears.

"Go home."

Not strong enough to put any emphasis behind his words anymore, he must have sounded as dead as he felt. Rose started to shake a little bit. Then tears rolled down her withered cheeks. Her sobs, choked and squeaked, whispered in the kitchen. She squeezed his hand as hard as she could, but he couldn't squeeze back. She fell to her knees in front of him, holding his hand. Then released him, to cry into her own.

Zack turned and walked into the living room. He stopped for a second to look at Lydia. She was sleeping in the fetal position, hugging herself tightly.

He turned to see John asleep on the floor. He was lying on the sleeping bag he always used when they went hunting.

Zack walked up the stairs quietly. He sat heavily on his bed, feeling sick in every part of his body. His eyes were raw and stuck to his eyelids. He had no energy because he hadn't eaten in a few days, but he felt too sick to eat. His skin felt sore, like it had been pulled or burned. He missed Sarah so much....

Everyone around him was suffering because of him. He loved his friends; these were the only people he had in his life.

But at the same time, he absolutely hated them. They weren't responsible for Sarah, not really. Yet he blamed them even more than S.W.O.R.D. If they had told him beforehand....

At least he wouldn't have had to watch her die... at least he could have died protecting her....

Everything was wrong.

He looked round the room again when his eyes settled on the metal cabinet in his closet. His eyes stared emptily at the grey doors. For a few moments his mind was finally quiet. For the first time in days his mind didn't buzz and hum like an overworked machine. He could feel his brain cool down as his thoughts slowed their violent thrashing inside of his head. It only lasted a short while though, then it seemed like the tornado of emotion in his heart changed direction and started spinning the other way.

Zack stood and crept over to the cabinet. The key was already in the lock so he just pulled open the door slow, which made the door creak loudly.

There were two rifles, a shotgun and his Diesel in a zipped up case. He pulled it out and sat back down on his bed. He unzipped the triangle case and bent the top back. The metal was a little worn, with scratches along the slide, but it was still in pretty good condition.

Zack remembered the first time this gun was put in his hand. The GSA did part of their training in boot camp. A short gruff man with a perfectly groomed mustache put the Desert Eagle .50 in front of him and a dozen other GSA on a firing line. At thirteen, Zack and everyone else in the GSA were already bigger than the average soldier. According to the Ranger in front of them Zack and the rest of the GSA were breathing walking tanks.

And tanks ran on diesel, hence the nickname.

After camp Zack, Daniel, Rose and John became IN-14 led by their non-GSA Commanding officer: Lydia. That was six years ago now... this gun had been an extension of him all these years. He'd fired it thousands of times.

...And now, he wanted to fire it one last time....

Zack slid the clip into the gun. It stuck a little bit. He pushed it a little harder and it snapped into place with a clack. He used his thumb to release the slide, loading a round in the chamber.

Zack's head jumped towards his open door, worried that they might hear him downstairs. He was still for a moment watching the door, one part of him hoping that in that moment someone would come check on him. Another part prayed that no one would see him like this, like it would be embarrassing for his friends to know he was thinking about killing himself.

He slowly placed the cool metal barrel against his cheek, rubbing it for a moment. Then he inched it up slowly to his temple.

Was this what he really wanted? For everything to just

stop? There was no going back after this. He couldn't be sure what was on the other side either. Maybe there was nothing at all. Or maybe fire and brimstone for the rest of eternity. Or maybe, if there was an afterlife, and there was any kind of charity in this universe he could see Sarah again. Maybe they would have a chance to 'live' the life that they were supposed to have.

Or maybe Zack deserved all this. Maybe Hell was where killers and monsters were supposed to go. Maybe it was finally time to face the music.

Zack felt himself start to cry again. His hands shook as his arm started to tremble. He took a deep breath, trying to settle down, but he just shook harder.

I don't want this. Not like this.

Zack leaned back and pushed his arm back behind his head, stretching his muscles out. His hand had been squeezing the handle so tightly his whole arm was flexed. He was pretty dehydrated as well, which was making him feel like he was about to cramp.

Zack thought it over one last time. This could be a chance to see Sarah again, to never feel pain ever again. Zack exhaled, shaking his head, as he brought the gun down.

But the way he brought the gun down he bumped it with his head...

And his finger twitched...

BANG!

7. I FEEL A LOT BETTER

Zack flinched forward as he felt something graze his head, a bang deafening him. There was a deep, constant ring in his ears as his eyes widened, staring at the floor, gun still in hand. He jerked up straight and used his free hand to feel the back of his head. At about his crown he felt warm blood on his hand. His hand twitched back a little, then moved in to feel the gash. He felt his bare skull, coarse like a wet brick.

Zack barely heard someone say his name through the ringing. Then felt the tremors in the floor as people stormed up his stairs. John and Rose appeared in the doorway, Zack meeting their blood soaked eyes. John tackled him on the bed, grabbing his arm with the gun so hard Zack thought he might dislocate his wrist. Rose was instantly on top of his free arm, jamming her knee into the inside of his elbow. Her hands shot to his head and began to jerk him around until she found his wound. With his head tilted he could see Lydia run into the room next, still disoriented.

Zack vaguely heard John yelling something along the lines of 'Drop it'. He let his hand relax and felt someone besides John pull the gun out of his hand. The way his neck was craned he could see Lydia fumble his gun with shaky hands. She popped the clip out and cleared the chamber, then turned to Zack. John repositioned himself to look at Zack's wound as well, mumbling something he couldn't understand through the ringing. Rose mumbled something back, before pushing Zack's head back to look into his eyes.

"What were you thinking?!?!"

Being able to see her lips helped. He could see Rose's eyes

soaked with blood and tears. He could see the way her lips trembled as if it was taking everything out of her not to sob.

He could see John leaning back on the bed pulling his hair back with his hands, trying to keep from crying himself. Lydia fumbling as her mind frantically searched for a way to help, but all she could do was stand there, panicking and feeling useless.

Zack couldn't find the words. Maybe shock put things into perspective, let him see something other than his own pain.

It hit him how much pain the people he loved were in as well.

"I'm sorry...." Zack started to cry too. "I'm- I'm so sorry...."

Rose's face scrunched up right before she fell into his chest sobbing. John moved and hugged both of them as his own chest started to shake and Lydia held onto his legs.

"I think..." Zack took a deep breath, getting control of himself. "I think I would like breakfast. And a shower."

* * *

Zack sat on the toilet in fresh clothes, as John bandaged his head.

"We could cut your hair, it would make this a little easier," John said, trying to get the tape to stick.

"Sarah cut my hair a little while ago," Zack said, playing with the edge of his shirt.

John was quiet for a moment. "Well, it helps hide this at least...."

John finished up and they walked down stairs. The thick smell of breakfast brought the first feeling of hunger in days. Daniel was moving around the table as they approached the kitchen; he must have made it back.

"Hey!" Rose said, over the stove cooking bacon while Lydia and Daniel set the table. "You feel better?"

"Yeah, my ears are still ringing a bit," Zack said, sitting down.

"You get it all wrapped up?" Lydia asked, walking over to

John.

"Yeah." John handed her Zack's first aid kit.

Lydia put it back in the cabinet.

"...I'm sorry," Zack said, after everyone was quiet for a few seconds.

"Do you wanna talk about it?" Daniel asked, sitting at the spot next to him.

"I don't know what to say..." Zack shrugged.

"You know we all love you, right?" Lydia said, hugging him from behind. "Please if you thinking anything like this, talk to us. We just don't want you hurt."

"I know," Zack said wearily. "I'm sorry for... everything."

"I'm sorry too...." Lydia whispered.

"Breakfast is ready!" Rose said, setting down a large platter of scrambled eggs and bacon.

Eating together with everyone, just being in their presence, did wonders for his mental health. Filling his stomach also made a world of difference, as if each bite brought him a little closer to life.

"Not to put any pressure on anybody but we need to start heading to Portland for evaluations here soon."

"How long does it take to get there again?" Rose asked, picking up the plates.

"Well, it'll take 32 hours to get there on the train from Joliet. It takes us about 4 hours to get to Joliet. So, the latest we can leave and get set up in our hotel is tomorrow night." Daniel sighed as Rose came back from the sink, drying her hands off with a towel.

"Do you think we could leave today?" Zack asked, scratching at his placemat. Everyone turned to look at him.

"Are you sure you want to leave this quick?" John said.

"Yeah, I, uh... I think it would be good to get away from here for a little bit," Zack said, rubbing his neck.

"Well, I can call ahead and see when today's train leaves. S.W.O.R.D has had all stations reserve one train for a direct trip to the capital this week," Daniel said, running his hands through his hair. "Can everyone get packed in time?"

"Yeah, I'm good," John said. "If you want, I can call the Hoosier boys to watch the house," he added turning to Zack. Zack nodded.

"I just need to pack," Rose said.

"It's fine with me," said Lydia.

"Alright, great. We can get there a day early, and don't have to worry about any mishaps," Daniel said.

The set up of the trip didn't take long. John stuck right by Zack and went with him to grab clothes and set up the house-sitters. Everyone seemed to have come to the conclusion that Zack wasn't really supposed to be left alone for a while. They wouldn't let him carry his gun or knife either. Zack didn't bother to protest; it was probably for the best anyway.

On the drive to Joliet they went over their old numbers from last year's evaluations. Zack zoned out for the most part, though. While he *was* feeling better, his mind was still kind of foggy.

When they got to the train station they were able to make it onto a late-leaving train for the capital. The first thing they did was get set up in the overnight cars. Lydia had a separate officer cabin so she went off without the rest of them.

"You guys hungry? I think I might go to the food car," John said.

"It's called the dining car?" Rose said, raising an eyebrow.

"I just drove all that way so I'm taking a nap," Daniel said, stretching out on one of the beds.

"Oh, a nap sounds so good...." Rose sighed.

"You know, the diner might not be open until tomorrow, it's already five," Zack said, thinking out loud.

"Oh, for Pete's sake. We missed lunch?" John looked like he might cry. "Why don't we ever fly?!?"

"Oh yeah, Moneybags? Have you been saving your entire pay for the last two years so we could afford five plane tickets?" Daniel asked.

"Not really. Your mom is hella expensive," John said.

"O-kay, no gross talk about people's moms please," Rose said.

"Relax, man. The lounge car should be open. They'll have bar food. I could go for some pretzels," Zack said, stretching out his back.

"Yeah, that'll work," John said, his mood instantly improving. "Alright, Zack and me will be at the bar. We'll leave you two to your hanky-panky."

"Oh my God, we're not gonna do that!" Rose said, flustered.

"Mhm, just remember these cabin walls are thin so try to leave screaming to a minimum," John said as they walked out the door.

"EW! Get out of here!" Rose said, throwing a pair of socks at him.

Zack and John walked down the cars until they reached the warmly lit lounge car, attempting to give it the feel of a restaurant. They got a bowl of nuts, pretzels, and a couple of beers and sat in a grouping of leather chairs by the window. They were halfway through their beers when Zack noticed two kids walk into the car looking lost.

"Hey." Zack caught John's gaze and nodded towards the kids. John slowly looked around the cabin, making it seem like he wasn't looking at them.

"Must be some newbies. They look about thirteen," John said, drinking his beer.

"First time on the train is always the coolest," Zack said, grabbing another pretzel. The first kid looked around pleadingly, until his eyes landed on Zack. Zack pointed at the kid, then made an "okay" sign with his hand while raising an eyebrow. The kid tapped his friend and walked over to John and Zack.

"Hi, excuse me, um, do they have food on the train?" The kid asked.

"Help yourself," John said, motioning to the bowls.

"The dining car will open up in the morning," Zack said. "It's just bar food 'til then."

"Oh okay," the kid said, looking relieved. "We thought that there wasn't any for a minute, and we were supposed to pack food."

John laughed. "No, there's food. First time heading to Portland, I take it?"

"Uh, yeah," the second kid said as they both sat down. "We're going for our first evaluation."

"Are you guys...?" The first kid trailed off.

"Yep," Zack said, knowing that he was referring to S.W.O.R.D. operatives. "Zackary Taylor, GSA, IN-14."

"John Henagar, GSA, IN-14 as well," John said, waving his hand.

"James Allen," said the shorter one with freckles.

"Evan Jones," said the taller, tanner one. "I'm not sure about anything else...."

"If this is your first time going in for evaluation you'll be unclassified until you meet standards," Zack said.

"Basically, you go pass an easy test then they'll give you a code off your state and a number that means... something...." John finished.

"Oh okay," James said, seeming more relieved. "Our instructor doesn't really tell us these things."

"Well, grab a beer and allow your upper class-men to enlighten you," John said with his typical grandeur.

The kids paused, looking at each other for a moment.

"...They let you have beer here?" Evan asked slowly.

"Yeah?" John said, raising an eyebrow.

"They said you have to be eighteen back home," James said.

"Ahh," Zack said. "Yeah, after you get thrown into a war zone that doesn't apply anymore."

"'If you're old enough to be out here when people are trying to stab you with pitchforks you're old enough to drink dammit!'" John exclaimed. "At least that was what one of the officers told us after crap went down in Texas during the food riots."

"You guys were there for that?" Evan asked. "Our CO said that was *the* moment the GSA was taken seriously!"

"Yeah, that's one way to put it...." Zack nodded.

"It's not a great memory...." John shook his hand, dismissing the subject. "Tell you what, first beer is on us. We will get you set up on the right foot," John said, tapping Zack on the arm. Zack got up and followed John to the bar.

"Nice kids," John said as they walked up.

"Yeah. You remember your first beer?" Zack said. "Two Milwaukees please."

"Seven even," the bartender replied.

John tossed the money on the bar. "Whoa." John said suddenly. "Hottie incoming."

Zack looked up at John, then turned to see who he was referring too. He locked eyes with a shorter woman in black business attire.

Her short blonde hair was pulled back into a bun.

She quickly exited the car.

"Ouh... she got one look at me and ran out of here," John said with a sigh. "Hey, I gotta piss, you okay to hang out with the kids a few minutes?"

"Yeah... no problem," Zack said, turning back to the bar.

Was that...?

John slapped Zack on the shoulder and headed to the bathroom. The bartender came back over and handed Zack the beers. Zack went back over to the kids and handed them out.

"Hey, thanks!" Evan said. "Is everything okay?"

Zack was silent for just a second.

I'm on a train heading to be evaluated by the people who had murdered the love of my life... I tried to kill myself less than twelve hours ago... and I suddenly remember that there was a woman claiming to be from S.W.O.R.D that brought this whole mess to his doorstep that I had totally forgotten about until I saw her on this train... No, everything is not okay.

"Yeah, everything's fine," he lied. "I'll be right back."

"O-okay."

Zack hurried out of the cabin after the woman, barely catching a glimpse of her as she hurried down the hallway. At one point she turned around to shut one of the car doors, looked up, and saw him two cars away. She quickly continued through the cars.

Zack felt heat rise throughout his body, as his vision got sharper and his eyes swelled with blood. He started throwing open the car doors to the surprise of the occasional passenger. The woman made it to the caboose, and began talking frantically. He was halfway through the car preceding the caboose when two men sprung out of their seats in front of him, pulling guns.

"Don't move," one of them said with a slight accent. Zack stopped his advance, mentally kicking himself for being caught off guard. He sensed movement behind him as well. He turned his head slightly to see two more men get up, guns in hand.

"Why don't you take a couple deep breaths mate?" The other man in the front said in a thicker accent. "You could make a fella nervous with all that blood in your eyes."

Zack stayed still for a moment, thinking. The gun the short guy in front of him had was a five-seven. If it had steel point rounds that could kill Zack pretty quick from this range. He had rushed off, not thinking at all a moment ago, but now he needed to use his brain. He quickly realized he probably seemed weird to the kids that he left in the lounge car, and John would try to find him pretty quick. Zack took a deep breath and put his hands up.

The man in front of Zack gave a nod and two other men got up from their seats and started to pat him down.

"He's got nothin'," one of them said, releasing him. "We're clear."

The caboose opened up and two older men walked into the car with the woman Zack had been chasing. The shorter, darker man came up first looking over Zack but keeping a little distance.

"Hello!" He eventually said with a little nod.

"...Hey."

"How are you feeling?" The man asked.

"I-" Zack let his hands drop. "What?"

"How are you feeling?" The man continued. "Any headaches, migraines, trouble keeping food down?"

"Well, I'm not sure, but I think I may have had a stroke," Zack said, feeling crazy. "Because I just..." Zack pointed back to the other cabins. "Saw the lady responsible for getting my fiance killed. Then I chased her over here." Zack pointed to the ground. "Then I got jumped by two British guys."

"Irish actually," one of the gunmen said.

"Oh, well, my fricking mistake, *mate*," Zack said, imitating his accent. "Then a strange guy comes out of nowhere and asks me how. I'm. Feeling." Zack slapped the back of his hand onto the palm of his other hand. "So you know what? At this point I feel pretty insane!"

Without missing a beat, the doctor grabbed a small pack out of his coat.

"Do you smoke?" He asked. Zack grabbed at his head like it might explode.

"WHAT!?" Zack felt confident he had actually lost it. The man just stood there, holding out cigarettes. After staring at him for a moment Zack realized that the man was not going to elaborate or continue. Zack shrugged, looking at the ceiling, wondering if he was actually going crazy. Then, he slowly reached out a hand and grabbed a cigarette out of the man's pack.

"My name is Salim Koury. I'm a doctor," the man finally said. "I don't think you are having a stroke. You'd be showing a lot of physical symptoms. I don't know about insanity though."

"Okay...." Zack said, putting the cigarette in his mouth. Then he noticed that the man was not reaching for a lighter.

"This is my dear friend Micheal Harris. He leads this little group. The young girl back there is Olivia. That is Joshua and Brian. And back there are Timothy and Lucas," Salim said, pointing to the various positions. "We are planning to overthrow S.W.O.R.D. and we'd like your help."

Zack stood slack-jawed, staring at Salim, completely dumbfounded.

"Wait, what?" Olivia said, apparently also dumbstruck. She looked to the other older man, Micheal, who also appeared to not be in on this.

"Uh…." Micheal coughed and moved next to Salim. "Salim. We did not talk about this."

"Yes we did," Salim said, facing Micheal. "6 weeks ago you brought up the idea that we do not have the personnel within the ranks of S.W.O.R.D. to adequately track the movements of the royal family. His name is on the list of possible suitors, but you crossed him off because you didn't think he would have reason to turncoat. Now the love of his life was taken from him by S.W.O.R.D. officials and he has lost a reason to live. He's perfect."

"That's not a reason to tell him everything Salim!!" Olivia whisper-yelled, coming up behind him.

"And you just tell this guy everything and our real names?!?" One of the gunmen… Brian? Added.

"I-I'm sorry," Zack said, feeling the air around him with his hands. "Can you just, um, go through that again? I'm confused."

"Certainly. This is my dear friend Micheal Harris, he leads this little group. This young girl is Olivia. This is Joshua and Brian. And back there are Timothy and Lucas," Salim said, pointing to the various positions once again, completely monotone. "We are planning to overthrow S.W.O.R.D. and we'd like your help."

He just went through it again, Zack thought. He stood there completely out of place. He, just moments ago, came charging through, dead set on killing this Olivia woman, but now he could barely move.

"What, uh… did you want me to do?" Zack asked.

"Ideally, assassinate the King of the American State and several other high ranking members of S.W.O.R.D. and the Monarchy," Salim said without missing a beat.

“Oh well, at least it's nothing unreasonable. Would you like a cup of sugar too, neighbor?” Zack asked. Salim looked out of the corner of his eye, then turned towards Micheal.

“Why did he ask if I needed sugar?” Salim asked.

“It's like a play on words. He's insinuating that you are asking quite a lot from him using sarcasm,” Micheal explained, rubbing his temples.

“Ah.” Salim nodded, returning his attention to Zack. “I don't care for sarcasm, can you be blunt?”

“You just- you can't-” Zack found his frustration finally kicking in. “Two minutes ago, I was going to kill her!” Zack pointed with an open hand at Olivia. “Then you come out of nowhere, and ask me to kill the King of America?! First off, you don't just do that! That's not how you recruit someone into a gang, or a cult after talking to you! I mean I-I hate you! Do you realize what you have done to my life?! Do you even know?! I lost my-my Sarah because of you!! You walk into my home, bringing some kind of fricking ink monster, which almost killed me, by the way! Then they say that Sarah was in on it! Like it was her fault!! And they tired her and they hung her in the middle of town like she was some kind of fricking animal!!! Her mom, oh my God, her mother sees the whole thing, and she-she tries to stop it and they mowed her down! Right there! Right there in the-in the streets!! I had to bury her! I couldn't even take the sack off her head 'cause I didn't want to see her face all black and blue and swollen!! And now you want a favor from me?!?! SCREW YOU!!”

Zack finally finished his stammering, screaming, and spitting, and was out of breath so he looked at the man with crazy eyes, finally getting the rage out of his body. Salim was quiet as Zack caught his breath.

“You seem to think I personally, or us as a collective, are responsible for the death of Sarah who was important to you?” Salim asked in the same tone of voice.

“Wh- Yeah, I guess, that’s sort of it.” Zack nodded, trying not to let his head explode.

"Well we aren't at fault, but I apologize that you feel that way."

"Oh my fricking God...." Zack looked at the man holding a gun at him. "I know you literally have me at gun point here but are you serious with this?"

"Micheal, please...." The gunman even felt bad now.

"Salim, if you don't mind, can I take it from here?" Micheal said, tapping on Salim's shoulder.

"No, go ahead, recruit him for us, I was in the middle of a crossword puzzle," Salim sat in one of the seats.

Zack suddenly felt a very strong urge to cry.

Micheal now stepped up in front of Zack.

"Sorry, Salim doesn't excel in social situations," Micheal started. "He's a brilliant doctor, just not a big people person."

Zack stared at Micheal. He couldn't think of anything to say anymore.

"The people around you here, our little group, all of us have been wronged or lost loved ones because of S.W.O.R.D. I understand in this moment it's not what you want to hear, but all of us know you're pain. I know all too well the anger and hate you have inside you, please believe me when I tell you it is misplaced. S.W.O.R.D. killed your loved one, simply because they could; there was no reason to ever hurt her because that office was visited by us," Micheal said.

"I-" Zack was stunned. Everything about this situation was a migraine, but maybe he had a vague point. Zack laughed a bit at the absolute insanity storming around him. "Okay, maybe you didn't tie the noose, but you are responsible. I didn't want anything more than to just live my quiet little life with the only person who made me feel alive. And you brought hell to my doorstep and-and you made it my home."

"Hell was coming for you no matter where you hid," Micheal said. "Don't tell me you thought you'd achieve your dream just by hiding away. You're a S.W.O.R.D. operative with GSA. You would have, and still will be, used and disposed of."

"Sarah would still be alive," Zack sneered back.

"And in all likelihood, would have ended up widowed around 30. Possibly raising a child also with GSA all alone, solely responsible for the family you would have left behind," Salim said, without looking up from his crossword.

"I know I can never fix the repercussions of our actions. Nothing I do or say will ever bring your loved-ones back, or heal your pain. But if you are searching for death, or revenge, or a way to make sure this never happens to anyone else then I promise that starting a revolution will mean far more than a fight on a train car." Micheal added.

Zack, emotionally drained, could no longer think of a reason to fight, or debate with the man.

"Hey!" A voice came from the door that connected to the other cars; one of the guys must have slipped out or maybe there were other people in the car. "His friends are freaking out looking for him. They'll be back here soon."

Everyone seemed to move and shuffle back to places like actors on stage. Joshua put away the gun that was trained on Zack. Salim slowly moved back to Zack for a brief moment.

"If you decide that you do want to help us, there is a bar in Portland on the southeast side called Wynn's Pub. If you go there alone around closing time, we can talk more about the role you could have," Salim said.

"Salim!" Micheal said, in an urgent tone.

"ARE YOU SERIOUS!?!" Olivia yelled.

"STOP TELLING HIM THINGS, SALIM!" Joshua yelled as well.

"Why are they all yelling at me? That is important information," Salim asked Micheal.

"Because it IS important information, Salim. Let's sit down for a moment...." Micheal explained, looking very tired.

Zack just stood there for a second, still holding the cigarette in his hand, looking at the floor. When his senses had finally somewhat returned, Zack shuffled to the door and walked out to the caboose.

The car was going pretty fast, but the half open walls only

kept the wind from hitting him too hard. The chugging of the cars was a bit louder, but not deafening. The caboose was a type of smoking/viewing car so he could see through Plexiglas all the way around. Zack leaned his elbows on the railing that was about two foot away from the glass, where one other man was leaning smoking.

"Need a light?" The man said.

Zack looked up to see the other gunman, Brian. Zack pushed out his cigarette as Brian flicked his lighter. "Never got why he did that to people. Always gives out cigarettes, never lights them."

They both leaned there against the rail, smoking in silence.

"ZACK?!" A door slammed open, and Rose yelled out his name. "Guys he's out here!"

In nothing flat, Rose was up on the rail to Zack's right.

"Why did you run off on your own?? John comes bursting into our room, freaking out saying he has no idea where you went! Oh my God, you about gave us all a heart attack!" Rose said in her typical motherly panic. Zack still hadn't looked at her; he took another drag off his cigarette. "You're smoking again?"

Zack exhaled slowly. "Yeah... Sarah was the only reason I quit in the first place." Another drag and slow exhale. "I'm sorry I freaked you guys out. I just uh...."

Zack stopped a moment. He realized that he had not had hardly any time to process this whole crazy situation. If he told them what happened, they would probably have to fight these guys and they were all armed. It's not like they would let them all go back and grab their guns. Zack also knew where they would be, how to find them again later, so they might not even have to go fight these guys. Maybe he should just stay mum until they got off the train at least.

"I kinda had a little freak out," Zack said, flicking his cigarette to emphasize the half-truth. Brain flicked his as well and walked back to the other cars.

"Freak out? What happened?" Daniel said, stepping to the other side.

"I just... I walked over to the kids, and I couldn't breathe, you know? I started getting shaky, like I was nervous or something, and I just wanted to run. I felt really hot and I think I started going red. I just- I had to get out of that tiny little car." Zack said, rubbing his hands together hard.

"It's gone now though?" Rose said, rubbing his shoulder.

"Yeah, yeah, I got out here and walked around trying to catch my breath, and it got better but my head was still all over the place. Then this guy offered me a cigarette and I got, like, totally calmed down," Zack said, still gazing out of the glass.

"Okay. Do you still need a minute?" Rose said.

"No, I'm okay now. I think I'm gonna go lay down," Zack said, tapping the rail.

They walked back to their rooms. Zack laid down in the narrow train car bed, his mind scrambled from the whole incident.

8. FOR KING AND COUNTRY

Zack leaned up against a wall outside some military outfitter. The rest of the trip went smoothly. After checking into the hotel this morning they had to make a run to pick up some new issue uniforms since the exams were apparently going to be some kind of show for the public. Zack packed a fresh pack of cigarettes as he looked down the street of unending buildings, the capital certainly was huge.

"Why are you hitting them like that?" Rose asked.

"To pack all the tobacco into the cigarettes so they're tight." Zack opened up the packaging and pulled one out.

"Ah..." Rose nodded along, a slight sound of disapproval in her voice.

Zack tried smoking before with John as kids, an event which ended with a ineffective lecture from Lydia considering she was a smoker herself. He started smoking for real shortly after their tour in Texas during the bread riots.

Rose had a bit of a problem with smoking, but she mainly kept to that thing girls did where they say words and ask questions in a different tone and wait for you to feel bad.

Come to think of it, Daniel always bites on that.

"I wonder what's taking so long..." Rose looked through the glass door.

They were waiting on Daniel to get the new issued uniforms and some other workout gear. There was an opening ceremony and speech thing tonight, then tomorrow they would have physical exams. Military personnel all did this at different times of the year, but each branch had different requirements and tests.

"You doing okay? You're being pretty quiet...." She asked, looking back at Zack.

"I'm... doing...." Zack sighed out a cloud of smoke.

"I'm sorry... I don't really know what to say.... I want to help somehow but I just don't know what I can do."

It would be one thing if Zack was only grieving. Maybe two if you counted being unable to sleep through the night without waking up with nightmares. However, his mind had been thoroughly scrambled for the last two days. Mainly because he was asked to be a major assassin in a military overthrow.

...And partly because he still hadn't told anyone yet....

I mean, screw it, right? Not like I give a crap if they overthrow the government or something. I could just let it go, act like nothing happened. It's not my problem. Good luck, spaceman, I hope you and your rebel cause do great!

"I'm back!" Daniel walked out holding four bags.

"What took so long?" Rose asked, perking up.

"Eh, bureaucracy crap. Sorry babe." Daniel gave her a quick kiss on the head.

Zack started walking back.

"W-we weren't trying to seem lovey-dovey in front of you!" Rose walked up panicked.

"What? No you're fine, I'm fine, chill out, Rose." Zack raised an eyebrow at her.

"Okay..." Rose nodded. "Okay...."

They were able to make it back to the hotel pretty quick. Zack took John and his own bag back to their room, which was made up of two beds, one TV, an AC unit, and a bathroom in a small 10' x 20' rectangle.

"How's the TV out here?" Zack asked, seeing John slouched on the bed.

"I'm watching some old guy explain why I can't see the hot weather lady back home," John said.

"What?" Zack laid John's bag by his feet.

"I don't know, something about how there is so much shrapnel in the air that we can't put up satellites anymore, and satellites used to let us send stuff all over the world, and that's why we can't get cell phones, and good TV, and I don't get to see the hot weather girl, and everything is trash." John shut off the TV. "Oh, and we are trapped on Earth forever or something."

"Oh my God, the walls are closing in." Zack rolled his eyes. "Wait, how does S.W.O.R.D. get calls and stuff? I feel like I've seen Lydia use a cell phone before...."

"Oh, sorry, there are like three satellites left, so like governments around the world can do stuff and talk to each other and we get that one government channel." John opened up his bag. "Calling it now, bunch of conspiracy nonsense. They just don't want people talking to each other. Oh, these fatigues are lit!"

Zack opened his bag as well. Along with some workout gear were a new set of crimson red pixelated fatigues. Crimson was the accepted military color for the GSA, which reinforced the name Bloods.

Well, that and some other nasty things Zack would rather not reminisce about.

Zack and John changed and got as clean as possible. Military ceremonies were kind of a pain: shoes had to be shiny, shave had to be smooth, hair and berets perfect. After checking each other over, they exited their room and walked down the hallway knocking on Rose and Daniel's door.

"Hang on!" Shouted a voice. The door opened and Rose walked out, her hair in the typical military tight bun. Daniel followed her out. "You guys ready?"

"Yeah, are we stopping to get Lydia?" John asked.

"Yeah, she's got to check us in or whatever," Daniel said. They walked down the hall to the elevator and clicked floor four. After a quick ride they exited onto the upper class floors.

"What room is she in?" Rose turned back to Daniel.

"Four sixty... eight?" Daniel hesitated, reached to his wallet and pulled out a card. "Four sixty eight, yeah."

"I'm right here," Lydia said, walking up to them. Instead of fatigues, her uniform was more formal, a cream suit set with crimson trim. Her hair was like Rose's, the insignia of a book, dagger, and pistol on her beret signifying she was a GSA instructor.

"Oh, we were about to come get you! We're heading out now, you coming?" Rose said, motioning her thumb at the elevator. Lydia stopped and folded her arms.

"A-ten-hut!" Lydia said sternly. Quickly, all four of them straightened their backs, clicked their heels, and stood in a perfect line.

Lydia walked up to Rose. She moved her head around checking Rose's hair. Then moved on to Daniel, checking his shave. She did the same with John and Zack before she finally dropped the drill instructor act. "At ease. Don't forget this is a S.W.O.R.D. event so we operate with proper behavior. At least until I lose this jacket."

"Yes ma'am!" They said in unison.

"Move out." Lydia said.

"Yes ma'am." They said, not in unison now. Lydia grabbed Zack's arm for a second.

"There's going to be a speech and a lot of nasty people here," she whispered to him. "Whatever happens, you are stone for the next two hours. After that, we can do whatever you need."

"Yes ma'am," he whispered back. Lydia reached down and squeezed his hand quickly before they got into the elevator.

Since the only explanation Zack gave for the train incident was having a panic attack, Lydia was worried about him during the ceremony. Panic attacks weren't super uncommon; Daniel had them a while back. Lydia had said that some soldiers got them after combat sometimes.

Letting S.W.O.R.D. know you were having panic attacks however, wasn't the best idea. If you were broken physically you could be fixed, but if you were broken mentally....

Well, they call it 'dead weight' for a reason.

* * *

They walked into a big building with Gymnasium in raised letters for check-ins. Lydia signed them in at a table and headed to the stadium to get ready with the other officers for the presentation. S.W.O.R.D. officials separated and ordered them alphabetically in several lines. After an hour or so someone in charge gave the march command and the line slithered like a giant snake out to the field that they had set up for the presentation.

They walked into the stadium, assaulted by the noise of a large crowd in the stands. Zack walked in a line with the other soldiers as they began to file into rows of ten, the national anthem playing over the crowd. Some government officials and spectators sat in the stands, while the officers had chairs at the front of the lines. All together there may have been at least two hundred GSA and many hundred non-military personnel in the stands. Once everyone was in position, the anthem stopped and a general saluted them and everyone saluted back in kind.

"Operatives of S.W.O.R.D.'s Genetic Systemic Augmentation Division and citizens in the stands, welcome the King of the American State: David Hudson, first of his name, and the royal family."

Thunderous applause erupted out of the stadium. Zack clapped with the other operatives as he watched the stocky man with the fancy suit walk proudly onto the stage accompanied by several body guards. The queen and their two daughters followed not far behind, the older daughter accompanied by a darker-skinned man that Zack didn't recognize. The king stood at the podium as the others took their seats off to the side. The applause continued to rage on for several moments as the king stood smiling at the mic.

"Good evening, my loyal subjects," The king said, causing the audience to fall silent immediately. "Thank you for coming to witness our opening ceremonies for the evaluation of our GSA division of operatives. As you know, we hold these tests every year to make sure our operatives are staying in peak physical condition, as well as study the effects of GSA, to improve the quality of life for our entire kingdom." King David looked over to his family.

"However, this year is a special case." He motioned to his family. "This year, in the fall, my eldest daughter, Eliana, is getting married!"

More applause. The older girl stood up, as did the darker man next to her. They both gently waved to the crowd.

"It has been becoming more and more difficult to protect my family," King David continued. "In order to keep my family safe, as well as cut down on the overall manpower, I have been advised to pick the cream of the crop from our pool of operatives to serve as the personal bodyguards for my family as well as a few guards for the royal palace!"

Zack was fading in and out of what exactly King David was saying. He hated having to stand at attention to listen to the heads of government and military, who loved to hear themselves talk. Blah blah blah, we are so awesome. Blah blah blah, pander to the peasants. Blah blah blah, stroke our egos.

"I understand that this is no easy task. After all we are cursed to live in such dangerous times..." Lights dimmed slightly, as several large screens lit up, playing some kind of video.

Blah blah blah, fear mongering, Zack thought.

"Filled with turmoil in every country around us, threatening our way of life..." The screens flashed to show a war zone.

"Horrific disease and biological warfare..." Flashes of hospitals with people disfigured and sick were next.

"And worst of all, the spineless, terrorist trash that seeks to destroy everything that we hold dear."

Zack went stiff, his attention becoming completely focused on the screen in front of him. For only a few seconds, Zack saw a video of Sarah, scared out of her mind. It was only a second, then it was onto someone else. Perhaps someone just as innocent.

Zack could only focus on the screen. After a few more

clips of different people, there was a deafening roar when it came to clips of people hanging and the the king said something to rally the crowd. For nothing more than an instant, Zack watched as Sarah's lifeless body swung by the neck to the cheering of thousands happy to see her dead.

Zack tried not to shake. He couldn't breathe. His chest, every muscle in his body, clenched as if trying to pop through his skin. It felt like he was having a heart attack.

A hand grabbed onto his, the soldier next to him seemed to notice what was happening.

"Deep breaths. Control your breathing."

Zack didn't even know who the guy was.

Zack squeezed the stranger's hand anyway, and tried to steady his breathing. After a long speech Zack couldn't hear over his heartbeat, they started to move back to the gymnasium. It didn't take long for John to run up to him, shortly followed by Rose and Daniel.

Leaning on them for support occasionally, they headed back to the hotel. Lydia ran up behind them. She went straight for Zack and hugged him tightly.

"I'm sorry," was all she could say.

When they got back to the hotel Zack changed and laid in bed staring at the wall. Every once in awhile someone patted his shoulder and asked if he was okay, if he needed anything. Hours went by as Zack stared at that ugly brown wall. He stared at it until it turned black, and then turned slightly blue from the neon lights outside. Focusing on it helped. He could put his mind on the other side for a while, not be paralyzed thinking, just focused on the wall.

Being focused was good. Being focused was what had always kept him going over the years. Anytime something bad happened, anytime he struggled, he used to focus on Sarah, on the happy life they would build. But now there was nothing to focus on except the wall. He didn't have a happy future plan; he didn't have a goal to focus on at all.

A goal to focus on... Zack got up.

He looked at the clock on the table: 1:19 A.M. John was asleep in the other bed. Zack grabbed his wallet and cigarettes and stuck out of the room as quietly as he could. Once he was outside, he lit a cigarette as started walking south.

On his walk he truly tried to look at the city, occasionally he'd pass a man or woman sleeping in a box. Every couple of blocks he'd see two or three girls standing under a light post. Some of them tried to flirt, others tried not to look at him. Every once in a while he'd pass a man who'd get real close and start begging, but the look on Zack's face must have told them to give up quick. They'd all scamper down the street to find the next person to try to get something. He was on his fourth cigarette when he got to a corner bar with a long sign that said Wynn's Pub in green neon lights. He pushed through the big wooden double doors.

Inside the pub was a bit bigger than it looked on the outside. Most of the space was taken up by the dining area, with a curved row of booths along two walls, tables everywhere else with big picture windows against the street to open the place up. Opposite of the dining area there was a long bar, a couple of customers sat in various places. Zack grabbed a stool somewhat in the middle.

"Haven't seen you before, stranger," said the bartender in a thick accent. Zack looked to see the man that had a gun in his face a few days before. "What brings you in?"

"Name's Zack. Just looking for a drink. Did I miss last call?" Zack asked after a pause. The bartender looked over at the clock.

"Eh, it's not quite two yet. What'll you have?"

"Whiskey neat, make it a double if you don't mind."

"Sure thing. LAST CALL!" The bartender grabbed a glass and poured Zack a full cup of whiskey. "You need anything else, screw off cause it's two in the morning. Name's Joshua by the way."

"Joshua...." Zack repeated, trying to remember it this time.

Zack took a mouthful of whiskey. He didn't know why but

whiskey was the only alcohol that didn't make him gag. It still burned like hell but the taste wasn't terrible. He thought about the one time Rose and Sarah had him try tequila at a restaurant and he about threw up.

Zack sat there drinking as Joshua slowly kicked the last few patrons out. Once Zack was the only customer left in the bar he locked the doors and walked over grabbing the last few dirty dishes off of the bar.

"Well?" He said, looking at Zack, rubbing a glass. Zack tipped back his glass, swallowing the last of his drink. He sighed as the heat coated his tongue and set the glass down firmly.

"I'm in."

9. MEASURING UP

Zack stepped out of the shower just as John woke up, his hair a mess, his eyes still squinting against the sun.

"You're up early." John groaned.

"Yeah, I woke up and couldn't get back to sleep. You want to get breakfast?" Zack said, pulling on his new compression shirt.

John squinted at him funny, cocking his head to the side. "Uhh... yeah actually."

"Good, I feel like I haven't eaten in days."

"Well you kind of haven't. Not much anyway," John said, getting up and itching his back. "I'ma brush my teeth and stuff then I'll be good to go."

"Ight, hurry up." Zack put on his new zip up hoodie with his squad's designation on the back and sat down to put on his socks.

The hotel had set up a Continental breakfast for the GSA in a large hall on the first floor. It was already about a third of the way full with operatives getting up too early with pre-test jitters. John and Zack sat at one of the smaller round tables.

"Well good thing we didn't get Daniel and Rose, looks like you are gonna eat the whole hotel down," John said, looking at Zack's two plates.

"I told you I was hungry," Zack said, digging in immediately.

John started eating too. "You feeling okay?"

Zack looked up to see how John was looking at him.

"You are a little chipper today."

"And that's a bad thing?"

"It's a jarring change of pace."

"I had a realization, or whatever." Zack rubbed his hands together.

"What's that?" John asked.

"It's like I became aware of something."

"Wha…." John started confused. "Okay idiot, I know what a realization is."

Zack laughed a little at his own joke, then dug back into his eggs. "I don't want to go home, John. I'm not going."

John sat there looking at Zack, letting his words sink in.

"O-kay… What do you mean you're not coming home?"

"I mean…." Zack shoveled more eggs in his mouth. "If I go home, and I have to see all the places I had all these memories of Sarah with…. I'm not- I can't do that right now. I'm not in the right place in my head. I can't go back there right now."

John stared blankly at Zack.

"This year they're going to keep some of us to work here for the royal family, yeah? So I'm going to give it all I have; I'm gonna try to get picked. If that doesn't work out, I'm gonna see if Lydia can get me transferred to a regiment doing a Canadian rotation-"

"A Canadian rotation is five to ten YEARS, Zack!" John looked at him in disbelief. "GSAs don't DO Canadian rotations; that's army territory! The GSA stays HERE, we do work HERE! On OUR soil!"

"Well if the royal family doesn't want me, and the army doesn't want me, then they probably wouldn't miss me if I was just gone."

"'Just gone'?" John repeated. "What do you mean 'just gone'? Gone where?"

"If they tell me I have to go back, there's no other option, I'm going AWOL," Zack stated firmly, looking into John's eyes.

"Whoa, whoa, whoa, whoa."

"I'm serious."

"Dude, you can't-" John looked around to check if anyone was listening. "You can't just desert."

"It's a last resort."

"Okay, no. Trying to win this little event so you can work for the king directly, that's crazy. Saying you're gonna go into the army is crazy AND stupid. Going AWOL is bats and brainless!" John whisper-yelled.

"Calm down, it probably won't even come down to that."

"I will not fricking calm down! You are way too fricking calm, that's the problem! I know you are totally fricking serious right now! Going AWOL is a death sentence!"

"Well, for me, going home is a death sentence too!" Zack fired back.

John sat back in his chair and rubbed his face sighing. "Will you please just think about what you're planning. Man, it's crazy."

"What do you think our odds are to win?" Zack said, changing the subject.

"What?"

"What do you think our odds are that we get picked for this bodyguard thing? Me, you, Rose, and Daniel?" Zack asked.

John began biting his nails. "I don't know, two hundred to one?"

"Think about it, if they need one bodyguard for each person in the royal family, plus the new guy that's five people. They've got to rotate people in - it's not gonna be twenty four hours a day, so let's say three rotations of eight hour shifts. Then you got to think sometimes people get sick and people would lose focus with no days off so add in one more group at least. That makes twenty positions. So right there your odds are twenty to two hundred, which makes it one in ten. And they most likely won't choose these young guys; they're too green, and some guys are going to go easy because they don't want the job. So I think we've got at least a one in seven chance," Zack said.

"You're fricking losing it, bro," John said, starting on his eggs.

Zack sighed, leaning back in his chair. "Yeah, maybe I already lost it...."

John looked at him for a few seconds before putting his fork down. "Alright, I'm with you," he said, rubbing his hands. "Screw it. Let's do it. Let's win."

"For real?"

"For real, but if we don't make it you talk to me before you do anything else, okay?"

"Right. Oh and maybe don't tell Lydia and Rose about this. You know how they get," Zack said.

"You mean worried? Yeah, yeah I do."

Most of those options were smoke and mirrors; an excuse to explain why Zack wanted or needed to win. While he didn't get much of an explanation from his new friends, there were a few things they did lay out for him. Step one: get accepted into this new GSA bodyguard position by any means necessary.

...Okay that was sort of the only step he knew.

There were a few other preparations like 'get your group to go all out' and 'be ready after the drug test'.

Whatever that means....

Zack just started getting nervous about the sudden choice he made last night when Rose and Daniel walked in.

"You guys are up early!" She said, leaning on a free chair.

"Yeah, I was starving," Zack said.

"Well don't eat too much, you'll get sick on the obstacle course. You guys ready to go?" Daniel jutted a thumb to the door.

They all headed back to the stadium, which had changed over night. On the field there was now a large obstacle course that was maybe ninety feet in the air at its highest point. There were timers on the track as well as a couple of benches and squat racks underneath the stadium.

There were a couple of different measuring events set up for today. There would be the typical bench press and squat tests for muscle strength and endurance. There was also the forty yard dash, high jump, and the obstacle course, to check on movement and agility. Then tomorrow they would have target practice and the gun course.

"Hey, I'm gonna head to the bathroom real quick," Zack

said.

"Hurry, we're gonna be up here in like, fifteen minutes," Daniel said. "Do you need someone to go with you?"

"No, I can hold it myself, thank you," Zack said.

Daniel silently gave Zack the finger and shook his head.

John giggled.

"Zack. Seriously, if-" Rose began.

"I promise I will be right back." Zack cut her off, holding out a pinky.

Rose wrapped her own pinky around his.

"You promised! Hurry back," Rose said, seemingly satisfied with that.

Zack headed into the inner workings of the stadium and headed to the older nastier bathroom on the south side. He walked in to another kid hunched over the toilet with his friend looking over him. Zack gave the kids a nod of sympathy and headed to the fourth stall in. He sat down so it would seem normal, and reached underneath the back of the tank, grabbing a little toothbrush holder. He opened it to reveal the medium sized syringe, mostly full of a dark, reddish-brown liquid.

The first thing Zack had to do was win the competition and make it into this new Royal Guard. Size-wise, he was already sure to be considered, and he was in a good age group, but to seal the deal he had to get high marks in all of the physical tests. So Salim snuck this in for him, a booster of some kind.

Of course, if he had known that it was going to be a giant needle of sludge-y looking blood, he might have asked for an explanation.

Zack sighed. "Hhooohh, this is gonna suck...."

He took the cap off, careful not to drop it, stuck the needle into his butt cheek and pushed down on the plunger quickly to get it over with. He put everything away neatly and hid it back in its spot.

Zack felt normal leaving the stall, but by the time he got to the field he was feeling a little hot and shaky. He walked back to his friends who were stretching in the grass trying to look calm.

"Do you remember your time from last year, Zack?" Daniel asked.

"For the Forty?" Zack asked.

Daniel nodded.

"Uh... I want to say four one nine?"

"See? I told you I was first last year!" Daniel said to Rose.

"Okay, you're right, I'm sorry! I'm just human, not perfect like you!" Rose said, flipping her hands about.

"Oh. My. God. Too bad there's not an event for overreacting," Daniel said, lightly irritated.

"*Excuse* me?!" Rose said, whipping her head around.

"We're doing the forty first," John told Zack.

"Ah, good that coffee has got me jittery," Zack lied.

"What is really the point of this one? I get the strength tests and marksmanship, but running? We have vehicles dude." John wondered allowed.

"Unit fourteen! Indiana! You're up!" A man yelled.

"That's us!" Daniel popped up.

They headed over to the table next to the track set up on the west side, and checked in.

"Go ahead and get your blood moving. Tenabalm, you're up first," the guy at the table said.

Everyone started their breathing exercises. Zack quickly felt the blood rushing in his body. His vision got sharp and his muscles tensed and burned ready for action. Rose shook her limbs out and headed to the starting block. The whistle blew and she took off, and she was through it in a heartbeat.

"Time: four, seventeen! Four, one, seven!"

"Not bad." John shrugged.

"Yeah, she'll top that on the second run through. Her first one is always about point oh five slow." Daniel nodded.

"Next: Henagar!"

John did a little jump-jog up to the block. He stomped his feet in solid, and nodded. The whistle blew again and John took off.

"Time: four, ten! Four, one, zero!"

"Wooo! That's what I'm talking about baby!" John hollered, as Rose came back out of breath.

"Awh dang it...." Rose whined.

"You'll get it next time, babe." Daniel kissed her temple.

"Slater, you're up."

Daniel headed over to the block.

"Knock 'em dead baby!" Rose shouted.

Daniel shook his head with a grin. The whistle sounded again and Daniel took off.

"Time: four twelve! Four, one, two!"

"Come on!" Daniel said, shaking his head as he turned back.

"Get good bro!" John yelled, his arms out.

"Bite me, Henagar." Daniel flipped him off in response.

"Taylor, you're up."

"Zack, please kick John's butt," Rose said as Zack walked up to the designated starting spot on the track. He scratched his shoes against the rough orange rubber.

Zack felt like he was about to have a heart attack. He was already breathing hard, and was shaking uncontrollably now. He shimmied his feet into the blocks, and got set into position. Everything around him seemed to slow down a bit as he focused, though, and his body tensed. The whistle blew and Zack took off, noticing he got a very good jump. He couldn't quite tell but it felt like he hit his top gear really early around the twenty five. He pushed all the way through the line and had to go pretty far past the line to slow down easy. The combination of the air rushing by his ears and how far away he was made him not hear his time. He turned and jogged back.

"What was it?" Zack yelled on his way back.

The man by the little scanning light machine looked back to him. "Three, nine, one."

Zack slowed to a walk on that.

"You beat the best time of the day by point one."

Zack stared at him for a second as he walked, then started doing the math in his head. He had almost beaten his own record by three tenths of a second. With his heart about to explode, Zack started to worry again about what the hell was in that needle.

Zack walked up to his friends out of breath, as they all stared blankly at him. Zack shrugged.

"I got a good jump."

"Uh, no. I got a good jump. That was insane," John said, looking him over.

"Seriously, Zack, what was that?" Rose asked, bewildered.

"No kidding. People don't make a three tenths jump in a year," Daniel said.

"Well I don't know if I ever went full out at these things before." Zack's mind frantically tried to think of an excuse.

"...And we need to win?" Daniel asked.

Zack looked at him still trying to catch his breath.

"John told us." Rose said, folding her arms.

Zack looked at John. John rubbed the back of his neck.

"Okay." Daniel nodded.

"Okay?" Rose asked. "What do you mean?"

"I mean IN-14 is going to score the highest out of any unit in the GSA." Daniel said. "Usually there's nothing really riding on these little yearly exams so there's nothing but pride on the line. This time it's different."

Zack looked at the ground, feeling slightly ashamed.

"From here on out, we are full-tilt-full-tassel, everything you got. We are one hundred percent serious." Daniel said.

"No more jokes. Not until we celebrate our new jobs." John nodded.

"Let's go win this thing." Rose gave Zack a thumbs up.

I've got some good friends.

* * *

The rest of the day's events went on like that. Zack beat personal best after personal best by huge margins. He wasn't sure how high he was ranking compared to everyone else, but he felt unbeatable in the moment. It was maybe five in the afternoon when they finally finished up.

"Holy crap my legs are killing me." Daniel sighed.

"No kidding, I hope I don't get a cramp tonight," Rose said, stretching out her calf. "How about you guys?"

"Eh, I'm not dead, but I'm sleepy as all get out." John sighed, leaning against the wall.

"I'm feeling kinda tense still." Zack grunted as he sat on the ground.

"Your body's probably still working off the adrenalin," Rose said, turning to face him. "You might finish in the top ten! I wonder if we'll all get to work in Portland for a while."

"Yeah, our odds have got to be pretty good after a performance like that," Daniel said. "It'll be nice to stay in the city for a while. Things with my parents have been getting kind of annoying lately."

"Plus, we never get to go to the beach. We are going this year!" Rose said, fired up.

Zack looked over at John.

"Yeah, I mean where else am I going to find a girlfriend. I need to find a pretty city girl who has a thing for country boys," John said, flexing.

"In what way are YOU a country boy? You've never done anything remotely country," Rose asked.

"Eh, minor details. Zack can come too, talk about raising chickens or whatever," John said, tilting his hand around.

"Why would Zack be with you picking up girls?" As soon as Rose asked the question she remembered Zack was alone now. The air went dead silent around them.

"It's okay guys," Zack said, picking at his shoes uncomfortably. "Thanks for the invite. Maybe later...."

"I'm sorry...." Rose said quietly.

"Don't worry about it," he said. "I just miss her a lot."

"Zack," Daniel said after a moment.

Zack looked up at him.

Daniel seemed to struggle finding a way to say what was on his mind. After a moment he seemed to find different words. “If me and Rose are making you uncomfortable with the whole-”

“Rose and I. Sorry,” Rose butted in.

“No, guys, hey, it's fine, I'm happy for you. If anything I'm sorry for the way I've been acting, I didn't mean to put that stuff on you guys,” Zack said, shaking his head.

“Hey man we're your friends. You can lean on us in times like this,” John said quickly.

“If anything I'm sorry we couldn't do more! I feel so responsible for everything that happened, and oh my God when we heard that gun go off at your house I about-!” Rose continued in a panic.

“Whoa, hey don't bring that up he doesn't want to talk about that!” Daniel said, cutting her off.

“Not talking about it is the exact opposite of what we should be doing!” Rose stood up, in a borderline panic. “Zack, I just- when John said you really needed to get away from home and hinted that you were still thinking about killing yourself, I have been in a nervous wreck-”

“Yeah, I told him not to do that.” Zack said to John, getting a choking 'don't look at me' expression in response.

“And I'm trying to be normal, because you seem like you’re doing really really well now, but the other day I got a book about it and it says that people having suicidal thoughts can-”

“You bought a book? What book did she buy?” Zack said to Daniel this time, but getting the same expression in response.

“They can act like everything's great because they are hiding their emotions and even when everything happened you just shut down, and I thought that you know you really hated me for everything and you still haven't talked about any of it and it is KILLING me, Zack. I don't know what you’re thinking or feeling. I have this pit in my stomach thinking 'Oh God is this they day I'm gonna find him dead' and I start panicking and then I can't breathe and I-I-I.” Tears were starting down her face as she started to hyperventilate. Zack grabbed her by the shoulder.

"IT IS NOT. YOUR. FAULT." Zack shook her. "Rose, I'm sorry, for putting this on you. I've just been going through a lot. But it is not your fault. And I know I'm the one who made you feel like that because I did blame you at first; I blamed everyone, but it is not your fault. There was nothing we could have done. And I don't want you to have to worry about me so I promise whatever happens if I go back to that dark place I was in I will talk to you. I will let you know what is going on with me, you have my word."

"Anytime? No matter what. You promise?" Rose sobbed.

"I promise."

"I just- I don't want to lose anymore friends...." Rose sobbed into Zack's chest.

Before he knew it, John reached out and hugged them both, then Daniel as well.

He wasn't the only one who missed Sarah....

"I'm sorry...." Rose said, pulling away and wiping her eyes.

"It's okay." Zack didn't know what else to say.

"We're all just worried about you man," Daniel said, patting him on the back.

"I know." Guilt started to make his chest ache a little.

"Hey, we got to go do the drug test," Daniel said, looking at his watch. "Then we can go home and relax. What do you guys say?"

"Sounds great! Maybe Lydia will take us out for steaks!" John said, pumping his fist.

"Yeah right. Maybe she'll get us a bologna sandwich you mean." Rose scoffed.

They headed over to the big square tents that had been set up. Zack looked around for a minute, as it dawned on him that he had no idea how he was going to pass this drug test. He was just starting to sweat, when he heard a voice behind him.

"IN, 14?"

Zack turned around to see Salim behind them wearing a white lab coat.

"That's us," Daniel said, walking up to him.

"Hello, my name is Dr. Koury. I will be administering your drug test today," Salim said. "If you'll just follow me."

Huh, well I guess that worked out, Zack thought.

"You know, your group did very well! Some of us had a small pool going on to see who would have the best team. I think you all might have won me a little money," Salim said as he walked. "If you are up for it, I'd like to give some back to you. I own a small pub and restaurant called Wynn's, it's on the southeast side. If you stop by tonight your dinner is on the house."

Micheal mentioned he would be writing Salim a script to recite.

Little on the nose Micheal....

"Oh no way, that would be awesome! We were just talking about that," John said.

"About Wynn's pub?" Salim asked, confused.

"No, like what to do for dinner," John explained.

"Ah, I see." Salim nodded, then he stared at Zack. "Well then, would anyone care to go first?"

"Yeah, I'll go first, I gotta pee anyway," Zack said quickly, picking up on Salim's hint.

"Right through here," Salim said, opening a tent flap.

Zack went in. Salim handed him a little screw lid cup which he filled and handed back to Salim. He quickly put it in his left coat pocket, and from his right coat pocket produced a different jar, which he wrote Zack's name on.

"Are you feeling jittery at all, Mr. Taylor?" Salim asked.

"A little bit," Zack said.

"Hmm. That's normal due to the amount of exercise," Salim said. "You should walk outside, perhaps to an area within twenty five yards of the stage at the center, so that your body will properly cool down."

Way to be discreet, Michael.

"Okay, I'll do that," Zack said, nodding. He turned to his friends. "I'm gonna walk around out here for a little bit."

"Okay, we will be there in a bit," Rose said.

Zack walked out into the open area and stretched a little. He looked around, noticing that Lydia was walking towards him. They locked eyes and exchanged a wave. He started walking to her when he bumped into someone.

"Whoa, sorry," Zack said, grabbing the person, only to see that it was Joshua from the bar.

"No prob. Get to the youngest princess, stop the event," he said coldly, walking away.

Zack looked around quickly, noticing that the royal family was behind Lydia on her right side. He jogged over to Lydia.

"Hey! I heard you guys did pretty well," she said, smiling.

"Yeah, I suppose so!" Zack said, looking behind her. They were maybe a hundred feet or so from the royal family's group. He noticed that the guards were looking pretty lethargic. On Lydia's right though, there was a man pushing through the crowd rather fast.

"Well I was thinking that maybe we could all go get-" Lydia spoke as the man drew a gun.

"Lydia, LYDIA!" Zack pushed her out of the way, and fell into a dead sprint. "LOOK OUT!" He yelled, as he ran. Joshua said to get to the youngest, who was also the most exposed. He ran for her as the man pulled the gun up at her a few yards away. In an instant he slid down and covered her as shots rang out. He did a single roll with the girl in his arms and positioned his body to defend her from any more shots. He heard someone yell, "GUN!" as chaos ensued. Zack scurried to his feet as two other soldiers ran over.

Zack turned slightly to see the man on the ground with several soldiers on him. He looked at the small girl he was carrying as she clung to his chest.

"Are you okay, Princess?" He said, out of breath. Two little brown eyes full of tears looked up at him, then went back into his chest with a nod before she started sobbing hard.

"Hey, hey. It's okay, Princess, I got you. Zack's got you kiddo everything's gonna be fine. I ain't gonna let anything happen to you," he said as soothingly as he could. He gently rubbed her back.

"Here, I'll take her," one of the soldiers said. But the moment he touched her, the little princess threw her arms around his neck.

"NO!" She yelled, as she cried more violently. The soldier pulled back a little, looking at Zack.

"It's okay. I got her for right now," Zack said.

"He's clear. He's one of mine," Lydia said, coming up behind Zack.

"Alright, this way," he said, escorting them over to the queen. Seeing her daughter she quickly walked over to them.

"Annabelle! Are you okay?!" She said, the panic coming through her voice slightly. When Princess Annabelle didn't answer, the queen turned instead to Zack.

"She's safe physically, your Majesty. She just seems to be shaken up," he said, bowing as much as he could with the girl on his hip.

"Well no wonder! You tackled her too hard! Why couldn't you go after that assassin instead!!" She yelled at Zack.

He quickly hit his knees and held onto the girl tightly. "Forgive me ma'am." He stared at the ground.

"And the rest of you, where were you?! My daughter could have been killed!!" The queen screamed, obviously in shock.

"Elisa! Calm yourself!" King David's voice shook out. Zack set Princess Annabelle on her feet and motioned for her to go to her mother. She quietly wrapped her little arms around her mother's waist. Hearing footsteps, Zack pushed himself down so his forehead almost hit the ground. King David stopped in front of him.

"Rise. Let me have a look at you," the king ordered.

Zack carefully rose, making sure not to bump into anyone. Strangely enough, Zack didn't look up to the king who he had always seen towering above him. In this moment, they were on equal ground. And Zack had to be a good four inches taller than him. This being the first time he had ever been this close, the magic was lost as he realized that the king was nothing more than a man. Zack stiffened like a soldier and made himself reputable.

"At ease son. You don't have to be so tense, this isn't a drill," King David said with a light smile.

"Yes, my Lord," Zack said, as he relaxed his stance a bit. "I just uh- I'm not sure where I'm supposed to look...."

The king chuckled lightly at that. "You may look me in the eyes as you would anyone."

"Yes, sir," Zack said, looking at him. Behind the king the older princess and her fiance had also appeared.

"Is he okay? His eyes are all bloody," Princess Eliana said, cringing.

"His people do that when they are under stress," King David answered. "You were very courageous son. Thank you for saving my daughter."

"Thank you my Lord, it was only my duty," Zack said, trying to think of the most groveling, pandering bull crap he could.

"So this is what a Blood is," the foreign prince said, approaching Zack. "It's one thing to watch from the stands, but to see one in action firsthand... you impress me."

"Thank you sir," Zack said, bowing again.

"Are they all so polite?" He asked King David, circling Zack.

"I suppose it would vary from soldier to soldier. What is your name son?" King David asked, tilting his head.

"Zackary Taylor, Indiana, county 14, sir," Zack said.

"You seem to be rather well mannered, Mr. Taylor. Is that part of your training?" King David asked.

This arrogant sap-head doesn't even know what we do, does he? Zack thought. "I don't believe it is in our official itinerary sir. However-"

Zack turned to Lydia who seemed to stiffen when he stretched his palm at her.

"This is Lydia, my commanding officer, and the woman who taught me everything I know about being a soldier. She could answer any questions you might have better than I can," Zack said, passing the buck. "...Also, getting the opportunity to speak in front of the royal family has me pretty nervous."

The king and foreign prince both laughed at that.

"I can't get enough of his accent," said the foreign prince.

"So you are the one who trained this young man? You have my thanks as well, Ms. Lydia." King David nodded at Lydia.

"Uh, thank you sir. Zack is one of the best," Lydia said, clearly as nervous as Zack was.

"Taylor, was it?" The foreign prince said behind him.

"Yes sir?" Zack answered.

"You seem to have been shot here. Do you feel it?" He asked.

Zack flexed his back muscles, and felt a slight twinge. He rolled his shoulder blades and felt it a little stronger.

"Now that you mention it sir, I do feel a slight pain in my shoulder blade," Zack said.

"Are you okay?" Lydia asked, turning her attention to Zack.

"I think so. What was the caliber?" Zack said, moving his arm different ways as the pain became slightly worse.

"Nine mil I think."

"Can you get it for me?" Zack said, pulling off his shirt. Lydia took out her knife and got behind him. She started digging around in his back. The prince came around to the front to analyze him more. He placed his hands on Zack's stomach, pressing his thumbs into his muscles. Then he checked around his neck, chest, and arms.

"Got it," Lydia said, pulling the bullet out.

"Are all the soldiers in the GSA like you?" The foreign prince said, continuing his examination. Zack started to answer, then stopped. Maybe this was a good chance to seal the deal.

"Permission to speak freely, my Lord?" Zack asked.

The prince's eyes moved up to his. "Of course."

"There's no one like me," Zack said coldly.

The prince started to laugh as he backed away from Zack.

"So, Prince Armando, what do you think of our GSA division?" King David asked.

"Well I can't speak for the whole division. But if the rest are at least close to operative Taylor here, you may color me impressed," Prince Armando said, with a nod.

"Thank you sir!" Zack bowed.

"Well it is time for us to be heading home. Thank you for your actions, Mr. Taylor. I shall be expecting great things from you," King David said, turning his eyes to Lydia. "Lydia, was it? Have Mr. Taylor brought to the top doctor and get him fixed up. This takes priority."

"Yes, my Lord!" She said with a bow.

They turned to start leaving, Prince Armando placing his hand around the older princess, Eliana's shoulder.

I should probably study up on them so I don't look like an idiot later. Zack thought. He was about to walk off when the youngest princess wiggled away from the queen and ran over to him. Zack dropped down to a crouch as quick as he could.

"Yes, princess?" He said, coming eye level with her. She then quickly placed her hands on his shoulders, and kissed him on the cheek. Zack froze, unsure how to react.

"Thank you for saving me," the little girl cooed, sweet as sugar.

Zack's heart melted at the innocence of this little princess, not yet tainted by the evil world. But he did not forget who she was. This was the Princess of North America who just kissed him. This honor was supposed to be unbelievably humbling. Zack pushed his forehead to the ground again.

"Thank you for being my princess!" He said, staying prostrated. Then an idea came into his head. He brought his face up. "My Lord, if you would have us, my team would be honored to escort you home!"

"Zack!" Lydia whisper-yelled at him.

The deep throaty laugh of the king rang out over the silence.

"I think we will be okay. Though I shall remember your

dedication son," King David said. "Come along now dear."

And with that they were off. Zack stayed still until they were a good distance away.

"Holy crap, I think I might have a heart attack," Lydia said, bending over to breathe.

"You? What about me!" Zack said, also having a small panic attack from the little princess.

"Come on," she said, pulling him to his feet. "We are getting you patched up, then I am getting SEVERAL drinks."

10. LET'S TAKE A LOOK AT YOUR RESUME...

"I still can't believe that flipping happened." Lydia shook her head and picked up her beer.

"Were you nervous?" Rose asked, glued to the story.

"Oh my God, when the queen yelled at me I almost pissed myself." Zack cringed, drinking his beer.

"I bet, that would be fricking terrifying." Daniel nodded.

"How are you all doing?" Salim asked, coming up to the table.

"Salim, everything is wonderful. Thank you so much for this," Daniel said sincerely.

"Did you have any trouble finding the place?" Salim asked.

"Not too much. We got directions from someone in the lobby of our hotel," Rose chimed in.

"Excellent! Well, everything is on the house tonight. It's not everyday we get a national hero in here," Salim said, turning to Zack and eliciting a few *woos* from his friends.

"You might end up regretting that Doc, you haven't seen our CO put them down." John teased Lydia, getting the finger from her in return.

"Please enjoy yourselves." Salim started to leave, but stopped. "May I give you all some advice?"

"Sure, what you got for us?" Daniel said, nudging his chin up.

"Well nothing is official, but there are a few rumors that your team might be a top pick for this new royal guard. If you were to be picked for said group, they will be bringing you all in for these psychiatric evaluations." Salim started.

"I take it you are not a fan of psychology, Salim?" Lydia said, with a laugh.

"I am not one for fake sciences, no." Salim continued. "It would seem that in these meetings they try to ensnare soldiers with their own words. If you wish to be accepted into this new unit, you may want to be on guard about what you say, as I've never seen anyone rejected for saying too little."

"Huh, we'll keep that in mind, Salim," Daniel said, nodding.

"Good. Enjoy your dinner!" And with that, he was off.

"Why do you think he'd tell us that?" John said after Salim was out of ear shot.

"I bet he's got money on us getting in," Zack lied, knowing that the message was really for him.

"What did he mean by 'fake science'?" Rose looked at Lydia

"It's this whole thing. Most *doctor* doctors I've met *hate* psychology." Lydia laughed.

"*Doctor* doctors?" Rose giggled.

"You know what I mean," Lydia said, drinking again. "Excuse me if my nerves are a little shot from the national hero here throwing me to the lions!"

"Sorry." Zack shrugged.

"Still..." Daniel flicked his glass. "We could really be staying here for a while."

"This place sure isn't like back home," John said, nodding.

"Did it take you long to get used to the big city, Lydia?" Rose asked.

"Eh, I grew up in Joliet so it wasn't that hard on me," Lydia said. "Besides, if you do get in they will probably rotate you back out after a year or two. Who knows, they might even let you guys retire early if you wanted to."

"I bet we would get to go all over the place too. I mean, it's not like we could really go out and see new places, but we'd still be working around the world," Rose said, almost excited.

"I wonder if they'll just keep us at the hotel," John said, grabbing another slice of pizza.

"You'll probably get an apartment," Lydia said.

"Our own apartments!" Rose said, excitedly. "I could get used to being a city girl!"

"You and Daniel gonna just share one?" Zack joked.

"I don't know if we would have enough room for all her clothes. Have you seen her closet?" Daniel said, dead serious.

"I don't have THAT many clothes!" Rose protested.

"Yes you do."

"Whatever. I guess I will just stay in my own apartment then." Rose folded her arms.

"Well, we have to wait for it to be official anyway. Maybe we should call it an early night," Lydia said.

"Tapping out already, Lydia?" John said.

"Yep, if we do get called in after the results are posted tomorrow, they'll start the whole psych evaluations right afterwards," Lydia said, getting up from the table. "You guys pound the water and get some sleep. I'll see you tomorrow."

"Night!" The group rang out.

"You guys want to head out too?" Daniel said, looking around.

"Yeah, might as well." Rose nodded. "I'm a little sleepy anyway."

"Yeah, fine, since you guys are gonna be lame," John said, flipping his hand about.

"I'll go get this boxed up," Zack said, grabbing the pizza. He headed up to the bar where Joshua was serving. He was busy with a customer, so a different secret rebel came up to him instead.

"Hey! What can I do for you?" Olivia said.

"Could I get this boxed up?" He said with a polite smile.

"Sure thing!" She said, disappearing in the back, then reappearing. "You know, you should come back tomorrow. Happy hour is at 9 and whiskeys are two for one."

"I'll be there miss...?" Zack said.

"I'm Olivia, but they call me Olive Oil," Olivia said with a smile.

"Good to meet you Olive Oil, I'm Zack," he said, taking the box from her.

"Yeah, we've heard about you Mr. Hero. You're good for business!" She said, scampering off. Zack turned, meeting Joshua's eyes as they exchanged a nod. Close to the door was Daniel leaning against the wall by the bathrooms.

"I think the waitress was hitting on you, *Mr. Hero*," Daniel said, with a smirk.

"You think so?" Zack raised an eyebrow.

"Yeah. Olive Oil, that's a cute nickname." Daniel nodded.

"You got a cutesy nickname for Rose?" Zack asked, leaning on the opposite wall.

"No, I could never think of one," he said. "Plus there's not a lot of good plays off 'Rose'."

"I guess not," Zack said with a small snort. John walked out of the bathroom and leaned against the wall next to Zack.

"What's up?" He asked, putting his foot on the wall.

"Not much. Waiting for Rose to get out of the bathroom. Watching Mr. Hero over here getting flirted with," Daniel said, almost aggravated.

"Mr. Herooo." John nodded with a grin.

"I swear to God, this nickname better not stick," Zack said, shaking his head.

"Was it the cute blonde?" John asked.

"Yep, her name is *Olive Oil....*" Daniel said, emphasizing the name in a flirty manner.

"Oh God, that is perfect. I love me some oil," John said, looking behind the bar.

"Ugh, you are nasty," Zack said, gagging. Rose walked out of the bathroom.

"Hey. What's going on?" She asked, looking around.

"John is perving on the blonde waitress," Zack said.

"Who has some oil for Zack," John said.

"Mm. No it's Mr. Hero remember?" Daniel corrected.

"What...?" Rose said, confused.

"The waitress was nice to me and dumb and dumber got jealous." Zack said, heading outside.

"You wish!" Daniel said, following him.

"I'll admit it, I wish hot blonde waitresses hit on me at bars." John nodded in agreement.

"You guys do know that waitresses flirt with everybody right? That's how they get good tips," Rose said, rolling her eyes.

"Forget the tip, she can have everything," John said.

"EW! URK! JOHN HENAGAR YOU ARE DISGUSTING!" Rose yelled in the parking lot.

* * *

The air was cool, despite the harsh morning sun shining in the middle of the stadium. The operatives came to the stadium, without any civilians in the stands this time. S.W.O.R.D. had put up a big screen that continued to cycle through each event, listing the operatives in order based on how well they performed. Occasionally, some group hooped and hollered at a ranking.

Zack had placed in the top ten operatives in every event, mostly landing in the top five. In the overall scores, he managed second out of all operatives.

When measurements factored in weight and age, pound for pound his name was at the top of the list.

"Holy crap," Lydia said, pulling her head back a little in surprise. "You've come a long way kiddo."

"Ladies and gentlemen, you know him, you love him, he's the pound for pound, champion, and the hero of the Unified American State! Zackaaarrry Taylor!" John used his best announcer voice.

"Yeah yeah," Zack said, rolling his eyes.

"Daniel you're sixth in the overalls, and seventh in the pound for pounds as well." Lydia shook her head. "You kids knock it off with all this impressive crap, or S.W.O.R.D.'s gonna start asking me to write up a- uh..."

"Curriculum?" Rose said, trying to help her out.

"Yeah."

"So Zack goes up in the pound for pound and I go down? I call hacks!" Daniel mumbled.

"Hold up," John said as the screen changed again. It was for the teams who were supposed to report in for further examination. IN-14 was second on a list of six teams.

"Why are we second?" John asked.

"John. It's alphabetical." Rose tilted her head. John took a second to analyze the board again.

"Ohhh." He finally said.

"Oh my God... you boys tire me...." Rose said, rubbing her temples.

"Come on, let's not be the last ones there." Lydia walked ahead.

They followed her out of the stadium to a building maybe a quarter mile away. They stood in the entry way for a while as the other teams came in as well. Everyone was quiet as a middle aged lady walked around making sure everyone was situated, though the silence despite the rather full room seemed to be unnerving her.

Then a team went in through double doors to what looked like a gymnasium. After about twenty minutes they called Zack's group in. They walked into the gym where a table was set up with many people in uniforms sitting behind it, as well as the king and queen. Lydia was directed towards the side of the table, a little in front. She looked rather nervous. Zack and the others were guided down a line in the floor and stood facing the table.

"Ten-HUT!" A voice hollered. IN-14 all saluted in unison.

"At ease!" They all assumed their relaxed positions.

"Rose Tenabalm, step forward," King David said. Rose quickly walked up to a little circle that a man pointed to. She stood for a moment trying not to fidget as some men were writing, others staring at her.

"Ms. Tenabalm, you finished last among your teammates, but you did do rather well among the GSA as a whole. You finished fourth among women as well," King David said, reading a file put in front of him. "How do you feel about staying in Portland for a time on the new personal service team that we are constructing?"

"I'd be honored sir- I mean my Lord." Rose stuttered. King David looked up from the file and flashed his trademark white smile.

"Not everyday you meet the king, huh? I'm sorry, my name is David. And I'm very impressed with you and your team," King David said in his loving fatherly voice.

Man, I might hate this guy but frickin' A' is he good at that. Zack thought.

"Thank you, King David." Rose smiled, relaxing.

"Well your file seems in order, the only thing is that in the notes we have it that you are in a romantic relationship with Mr. Slater, is that correct?"

"Uh, yes my Lord." Quietly this time.

"Well there are no regulations for the GSA on fraternization, that's not what we are worried about. Are you two-" King David spun a pen through his fingers. "Is there any possible chance you could be pregnant?"

"I- um." Rose fidgeted, her face starting to get red. "I don't believe I am...."

"Of course. I understand this is embarrassing for you. But understand I simply would not want to put a pregnant mother in harm's way. I would like to have you take a test at the hospital for sure, as well as be given a temporary block to ensure you would not conceive while your tour with us is ongoing. There will be someone to pick you up tomorrow to get everything sorted out," King David explained.

"Understood." Rose nodded, still embarrassed.

"Now, Commander West, Lydia was it?" King David asked, looking over at Lydia.

"Yes, my Lord!" Just a little too quick and loud. She was

nervous too.

"You mentioned in your evaluation that Ms. Tenabalm was a very sweet girl with a 'good bubbly personality'." The table laughed lightly. "The only concern I have is having her in a high stress, life or death situation, she failed the GSA exam the first time, and has a relatively low kill count. In your opinion will she hesitate in killing someone if it's the easy way to protect my family?"

"No, my Lord," Lydia said. "Rose is a sweet girl, but she's also tough as nails when stuff hits the fan. I would attribute the kill count to our location and Rose's not being in the same positions as the boys more than anything."

"Alright, anything else." King David looked around the table. Various people shook their heads. "You may go back to the line. Mr. Henagar, step forward."

Rose bowed and came back to the line. John walked up to the circle as King David handed a folder to the queen.

"Mr. Henagar, you did rather well in the events. But it's not your skill that I am worried about," Queen Elisa, said. "Your CO stated in her evaluation that you have something of a mischievous side. Would you say this is accurate?"

"I- uh. Yeah I mean I sometimes I- Well I mean I used to get into a little trouble." John stammered.

"Mm." The queen nodded, looking at the folder.

I wonder if this is where the term ice queen comes from. Zack thought as he shivered.

"Could you go over in detail one of these events?" Queen Elisa asked. "There is one in a report from your first visit to Portland. Something about a gentlemen's club?"

Oh Christ.... Zack thought.

"Uh... yeah so...." John took a deep breath and rubbed his neck. "So the very first time we came here it was crazy, you know? Like, this ain't nothing like home." John coughed a bit in his hand, obviously embarrassed. "Anyway, back home we had heard a story about these places where you could... pay a certain amount for certain things."

"Certain things? Please be clearer, Mr. Henagar." Queen Elisa tilted her head to the side in an almost mocking manner.

"Uh... Adult things." John mumbled. "So I was a little curious and I wanted to know if that was true and what it was all about."

"And Mr. Taylor came with you, correct?" Queen Elisa said, looking in the file.

"Yeah I sort of sprung it on him though. He was not aware we were going there ahead of time," John said.

"Mm."

She's way less nice than David, Zack thought, shivering again.

"So we got there and uh... it was a little more than I expected. Like, I was not mentally prepared for what all was going on. So... we just ended up sitting back and um... watching...."

And this story is so cringey.... Zack tried not to make a face.

"Anyway we had been there maybe ten minutes when this one guy starts to really, like, be rough with one of the girls. So I speak up and tell him to knock it off, and he shoves me and I tripped."

"Mhm. Then what happened? Be as specific as possible."

"That's when Zack punched that guy in the stomach then threw him onto this glass table which broke apart. Then we got into a brawl with, like, three other guys and we, uh... won. But the cops were on their way already and we got detained for a little bit." John finished quickly.

"Mm." Queen Elisa clicked a pen in the silence. "This was a bit of an ordeal at the time but now it's not that big of a deal. The part I would like to know about has to do with the men you fought. Were you aware later on that one of those men ended up dying from internal bleeding? Were you, or Mr. Taylor responsible for that?"

I didn't know that...

"Uh, no I never heard about that....Well, it all happened so fast, I'm not sure...."

"Do you believe you killed anyone?"

"I mean, I don't think so...."

"That will be all Mr. Henagar."

John seemed to freeze out of confusion for a moment, then turned and walked back to the line. As he walked he stared at Zack raising an eyebrow at him. Zack raised both of his in response.

Don't ask me, I don't know what that was about. Zack thought.

"Mr. Slater, would you step forward please?" King David asked, grabbing a new file. Daniel walked up to the circle and waited as the king read his file.

"Mr. Slater, you have a very nice record. You also were elected to captain in charge of IN-14 during Commander West's absence in accordance with GSA's current self-sustaining procedures." King David started. "Do you have the respect of this unit?"

"Yes, my Lord," Daniel said without hesitating.

"Good to hear. Your relationship with Ms. Tenabalm hasn't brought up any internal problems?" King David asked.

"No, my Lord." Again no hesitation.

"Really? No hiccups at all?" Queen Elisa chimed in.

"No, my Lady. Our unit is in a rural area and we have a bit less structure than the traditional military in GSA, but our relationship has always been secondary to our duty."

"And you can confirm this Commander West?" Queen Elisa asked.

"Yes, my Lady. Because our unit is so small and is not always in large battalions or other members of the military there are less problems between members," Lydia explained.

"Well, as long as it continues to not cause problems I have no objections. That will be all Mr. Slater," King David said. "And please continue to be a shining example for the GSA. We might put you on a poster."

The table laughed as Daniel walked back to the line, but Daniel couldn't hide the huge grin on his face.

"Mr. Taylor, please come forward," King David said.

Zack took a deep breath, shaking out his hands as he walked up, more nervous than he would like to admit. Zack stepped up to the circle with the king smiling at him. Zack noticed now how friendly his face was. His smile showed off big dimples, and he was a bit bigger, somewhat like a smaller Santa Claus. He was warm in the most simple sense, and quickly Zack felt his nerves loosen.

"Mr. Taylor, how is your shoulder?" King David asked with genuine concern in his voice.

"It's healing well, I should be at one hundred percent soon sir," Zack said, smiling back.

"Good." King David, nodded his head quickly.

"Mr. Taylor, I believe that I am in the uncomfortable position of asking you for forgiveness," Queen Elisa said out of nowhere.

"For what, my queen?" Zack said, more caught off guard that *she* wanted to apologize then the fact she was a queen apologizing.

"It seems in the chaos the other day, I completely forgot to thank you for saving my daughter. She can't stop talking about Mr. Hero," Queen Elisa said with a smile.

"Yes, she's been having a bit of fun with your name as well. She asked me this morning why your name was Taylor, 'that's a girl's name!'" King David said, creating laughs around the table.

Oh go suck a railroad spike, Zack thought, as he chuckled along with them.

"Mr. Taylor, how would you describe yourself?" King David asked, folding his hands. Zack roughly rubbed his forearm, trying to think.

"I would say I'm a fine soldier," Zack said flatly.

"Anything else?" King David asked.

"I'm sure there are other things about me, but I think that I'm a little biased," Zack said.

King David chuckled again.

"Yes, I suppose you are." King David nodded. He then tapped his finger on the table. "Tell me, how do you get along with your teammates? If you were to tell us about them, what would you say? You may be as plain as you like; speak freely."

"Yes, my Lord. I would say that Daniel is a hell of a guy, and he's always worried about us in his own way. He's responsible and honorable, and Rose is a lucky girl. Rose ,I would say, is a mother hen in the best way possible. She's always there to make sure we're eating and doing okay. John is the excitement in my life, I suppose. He's a good friend, and no matter what his personality shows on the surface, he will always have your back. I trust all of them with my life," Zack said.

"Mm. And what about your CO? Do you get along with her?" Queen Elisa asked.

"Yes. Lydia and I have always gotten along pretty well. She's the one who taught me how to be a soldier, after all," Zack said, glancing over to Lydia. "You could say I look up to her."

There was a long silence. Zack started to feel uneasy as the king and queen exchanged glances. After a moment, one of the people next to the king leaned over and whispered, and the king nodded.

"Mr. Taylor, General Williams," he said, introducing himself. "Do you have any comments about your military history?"

"I'm sorry? I don't understand the question, sir," Zack said. The general pulled out a piece of paper.

"Your confirmed kill count throughout your military career according to our record is at 36. We also can assume with Mr. Henagar's testimony that you were responsible for one more death at a gentlemen's club a few years ago, bringing your total kill count to 37," the general said, working it out on paper. "You passed your requirement test to be made an official GSA on your first attempt. During your six-year career, you have had 19 missions, received honors in many including the bread riots in Texas, and putting down some insurgents along the nuclear coast.... You lead your team in kills in action with the next closest being John Henagar with 15. Not to say you were ever in the wrong with these actions, but a count this high is... concerning."

"I-" Zack stood stunned. He had never really thought about that before. Most of the missions they split up. They had all killed people firsthand. After a while it had stopped being a big deal for all of them. And when they got home it's not like they sat around bragging about kills; they all dealt with it in their own way. He never knew that he more than doubled everyone else in kills.

"I never realized any of that. I'm told to do a job and I do it as efficiently and as quickly as possible, like we were taught," Zack said.

"Yes, but do you take pleasure in killing someone?" The general asked.

Zack gritted his teeth. "No, it's just a job."

"Would you say you feel nothing at all, Mr. Taylor?" A different man next to the queen asked. "No remorse, or guilt?"

"I didn't realize I should feel remorse or guilt about killing bad people, sir," Zack said, trying not to sound curt.

"It's rather interesting you say that, Mr. Taylor" the first general said. "You were raised by your step-father, correct? It would seem that your mother left you and her late husband when you were rather young, yes?"

"Yes that's correct. She left when I was eight." Zack said through his teeth.

"Then your step-father ended up overdosing on heroin it would seem. How old were you when that happened?"

"I was 15, sir," Zack said.

"After the events in Texas, correct? And since your mother could not be located at that time, and you moving would be difficult for your team, the house was deemed yours. Tell us, was your step-father a bad person?"

The worst you ignorant... you don't even know, Zack thought, clenching his teeth.

"Are you accusing me of killing my step-dad?" Zack asked.

“No, Mr. Taylor, we are trying to see why your CO filed for an official investigation and labeled you a possible Code 17,” the general said, staring at him.

“What?” Zack said, bewildered. He turned to look at Lydia who didn't meet his gaze, then back to the table. “Code 17?”

“Code 17 is a sanction for soldiers over exposed to trauma, becoming desensitized and more violent as a result. It mostly affects old soldiers who have been doing what we do too long. They start to rationalize murder, become bloodthirsty” the second general said.

“While you were not officially given a sanction, and your step-father's death was ruled as self-inflicted, it's troubling that your commanding officer would put this forward at all,” the first general said.

Zack processed what they had said. Lydia tried to throw him under the bus after his step-dad died. She assumed immediately that Zack murdered him.

“I couldn't tell you why she did that, sir....” He finally said.

“Perhaps you could explain this rational, Commander West?”

Lydia folded her arms and looked at the table, rocking herself a little. “I put forward that motion knowing full well that both would come up negative sir. I thought that it would be better to file the motion immediately so that in the future there would be no questions like this, but it would seem it had the opposite effect.”

Lydia looked up at Zack, her eyes seemed to ask him to believe her. Zack turned back to the table.

“Would you say you're an angry person, Mr. Taylor?” Asked another voice from the table.

“Sometimes.” Zack was out of it now. “When your life's on the line, or the lives of your fellow soldiers, being angry is better than being passive or afraid.”

“The main question we are trying to get to, Mr. Taylor, is this: are you of a sound enough mental state to protect the king?” The General asked.

"Absolutely," Zack said. "I won't claim I'm a good man sir, I won't lie to you. But I am a good soldier. And while I may not have had a good family situation, and I'm sure I have a stigma that comes along with that, but I have always had a king. And I have always had this military. That is my family sir, and I'd give my life to protect it."

"Well said," King David said at last. "Zack, I have no question in my mind about your loyalty, or your ability to do your job. However, just to be on the safe side, all of our applicants have to pass a mental evaluation. I hope you understand."

"Yes sir. If I am unfit to serve you I'd rather that be found out before I would even be given that chance to fail. But I assure you I won't," Zack said. He would pass these tests at any cost. He didn't have any family left.

His family was buried under a tree back home.

"Good. Tomorrow at eight o'clock you will each be brought in to start your individual vetting process. Feel free to use the rest of the day as you like, but get some rest. You are dismissed," King David said, pointing open handedly to the door.

They all bowed and headed out the door. Zack walked through the lobby and exited out the building and hopped down the steps, pulling out a cigarette. He lit it with shaking hands and took a long drag as he paced in front of the steps. Lydia quickly walked down the steps after him, but slowed as she got to the bottom. She leaned against the railing on the last step, only daring to steal glances at Zack as he paced.

"So uh..." Daniel started from the middle of the steps, with John and Rose coming down behind him. "Crap, I don't know what to say."

"I'm sorry about the club thing." John said.

"Don't worry about it." Zack exhaled, then dragged again.

"I wrote that report a long time ago," Lydia said.

Zack waited for her to continue, but she didn't.

"Why?" Zack finally asked.

Lydia folded her arms across her chest and rocked a little. "I thought that maybe if S.W.O.R.D. found out that your step-dad was abusive and thought you couldn't handle what was going on, you'd be in more trouble than if they thought you just snapped after Texas."

"Bullcrap," Zack spat.

"What?" Lydia said, whipping her head up.

"Bullcrap. I don't believe any of that," Zack said, walking up to her.

"Why would I lie to you?" Lydia said, standing up straight.

"I don't know, maybe the same reason you lied to me about Sarah? You were trying to cover your own rear?" Zack said.

"The hell would you know about that! You know how many times my butt has been on the line covering for you when you screw up?!" Lydia spoke louder, getting in his face. "And don't you put what happened to Sarah on me for one second! I did everything I could for that girl!"

"Also, why the hell are you making it sound like I killed my step- dad?!"

"I don't know. Did you?"

Zack couldn't believe what he was hearing right now. She knew the situation better than anyone.

"Guys let's not fight-" Rose tried to break it up.

"Let him answer, Rose." Lydia didn't break away.

"I don't know. You turned on me the second you thought you could get in trouble. Were you the one who ordered everyone who worked at the office killed? You're S.W.O.R.D. through and through anymore. Results at any cost, right!?"

SMACK!

Zack's eyes watered and his ear burned. He rubbed his face turning through the direction his body had turned. She had hit him pretty hard; he thought he felt his neck crack a little. He didn't want to cry but your eyes water pretty bad when you get slapped. It's like pulling nose hair, it just happens. He didn't bother looking at anyone, or saying anything. He just pulled out another cigarette and started walking away.

"ZACK!" Rose bellowed as he walked.

But nobody followed him.

11. WANT TO TALK ABOUT IT?

"Hey, what can I get you?" Joshua asked as Zack sat down at the bar.

"What's your favorite drink with whiskey?" Zack asked. resting his head on his hand. Joshua looked at him for a moment, leaning against the counter.

"Well after a girl slaps me in the face, I like to add to it with a whiskey sour," Joshua said, looking up at his eyebrows as he thought.

"Ha. One of those then. How bad is it?" Zack asked, feeling better already.

"Well, I don't think you'll get a black eye, but you're gonna have a mark for a while," Joshua said, mixing the drink. "What did you do anyway?"

"Oh, I called my CO a liar to her face, then blamed her for getting my girlfriend killed," Zack said, tapping the table.

"Jesus Christ, that's depressing. You couldn't lie to me and say you grabbed the Queen's arse or something?" He said, turning back to Zack with the drink.

"Ha! You think I'd get just a slap for that?"

"No, but I think it would make a better story," he said, setting the drink down. Olivia came behind the bar, from the table she just wiped down.

"Hey, I was hinting that you should be here at nine," she said. "Ouch, what happened to you?"

"Eh, I grabbed the queen's butt," Zack said, picking up his drink.

Olivia turned as white as a ghost. "...You what?"

The men chuckled lightly.

“Joshua said my real story is too depressing,” Zack said.

“Jesus don't scare me like that,” Olivia said, putting her hand on her forehead.

“Anyway, what's up?” Zack said, setting his drink back down.

“Salim, and the others want a break down of what happened and have a game plan for you to look over,” she said. “They're in the cellar. Whenever you're ready.”

“Sweet. I thought I might have to wait until two in the morning again,” Zack said, standing up.

“Nah, place is usually pretty dead during the day. We won't start getting people in here until at least six,” Joshua said, holding up the bar's little door.

“By the way, is that Olive Oil thing real? Or was that just acting?” Zack asked as he walked through the door to the cellar, that was off the bar.

“Yeah, it's real. Lucas gave me that nickname and the bar flies think it's cute, so, you know,” she said, walking behind him.

“Right. Which one is Lucas again?”

“He's the cook. He's got the stupid goatee,” Joshua said.

“No, no. It's a 'soul patch' remember?” Olivia said.

“Well whatever the heck it is, it's stupid,” Joshua huffed.

They walked into the cellar, where Micheal and Salim were working on something by a table in the middle of the concrete floor, in front of the giant metal doors of some kind of cooler. Zack had to duck to keep from hitting his head on exposed beams.

“Hey, I'm back,” Zack said, walking over.

“Hey. That didn't take long, how did it go?” Micheal said, looking up from the table. “Owh, I hope that wasn't from the therapist.”

“Nah, me and my CO got into it a little. And they aren't starting the psych evaluations until tomorrow. Today it was just the king and queen doing this little mini interview thing with the generals,” Zack explained, pulling out a chair by the table.

“Mini interview? That's different, isn't it?” Micheal asked, turning to Salim.

"Yes, that's not typical of royal guard vetting. But then again there has never been a guard from the GSA, so they are most likely being overly cautious due to the stigma of the 'Bloods'." Salim made finger quotes at the last word, still looking through papers.

"Well I don't know about overly cautious. I mean, the end game here is me killing the whole royal family." Zack shrugged.

"Fair point. How did it go?" Micheal asked.

"Well I wouldn't say it went badly, but I did have to maneuver a few obstacles," Zack said, rubbing his face.

"They had you run a course while you answered questions?" Salim said, looking up confused.

"What? No I mean, like, I had some previous actions that I had to explain."

"Ah." Salim nodded, going back to the paper.

"What was it?" Micheal asked.

"Well apparently when my step-dad OD'd, my CO filed for an investigation into his death, and tried to sanction me with an Article... crap what was it.... The one saying you enjoy killing people too much or whatever," Zack said, flipping his hand about.

"That's why you and the old lady got into a fight?" Joshua said, standing on the other side of the big round table.

"Yeah." Zack nodded. "King David wasn't too concerned, but the generals got kinda crappy with me."

"Hmm, I wouldn't worry about it too much. As long as you can pass the psych test you'll be fine," Salim said.

"See, that's the stuff that pisses me off about 'normal' people. None of them want to admit it, but they all want a soldier who's fine with killing. And you can't explain to people who have never done it that killing someone sometimes isn't that big a deal," Joshua complained.

"What do you mean?" Olivia asked, sitting down at the table.

"Like, if you got a chance to kill the king, would you

struggle with the decision? Would that haunt you for the rest of your life?" Joshua asked.

"No, but the king is an evil monster," Olivia said.

"That's my point. Most people are evil. Now if I was forced to kill a kid, or some lady that was crying and just defenseless then yeah that might mess me up. But killing the average schmuck isn't really keeping most soldiers up at night," Joshua said.

"You ever think maybe YOU'RE a jerk?" Olivia cocked an eyebrow.

"When have you had to kill people, Joshua?" Zack asked.

"I served eight years with the Guard. I did a tour through the south after the bread riots," Joshua said.

Zack winced at the mention of the bread riots.

"Alright, alright, if you all are done, Zack, we have the files on the royal family we wanted you to go over," Micheal said, handing him a stack of envelopes.

"Right." Zack set them down and opened the first one. "King David Hudson. Age: 47. Height: 6' 0. Weight: ~295 lbs."

"King David wasn't born into royalty. His father created the kingdom when David was 13. When he was 22, he married Queen Elisa but held off on having children for a few years," Micheal said. "The fact that he wasn't always royalty causes him to be seen as a kind of king of the people. He took over as king at 26 when his father passed away, and has been running the country ever since. We left some cuts of his speeches and decrees so you could get a feel for his mindset, albeit we can't really tell you who he is in private. There are rumors that he is something of a womanizer, though."

"Men with power I guess," Zack said. He put down the file and picked up the next one. "Queen Elisa Hudson. Age: 42. Height: 5' 9. Weight: ~165."

"Mm. The queen regent is originally from Canada. She was arranged to marry David to secure peace between the nations. It's worked for the last twenty years going strong. She's lost her smile over the years it would seem, and is rather icy to most people. She's pretty guarded, or she's been told not to speak too much. Either way, we don't have much on her," Micheal said.

Zack nodded, moving on to the next file. "Okay, next is Princess Eliana Hudson. That's the one I didn't know. Age: 21. Height: 5'7. Weight: ...Various?" Zack read, raising an eyebrow.

"Yes. Princess Eliana is a... difficult study. She was born the same year that David became king. There's rumors that she and her mother don't seem to get along. She was particularly close to her late grandma who passed away when she was 14. Before then she had been a bit heavier, but now her weight is kept in check through a strict weight control team she's been provided with. She has recently begun a courtship with Prince Armando Cortes from Mexico in an attempt to unify the entire Continent. They plan to be married this year. She's never known any other life but that of a princess, so stay calm around her, as she is the most likely to abuse her power over you simply because it's 'fun'," Micheal said.

"Noted. On to Prince Armando then," Zack said, opening the next folder. "Prince Armando Cortes. Age: 23. Height: 5 '11. Weight: ~185."

"Prince Armando hails from the Mexican royalty where his family has held power for generations. Not much there, but there is plenty of good soil for crops so the population has been able to keep growing. That population is the reason for the marriage to Eliana. If they were to attack they might be able to overtake us with sheer numbers," Micheal said. "There's a lot of rumors on his family, less on Armando as an individual. His family has a pretty tight squeeze on the Mexican people."

"Watch yourself around him too. Word in the palace is that he's taken an interest in soldiers of the GSA," Olivia said.

"Why?" Zack asked.

"Don't know. I did get some intel from one of my friends, though. Apparently he's either up King David's tail or trying to get tail of his own." Olivia folded her arms.

"I wouldn't worry about it much; if you'll go to the next one." Micheal waved his hand.

Zack shut the envelope, and opened the next one. “Princess Annabelle Hudson. Age: 7. Height: 4'5. Weight: ~95.”

“This will most likely be the one you will be assigned to. Princess Annabelle is the one you saved earlier. She’s quite young yet, and is supposedly very shy, possibly from being so sheltered. We don't have much more to go on than that,” Micheal said, stretching.

“And this last one?” Zack said, picking up the last file.

“That contains information on the King's late sister's daughter and her new husband. They will be staying at the palace as well, but they are on a honeymoon right now,” Micheal said.

“Duchess Josephine Hudson, and... Comrade Dmitri?” Zack asked.

“Yeah, he's from the New Proletariat World. He's a communist.” Joshua explained.

“What's a communist?” Zack asked, dipping the folder.

“They think if everyone's a slave, everyone is equal,” Olivia said, shaking her head.

“If everyone is equal, how can anyone be a slave?” Zack asked, confused.

“If you scare people enough they don't ask questions like that, it seems,” Micheal said. “Anyway, take some time and brush up on your politics. I'd like you to get back before it gets too late, and after this I want to run through some things you might run into tomorrow during your psych tests.”

Zack spent an hour or so going over the files and asking questions. Then another hour or two going over some of the tricks the psychiatrists might use to trip him up. They also worked on what to avoid as well as how to change the subject and avoid questions without looking like he's avoiding questions.

“So remember the key to beating the psych test is not to try to make them think you’re innocent or that there's nothing wrong with you at all; that would make it seem like you’re hiding something. You want to make them think that you have some problems but you want to make sure the problems you might have aren't going to be a problem for them," Micheal said.

"Right, right. So I'm supposed to mention I have a slight gambling addiction, right?" Zack said, ashing his cigarette.

"Yes but don't just come out and say that; wait for them to ask you about something you can work that into," Micheal said.

"Got it." Zack nodded.

"You know, he could get a tattoo," Olivia said.

"How would that help?" Joshua asked.

"Tattoos are a form of artistic expression. And you can't make art without emotion. That's what they're worried about right; him being emotionally detached?" Olivia said.

"Well I guess it couldn't hurt." Micheal shrugged. "To be honest, this is all second hand knowledge I've been hearing from other soldiers. Maybe we will get lucky and they'll just pass you after looking you over once."

"I don't have a problem with getting a tattoo, I guess, but what would I get?" Zack asked. Everyone was quiet for a second until Joshua slapped the table.

"Got it. Your cell's call sign is IN-14 right?"

"Yeah?"

"I, N, 1, 4," Joshua said, tapping down Zack's knuckles. Zack picked up his hand visualizing. "It's small, but noticeable. And it's a statement about loyalty and remembering where you're from!"

"Yeah, that would look pretty good I guess." Zack nodded. Behind him someone came down the stairs.

"Hey, someone's looking for you up here," Timothy said, walking down the steps.

"Who?" Zack said, taking another drag.

"Tall, short black hair, was in here with you before," Tim said.

"That's John." Zack exhaled. "How long have we been down here?"

"A good, long time," Olivia said, rubbing her face.

"I think we've covered everything we need to cover, so

we should all probably get back to our positions," Micheal said. "There's a tattoo place about 4 blocks east of here; they do pretty good work if you decide to get it done. Otherwise, come back and keep us up to date next time you get the chance."

"Got it," Zack said, standing up. He let Olivia and Joshua head up first before he walked up the stairs. Sitting at the bar was John, looking out over the mostly empty restaurant.

"What's up?" Zack said, sitting down next to him.

"Hey, I've been looking for you. They let you down into the cellar here now?" John said, turning back to the bar.

"Yeah, Salim wanted to check my shoulder, make sure I won't get an infection," Zack said.

"Ahh. Your face doing okay?" John asked.

"Yeah, it's not red anymore," Zack said, picking his nails. "Lydia still upset?"

"Well she didn't really say anything all the way back to the hotel. But when we didn't hear anything from you after two hours, she started freaking out," John said, rotating his hand out.

"I shouldn't have said all that. I was just pissed." Zack sighed.

"Yeah...." John agreed. "You okay now?"

"Yeah, I should probably go apologize, huh?" Zack said.

"Probably." John nodded. "She'll probably apologize too."

"Hey, before that. You up for an adventure?" Zack grinned.

"An adventure?" John asked, skeptical. "You know every time we go on an adventure we get in trouble right?"

"Come on, don't be a wuss," he said, slapping John on the back. Zack started walking out the door.

"Where are we going?" John asked, following him.

"Come on, it's a surprise," Zack said, as they walked. They headed east down the street walking past the different buildings. When they came across the tattoo parlor.

"I'm not getting a matching tattoo with you bro, that's weird." John laughed.

"Nahh, I'm just getting one," Zack said.

"For real? Since when have you wanted to get a tattoo?"

John asked.

"Eh, I've thought about it on and off. There just aren't any good spots to get one back home," Zack said.

They headed into a crusty, paint chipped building with L-Inks over the door. A man with face tattoos and full sleeves took Zack's 'order'. He picked a design and watched the guy chain smoke with one hand and tattoo Zack's knuckles with the other.

John watched, rather interested in the process, as the artist filled in the design made on his knuckles. Zack thought it was odd that some parts he didn't feel anything, while at other points he felt a sharp sting. It only took maybe half an hour, and it was done.

"You know, I got to say that looks pretty sick." John nodded. "Did it hurt a lot?"

"No, not really, just every once and a while it stung a little." Zack shrugged, as they walked back out of the shop as the sun was starting to set. It wasn't long before they got back to their hotel. Lydia was standing in the mostly empty lobby with Rose and Daniel.

"Hey," Zack called out.

"Hey man, you had us worried," Daniel said.

"Yeah." Zack sighed, and turned to Lydia. "I'm sorry about all that stuff. I shouldn't have acted like that."

Lydia rocked on her feet for a second. "Don't worry about it. I'm sorry too."

Zack nodded. After a second he reached out and hugged Lydia. She sighed and hugged him back.

"Did..." Rose stammered, making Zack look up. "Did you get a tattoo?"

"What?" Lydia said, pushing away.

"Oh yeah," Zack said, showing them.

"Oh my God! Zack!" Rose said, grabbing his hand. "Is that permanent!?"

"Of course it's permanent, it's a tattoo!" Zack said.

"Since when did you want a tattoo?" Lydia asked, feeling his knuckles. Rose did the same.

"I don't know, I always thought about getting one." Zack shrugged.

"It's so raised," Rose said, running her thumb over it.

"It flattens out later," Zack said.

"IN-14, huh?" Lydia said, tilting her head. "At least it looks really good."

"That is pretty sick," Daniel said, looking over Rose's shoulder.

They stood in the lobby like a bunch of idiots for a while before they headed into their rooms for an early night. Zack lit one last cigarette out on the terrace. He leaned against the corner of the railing looking up at the stars.

"Man, you can barely see the stars out here," Zack said, wondering why that was.

"That's because of all the lights in the city," Daniel said from behind. Zack turned, startled to find Daniel standing up out of a chair that was hidden before.

"God, I didn't see you. Don't spook me like that!" Zack sighed.

"Sorry, I thought you were talking to me!" Daniel laughed.

Zack turned back the other way and put his leg up on the rail.

"I would have figured you and Rose would be in bed by now." Zack ashed his cigarette.

"Nah, she went to call her mom," Daniel said. "Hey, I've been meaning to talk to you about something."

"Yeah? What's up?" Zack coughed.

"What do you think about... Rose and me getting engaged?" He asked hesitantly.

Zack ran his thumb over the filter of his cigarette. "Well you guys have been together a long time. It's about that time, isn't it?" Zack shrugged.

"No, yeah, it's just- I didn't want to make you feel bad or anything since... you know...."

"I'd feel even worse if you guys put your lives on hold just for me." Zack sighed. "I'm happy for you guys. I mean that."

"Thanks, Zack," Daniel said.

Zack heard him push off his rail and start walking. Zack looked back up at the sky. He could still kind of see the stars, but there was this, well he wouldn't call it fog exactly, but fog like substance over, or under the stars.

"Hey um...." Daniel's voice came back. Zack put his foot down and put his other foot on the other railing so he could see him. "When you asked Sarah, or when you were going to ask her, did you feel... weird?"

"Weird?" Zack repeated, raising an eyebrow. "What do you mean? Like, nervous?"

"No, not really," Daniel said, hanging his head. Zack waited for a few seconds to let him explain. "It's like... I don't know.... Rose is just so super excited for this. She went and picked out her own ring and everything. And she's making all these plans.... It's just...."

Daniel sighed, letting his shoulders drop.

Zack exhaled. "Like she's pushing you into it?"

"Well...." He started fidgeting with the railing. "It's not like I don't love her or anything. And I do want to marry her one day. But it's just, you know how she is, she's so pushy about it! She wants it done her way on her time, and it's like I'm an afterthought!"

"Mmm." Zack hummed behind his cigarette.

"I don't know man.... Am I just freaking out over nothing?" He said, rubbing his forehead.

"Well." Zack put his cigarette out on the railing and flicked it out into the street. "I would say that women in general are pushy like that. And you can't explain that to them either, it's like the time I told Sarah I didn't want to spend my weekend doing that corn maze thing a while back. Jesus Christ, it was like I told her she was too fat to be seen in public with me or something! 'You never want to spend time with me! If I'm such a burden I'll just find someone else to take me, and you can forget all about me!'"

"Yeah I remember that, you were pissed." Daniel laughed.

"But I would say on the other side of that is, if she gets pushy like that, it's only because she's so excited to be your wife," Zack said, smiling. "It might not be the best way to go about telling you how much they care about you, but that's how they do it."

Daniel nodded, scratching the railing with his fingernail. "Yeah, your right. Thanks, Zack, I feel better."

"Any time!" Zack gave a wave and headed into the room. John was already in bed. Zack clicked off the lamp on the bedside table.

He laid on his side facing the wall. He tried to cry as quietly as he could as he thought about how crappy he had been with Sarah about that stupid corn maze.

12. IT ALL STARTED WHEN I WAS BORN...

Zack was led into a reception area by the soldier who came and got him from the hotel.

"Thanks." Zack nodded.

Zack looked around the room. The waiting room was small with a small couch and a few chairs in the corner. There was also a small bookcase and today's paper. Zack walked across the room to where there was a little man sitting behind a glass window that was open.

"Hi!" The kid said in a squeaky voice. He was an adult, but had a very young look about him, almost cutesy. Zack was a little put off by the lack of masculinity.

City-boy... Zack thought.

"Hello. I'm here for a psych evaluation?" Zack said, leaning on the counter.

"Oh, yeah, Mr. Taylor, correct?" He squealed with a smile.

Kid it is wayyy too flipping early for you to be so animated. Zack thought, rubbing his face. "Yeah, that's me."

"One sec." The kid picked up a phone and held it with his chin. "Hey Jewels, he's here. ...The guy from S.W.O.R.D.. ...m'kay."

The kid hung up the phone. "She'll be right out."

Zack knocked on the wooden counter he was leaning on and turned towards the door that led to her office.

"So... You're in S.W.O.R.D. huh?" The kid asked.

Zack turned back around, giving him full attention. "Yes sir."

"*Sir* oh boy you don't have to be so formal about it. Call me

Nathan." The boy smiled... oddly....

O-kay... "Yes I am in S.W.O.R.D. Mr. Nathan."

Nathan began to laugh at that.

The door opened up, revealing a young blonde woman. Her hair was tied up in the back as her bangs started short to the left of her face and grew longer towards the right. She wore a pinstriped skirt with nylons underneath, and a clean violet blouse with frills covered her rather noticeable chest.

"Mr. Taylor? Sorry about that, I was filling out all those forms," she said, walking up to him and extending her hand. "My name is Julia Crane; I'll be picking your brain for a little while."

"Zackary Taylor. It's a pleasure ma'am," Zack said, straightening and shaking her hand gently.

"Ma'am? Oh God don't call me ma'am you'll make me feel like an old maid." Julia smiled while she tilted her head in an almost flirtatious manner.

"Oh, I didn't mean to offend..." Zack said, rubbing his neck. They finally broke the hand shake as she moved her body to the side, showing him into the office.

"Don't worry about it! You ready to get started? After you," she said.

Zack walked into her office and looked around. On one side there was a desk that was neatly kept. Behind it on the wall there was a clock and some sort of diploma. Painted on the wall with the door in very nice handwriting was: *Be the person you needed when you were younger.*

On the other side was a funny little couch, a comfy looking chair, and a desk chair. There was a little round coffee table in the center with a notebook lying on it.

"Are you nervous?" She asked, shutting the door behind her.

"No? Why?" Zack asked, turning to her.

"Eh, sometimes first timers get a little nervous. You almost seem on edge. Am I really that scary?" Julia said, with that same head tilt and smile.

Lady you have no idea... Zack thought.

"No, I guess I might be a little nervous. Never had to talk to a psychiatrist. You're not gonna make me remember I got molested a long time ago or something are you?"

"Ha, that's a little dark," Julia said, searching his eyes.

Zack did his best not to seem uncomfortable, standing with his hands at his sides and smiling lightly.

"Please, sit."

Zack headed over to the chair and leaned towards the coffee table. Julia sat in the desk chair and picked up the notebook.

"So, Zackary Taylor, that's a cool name. Is it okay if I call you Zack?" She asked, flipping open the book.

"Yeah, that's fine." Zack nodded.

"Oh, Julia is fine. Lots of people also call me Jewels, I like that as well. Just whatever you're comfortable with." She smiled.

"Um- would Dr. Crane be alright?"

"That's kind of a little formal...." Julia raised an eyebrow. "You don't have to worry about seeming disrespectful or whatever. I'd rather us be able to talk like we are friends, not, you know, formal."

"I'd feel more comfortable with Dr. Crane." Zack rubbed his hands together.

"Well, it's fine for now. We will get there at your pace!" Julia gave him a thumbs up.

...*This is weird,* Zack thought.

"Any-who, you are being considered for a position as a bodyguard for the royal family! Kudos!" Julia squealed.

What is up with the way she talks? Zack thought.

"Yeah, I'm pretty excited! It's going to be fun to live in the city for a while."

"You don't like the country?" She asked.

"No, I like it alright. It's just, this is like a big adventure, you know?" He said, wringing his hands.

"Ah, right. It's got to get kinda boring out there with nothing to do, huh?" Julia nodded. "What do you do for fun back home?"

"Oh, well I tend to do a little bit of gambling. Though I'm thinking maybe I do it a little too much," Zack said, seeing an opportunity.

"Oh yeah? What's your game?"

Crap.

"Uh, mostly poker with the boys."

"Fun fun! I wouldn't worry about it too much. Everyone needs to blow off some steam somehow," Julia said, dismissing his entire case.

"Oh, okay...." Zack tried to think of something else to say.

"What about family? You don't have anyone back home you'll miss?" Julia asked suddenly.

"Uh, no not really...."

"Really? That's a little unusual...." Julia clicked a pen. "What was home like for you growing up then?"

CRAP!

* * *

Zack grabbed a suitcase from the back of the van and handed it to John.

"Thanks. Not a bad little place is it?" John said, poking his chin out towards the apartment complex they had been brought to. Zack grabbed his duffle bag and shut the van.

The complex was only about two blocks away from the palace. It was a nicer building which had been renovated specifically for the GSAs. It was white and three or four stories tall.

"Yeah, it's gonna be nice not to have to mow the yard all the time." Zack nodded. They followed an officer into the building as he slid a card through a reader by the door and walked in. They headed to the desk in the lobby first as a girl in a military uniform stood and slid out 2 envelopes. The officer grabbed them and handed one to John and Zack.

"These are your key cards. You get two of them just in

case. Don't lose them, but if you do tell whoever is working the desk immediately so we can have them deleted off the system. Should you need anything during your stay here, come to the front desk and they can help you get it sorted out. Clear?"

"Yes, sir!" John and Zack said together. The officer led them toward the stairs.

"This will be where you stay during your service for the royal family. Your neighbors are the other GSA bodyguards. You're concentrated here so that information between the crown and its soldiers are easily connected." He walked up the stairs quickly while he talked. "You have been given an e-mail address, landline phone, and television for both off-duty entertainment as well as a way to receive video messages as well as send them. Clothing has been provided for you as well as a sum of money for personal affects. You are not required to stay here every night, your personal time is up to you, but you will be getting several messages mostly everyday. Failure to respond to them will bear consequences, so make sure you check in at least once every few hours. Clear?"

"Yes, sir!" They said as they stopped in front of two rooms.

"These are your quarters, Mr. Taylor in 210, Mr. Henagar in 212. These are also for you," he said, handing them both a cellular phone. "These are your cell phones; carry them with you at all times, have them charged at all times. You have a charger in your rooms, if you lose it or it breaks, talk to the front desk and they'll get you a new one. You have manuals in your room detailing how to use all the tech stuff as well as instructional videos. Take the weekend to become acquainted with all of them, as you'll likely use them every day from here on out. Clear?"

"Yes, sir!" The officer saluted and they saluted back, afterwards he quickly left.

"Duuuddddeeee...." John said, shaking Zack while looking at his new phone.

"Let's check out these rooms!" Zack said, trying to contain his own excitement.

Zack slid the keycard through the scanner and walked into his room. Right off the door there was a bathroom with all the amenities. Walking past the entryway there was a living room with a couch, a TV on a stand, and a few chairs and lamps. To the left there was a little kitchen, complete with a fridge, stove with an oven, microwave, sink, and cooking utensils. Then to the left of the kitchen, what would be behind the bathroom, was the bedroom, with a queen size bed, a desk with a lamp which held all of the manuals and other papers, and a big dresser next to a smaller closet.

"Well heck, this is pretty nice...." Zack mumbled.

"Dude!!!" Zack heard John bellow, then the door clicking when it opened. John came flying around the corner. "Bro! Our rooms? Are connected!!!"

"Shut the hell up...." Zack said, tilting his head. Zack came to look at the door on the other side of the bathroom was a little private hallway to John's room. "That's awesome!"

"Oh man, this is the tops," John said, plopping down on Zack's couch. "Living in a sick penthouse in the big city; this is the life."

"Man I want to hang out and get this place set up but I've got to go to therapy soon," Zack said, testing out a chair.

"Yeah this is the last day though," John said. "I got to go here soon too."

"Alright, I'm gonna get ready, what are we doing after this?" Zack said, standing up again.

"I dunno, Rose and Daniel aren't moving in till later so we should probably ask them first," John said. "I'm gonna go check out my stuff. Man, this is awesome!"

"Alright I'll see you later."

* * *

"So you don't really have any sort of stories on your step-dad, huh?" Julia said, exasperated. "You're telling me you lived with a drug addict stepfather and you never knew it?"

"Ehh, I was kind of busy, you know? Training and what not. It's always been my dream to be a soldier."

Zack had to struggle not to laugh right in Julia's face as he mentioned his 'dream' for maybe the hundredth time that week. The gambling thing failed immediately and she never noticed the tattoo, so stone-walling it was! Julia sighed heavily, flipping her notebook on the table and leaned back rubbing her face.

"Can I just..." Julia shook her hands above her head. "What is the deal with you people?! I have six GSAs that come in for these interviews and magically all of you act totally oblivious to your own lives! Don't you realize that I'm trying to help here!?"

Zack was taken aback. He had guessed that Julia was getting irritated, but he wasn't expecting her to flip out like that.

Apparently, Zack and his 'people' were being unreasonable.

"I'm sorry... I shouldn't have blown up like that," she said, leaning forward. "Is there anything at all that you could tell me about your life?"

She looked up at Zack. He didn't know what kind of face he was making, but it must have been concerning.

"What?" Julia said, searching his face.

Zack couldn't hold his tongue anymore. For six days he had put up with her stupid mind games, always being on his best behavior.

"You are trying to help us," Zack repeated slowly. "That's what you really believe?"

"I would like to think that I can help people overcome emotional problems, yes," Julia said.

"Mmm. Not people. Us. You think you are helping us, Bloods, with what you're doing." Zack stared at her.

"I didn't think there was a difference between the two. Do you not view yourself as a person?" Julia said, trying to change the topic.

"Stop trying to lead me with these stupid questions," Zack said

"I'm not trying to lead you anywhere, Zack. I genuinely want to know," Julia said carefully.

"Bull! How many of the Bloods that you get from S.W.O.R.D. keep coming after the mandatory period?" Zack was getting heated now.

"We're not here to talk about other people, Zack, we're here to focus on you," Julia said evasively.

"YET YOU ASK ME WHAT IS WRONG WITH MY PEOPLE!" Zack shouted.

Julia jumped.

Zack sat still, letting the silence drill into her.

"...I apologize for that. It was unprofessional of me," Julia said quietly.

"How many GSA operatives come back to see you after the mandatory period?" Zack asked, calmer. "How many GSA's that you've deemed unfit for service go on to live rich fulfilling lives, huh? You think you helped them?"

"...I'm not allowed to disclose information about past clients," Julia said.

"No, of course not. I'm sure you know though. Since you care so much," Zack spat.

"Is there some point you're trying to make, Zack?" Julia said.

"My point is I don't like you acting like you're some kind of saint," Zack said.

"I do NOT act like I'm a saint!" Julia raised her voice.

"No, of course not. And on behalf of my people, I apologize for being so difficult to the woman who will single handedly decide if we live or die."

"You're being dramatic." Julia folded her arms.

"YOU are choosing to be ignorant!" Zack spat back. "You don't get it at all, do you?"

"What don't I get?" Julia asked, skeptical. "Enlighten me."

"You ever seen a GSA doing anything else besides being a soldier?" Zack asked.

"Those affected with GSA make up a very small percent of

the population."

"You don't see them anywhere else because there is no other job for us," Zack said. "Do you know what happens to a GSA who can't pass an evaluation like this? They're deemed useless."

"What do you mean 'useless'?" Julia asked.

"I mean if a GSA soldier can't fight, he dies. If a GSA soldier likes killing too much, he dies. And If he doesn't watch himself and answer your questions right, he dies," Zack said.

"So you think that if you don't give me the 'correct' answers, and I say you are unfit for duty, you'll be killed?" Julia said, spinning the pen in her hand.

"I think that if you say I'm unfit for duty, I won't have to be killed. I won't have any way to live. WE don't get choices like YOU," Zack said.

Julia flicked her pen around in her hand for a while.

"If you didn't have GSA, what would you do with your life?" She asked.

Zack leaned back and sighed. "I don't know, maybe just be a farmer?" Zack rubbed his eyes. "I've got the chicken house back home which would give me a little bit of stability. I'd probably just go be a sharecropper out there somewhere."

"And you don't think you can do that now?" She asked.

"No."

"Why not?"

Zack sighed again. "See this is the thing, you just wouldn't know living in the city."

"Is it a lot different in the country?"

"Oh yeah. See, people here they don't really like us, but they love money so they could give a crap if you were a space alien, they don't turn you away," Zack said

Julia smirked slightly at his comparison.

"But back home everyone has their own morality, you know?"

"I don't. What do you mean by their 'own morality'?" Julia asked.

Zack tried to think of what he wanted to say.

"Okay, so back in my home town we barely got anything, yet somehow we maintain three different bars and four different churches," Zack said. "And it's like that almost everywhere. So you end up having these people who will go get drunk all the time because they hate their job and their life, then they go to church on Sundays and get forgiven, rise and repeat."

"Okay, I'm following," Julia said.

"Then, these people are all at the bar for the same thing, to whine about their lives. So whenever that happens people start looking for someone to blame. And almost universally that is whoever is employed by the government," Zack said, pointing to himself. "Then you get all the stories about us. You know on three separate occasions I've been asked if I drink blood? They sometimes think that's what fuels us when we open up our adrenalin."

"Yeah, I've heard that one." Julia nodded.

"So now you have angry people blaming you for their problems, people who are really scared of you, and people who are jealous you have some government job you 'lucked' into. Suddenly, without ever doing anything to anybody, I'm hated by almost everyone," Zack said, sighing again.

"Well, that would be envious- you know, not the point." Julia waved a hand. "Is it really that bad out there? I mean, not everyone can hate you guys."

"I mean, there are some people in our own town that treat us kinda normal." Zack shrugged. "There was this one time that we were down in Tennessee, when we got sent there to stop this small riot from a coal mine community. Anyway, we got to tear gas these miners and hold this line. There was this one group that got John, knocked him to the ground, and this one girl kept trying to kick him in the balls so I had to throw them off of him. Then this other lady spat in Rose's face and called her a 'baby murdering,' you know..."

"That's awful...."

"Yeah...."

"Did you have to kill anyone that time?" Julia asked.

"No, I didn't want to excite the crowd. Killing someone would have only made things worse."

"Even after they did all that to you and your friends?"

"There were other soldiers, just the regular guys, who had killed a couple of civilians the day before we got there; that's why we got sent in. I wasn't looking for a fight or to kill someone, I was just a seventeen year old kid who wanted to go home," Zack said, sitting up.

Julia was quiet for a while.

"If I really did want to help people with these sessions, how would you say I should go about it?" She finally asked, putting away her notebook.

"I don't know. I don't think you will be able to help everyone. But I don't think having people's lives riding on the answers is the right way to go," Zack said.

Julia nodded. "Well, our time is up. I have to make up reports and I don't want to keep you here longer than you need to be." Julia stood up and Zack stood with her. "And thanks for being honest with me; it was refreshing."

They shook hands and Zack headed out. He lit a cigarette as he walked, and hoped he didn't just blow it.

13. ONTO PHASE TWO

Zack walked into his new room and sprawled out on the couch. He let out a deep sigh as he tried to calm the nervousness in his stomach. Flipping out and yelling at his therapist seemed like a pretty good way to get failed.

Zack sighed again, sinking as deep into the couch as he could with the minimum amount of movement. He looked over at the TV and noticed a little red light blinking every couple seconds.

Was it doing that before? Zack thought, staring at the light, too lazy to move. *Maybe it's recording me. Eh... screw it, not like I'm going to be talking about assassination or treason aloud to myself anyway. Probably a buttload of cameras in here.*

Zack laid there watching the light blink for a few minutes. He stretched out and grabbed the remote without moving his torso and read the buttons on the remote for a bit, then pressed the power button.

The TV turned on to a news program that was playing too loudly. Zack turned it down so he could focus on why it was blinking. In the top right corner, there was a little envelope with a stop sign thingy with a number four in it. Zack looked at the buttons again, and found a matching little envelope button.

Pressing it, the TV took him to an inbox menu that stopped the old program. Four messages came on the screen: two were from S.W.O.R.D., one was from Daniel to Zack, and John, and one was from John only sent to Zack. Zack went down the list until he reached Daniel's message, and clicked on it.

A video prompt came up on the screen and Zack clicked on it. A black box filled the screen and then all of a sudden a naked woman popped up and seemed to be clicking around on a remote. Zack's eyes went wide. He could clearly see the woman in her... entirety.

"Hey honey? How do I know if it's on?" A familiar voice asked.

Zack flipped up quickly off his back to a sitting position.

"Oh, no, no way...." He gawked.

"There's a little red dot that comes up with a bar at the bottom." Another familiar voice said from what sounded like the bathroom. Zack could hear shower noises about the same volume.

Sure enough, the woman leaned forward, bringing her face into the camera's range, revealing it was Rose. She straightened and put the remote by her mouth.

"Hey guys, it's Rose. We got all moved in and we were thinking about going out tonight to celebrate. Sooo... I don't know, let say around seven? Just email us back, if you two can figure it out. Okay so let us know."

Zack tried to avoid his eyes. He couldn't help himself from peaking just a bit, causing himself a bit of guilt. The light from TV Rose was standing in front of caused his eyes to become aware of two piercings he was not privy to before.

"Oh my God, no fricking *way*!" He repeated, flinging himself back and holding his head together to keep it from exploding.

"And... send," Rose said, hitting a button. The video collapsed down into the message box. Zack sat flabbergasted, not knowing how to react. He eventually grabbed the remote and looked at the message John sent him. This one was not a video but text.

dude i can't even right now... come find me once you see it need to talk

Zack shook his head as he thought about John's reaction. He got up and went through the little hallway that connected to John's room. John was sitting on the couch watching TV.

"Oh my God, did you see it?!" John said, muting the TV.

"Yes I did." Zack nodded, running his fingers through his hair.

"Did you see the nipple rings?!"

"Yes, I saw the rings."

"I never would have imagined the nipple rings! Did you ever think she'd have nipple rings?!"

"Stop saying that!" Zack laughed.

"Oh my God, I don't know if we tell her or if we act like nothing's wrong!" John said, holding his head.

"Hell if I know." Zack laughed and sat down. "We're still going though, right?"

"Hells yeah! I'm ready to relax," John said, spinning the remote in his hand. He hit the message button and hit reply to Rose's message, and told her they were in.

* * *

"You guys don't want to try someplace new?" Rose asked, sitting at the table.

"I don't know, I think this should become our regular spot," John said.

"Yeah, I like Wynn's," Zack said, looking around the busy, yet not crowded, bar. The theme, Zack assumed, was an old Irish town bar. Almost every surface was beautiful dark wood. The floors, tables, bar, even the ceiling had what looked like unfinished wood with ink stamps like the bottom of a barrel. "You guys get ahold of Lydia?"

"Yeah, she'll be here shortly," Daniel said.

"Hey guys! What can I get you?" Olivia said, coming up to their table with a pad of paper.

"Hello, can we get a pitcher? There's going to be five of us," Daniel said.

"Sure thing, any appetizers?"

Everyone quickly did the 'speak now or forever hold your peace' look around the table.

"Nah, I think we're good," Daniel said.

"Okay, one pitcher coming up." Olivia put her pad into the little waitress belt and turned to Zack. "Hey, how did those exams go?"

"Not sure; they haven't sent us the results yet," Zack said.

"Well how did you think you did?" She asked.

"Honestly, I'm a little worried," Zack said, twiddling his thumbs.

Olivia gave his shoulder a squeeze. "Don't worry so much Zack, I'm sure you did great."

"Yeah. Thanks, Olive Oil."

She turned and headed back to the bar. Zack looked up to see Rose smiling with raised eyebrows, while the boys shook their heads.

"What?"

"Nothing. Just didn't realize the cute waitress had a crush on you." Rose giggled. "Wait! Is that the one from before?!"

"She was just being nice...."

Actually, she was asking for an update, Zack thought.

"Mmhmm. Olive Oil, is that her real name?" Rose leaned out from the booth to look at Olivia again.

"No, it's Olivia."

"So you talk with her enough to know her real name." Rose pressed.

"I'm pretty sure she was wearing a name tag one day."

"How'd she get your name then?" Rose asked.

"I... how did this become an interrogation?" Zack said, flipping his hand.

"Come on! She's cute!" Rose teased.

Zack sighed and started spinning his glass of water. "Yeah she is, but... I don't think I'm ready for that yet."

"Oh. Oh..." Rose said. "I'm sorry...."

"It's fine," Zack said.

"No it's not, I'm really sorry. That wasn't cool," Rose said, her eyes falling to her feet.

"Rose, chill, I'm okay right now," Zack said, trying to laugh it off.

"Hey, um... have you been doing okay man?" Daniel asked, breaking in. "I mean, when we aren't around and stuff."

"Yeah, yeah, I'm doing a lot better." Zack nodded, trying to quickly get through the mandatory 'please tell us your not gonna kill yourself bit'.

"Hey guys," Lydia said, pulling up a chair.

"Hey," the team said in unison.

"Well, I have some good news!" Lydia said, holding up a manila envelope. "Fricking finally...."

"Everybody passed their evaluations?" Rose asked.

"Yep! Only thing is that John is going to have to be chemically castrated, but oh well," Lydia said. "Hey, did you guys get beers?"

"Wait, what am I doing?" John asked.

"Yeah we got a pitcher," Daniel said.

"Oh, okay, screw you guys," John said, flipping them off.

"Chill, Johnny, your boys will be fine." Lydia laughed as she sat down. "God, I need a drink today."

"Why is that?" Zack asked.

"All this junk that I have to deal with from the Ups. I'm so proud of you kids for making the cut, but good God are they all over me lately. 'Are your guys gonna be able to adapt to city life? Are they well mannered enough for his majesty? One of them isn't gonna go crazy and bite the head off a chicken are they?'" Lydia rubbed her eyes.

"To be fair, I have done that once or twice." Zack nodded along.

"Here you go guys," Olivia said, bringing over the pitcher. "Can I get you anything?" She asked Lydia.

"Nahh, I'm good for now. Wait, what did you guys order?" Lydia asked the table.

"A giant, thick, meat lovers. We all ended up passing our exams, by the way," John said.

"Ah, see? You were all worried for nothing!" Olivia smiled, gently putting her fist to Zack's shoulder. "Well, let me know if you guys need anything else."

"Yeah, thanks, Olive," Zack said as she walked back to the bar.

"Well hell, she was all over you," Lydia said once Olivia was out of range. "You were worried?"

"Well, a little bit. I mean it's S.W.O.R.D. so you know...." Zack poured himself a beer.

"Ahh you had nothing to worry about, you had, uh...." Lydia looked at the wall, trying to remember a name. "Oh balls, it was some kind of bird."

"Crane?"

"Yeah, Crane." Lydia nodded, taking a sip of beer.

"There's no bird called a crane." Daniel squinted at Lydia, causing Rose to tilt her head at him.

"What? Yes, there is. The whooping crane," Rose said.

"The whooping crane? Seriously?" Daniel said skeptically. "You expect me to believe that there is a bird out there going round yelling 'WHAT WHAT!'"

"Oooohh my God...." Rose said, rolling her eyes as everyone laughed.

"Why was it a good thing I had Dr. Crane?" Zack asked, playing with his glass again.

"Hm?" Lydia said, looking up from her beer. "Oh, she's kinda new. Her mom was the one who got her the job, so she's got some connections. She was the royal family's wet nurse or something or other."

"So what if she's new?" Zack asked.

"Well she's not all that jaded enough for the old guys; she's kind of a pushover. You know how it is, any time a new kid comes in they have to deal with a few years of bullying," Lydia said, drinking again. "Only thing that sucks is that she's on thin ice. Some people don't think she's qualified so she needs to hit this one out of the park."

"So Zack better not bite the heads off any chickens, huh?" John laughed.

"Well it's not like her career is riding on me." Zack laughed as well.

"Eehhh... well I mean, not entirely," Lydia said, tilting her hand from side to side.

"Wait seriously?" Zack said, raising his eyebrows.

"I guess that makes sense. I mean heck, we are gonna be guarding the royal family now, not breaking up drunken fist fights." Daniel nodded.

"Yeah, we've got to be a hundred miles from the nearest cock fight." Rose sighed.

"Wait, we can't go see cock fights anymore?" John said, putting down his beer.

"You and Zack were the only ones to go to those! It was disgusting!" Rose said.

"To be fair, Zack only went to buy big roosters for his chicken coup," John said.

"Big roosters, big eggs." Zack shrugged. "Hey I'll be right back."

Zack walked outside and lit up a cigarette. He took a long drag in the shade, not close enough to the street to watch the sun set. Soon enough a cook with a soul patch came out and lit a cigarette next to him.

"How's it going?" He said, thrusting his chin out.

"Not bad, Lucas, right?" Zack said.

"Yeah." He nodded, looking at the clothing store across the street. "Good job on passing your exam by the way. Salim says good job too."

"Thanks." Zack nodded. "Lydia says that my therapist's career is probably riding on me."

"It is," Lucas said. "No pressure though. When we get done there ain't gonna be anybody *to* fire anybody."

Zack flicked ash off his cigarette, and dragged again. "I was thinking about going back."

"To where?" Lucas asked.

"Back to the therapist. I was thinking it might take some heat off me if it looks like I'm getting help."

"Or it could look like you need help."

"Maybe, but I'd still like to do it."

Lucas was quiet for a minute while they both smoked. "I'll run it by Salim. He'll probably want to look into the guy, make sure we know where he stands, and have some info on him."

"It's a woman. Julia Crane," Zack said.

"You ain't getting honey-potted right?" Lucas said.

"I... don't know what that means," Zack said.

"You aren't just going back to get with her are you?" He said. "Because they could have her trying to do that on purpose."

"...No, I'm not trying to do that with her." Zack mumbled and blushed. He couldn't believe how open with this stuff city people were with people they barely knew

"Allllllright...." Lucas said, stepping on his cigarette. "Sick ink by the way."

"Thanks." Zack put out his cigarette as well. He walked back into the bar.

"Hey, Zack, are you free tomorrow?" Daniel asked.

"Sure, what's up?"

"We're gonna go and get our new uniforms for work, you wanna come? There's a place on the north side of the city," Daniel said. "We also need to finish reading those tech manuals."

"Yeah, the billion-use-TV is ridiculous. It took forever to figure out how to send a message," Rose said.

John choked on his beer.

"What, like you're some kind of tech wiz?" Rose glared at him.

"No, no I am not." John looked out of the corner of his eye at Zack.

Zack smirked and shook his head.

"What? What is that about?" Rose asked, shifting her eyes between them.

"It's nothing," Zack said.

"No, don't say it's nothing! You guys are making fun of me!" Rose said.

"Here's your pizza guys!" Olivia said, walking out with a big pan.

They ate in between their banter, Rose giving up on John and Zack's inside joke.

Zack felt a little out of it, his mind starting to wonder what would happen to the people he'd leave behind when he reached his goal. The entire government would be toppled just by killing a few important people, after all. Rose, John, Daniel, Lydia, and now even people who weren't really involved like Dr. Crane would be affected. Would people back home feel the repercussions of his actions? Waiting seemed like the worst part; wasn't revenge done best in the heat of the moment, so it's impossible to think about the people that will be hurt?

"Ugh, I'm stuffed," Daniel said, leaning on Rose's shoulder.

"Ready for bed?" Rose asked, stroking his cheek.

"Yes!" Daniel puppy-talked back.

"Oh God, gag me..." John rolled his eyes.

"You sound ready for bed too, Mr. Grumpy Gills." Lydia mock-puppy talked.

"I am. You guys ready to go?" John said, getting up.

"Yeah I got to head to the bathroom," Zack said, heading to the men's room. He was washing his hands when Joshua walked in.

"Salim and Micheal said it's fine you keep going for appearances, just don't let her talk you into spilling your guts," he said, entering a stall.

"Got it. Anything else?"

"Nah. Not right now at least. Just work on memorizing your daily routine, getting people to like you. Give us an update when you have something important or in two weeks."

"Ight," Zack mumbled heading out.

14. FRESH STARTS

Zack walked into the therapist's little office in his new uniform. Nathan looked up from behind the desk and smiled.

"Well hey there, Mr. Taylor!" He whistled. "Lookin' fannnncy...."

Zack looked down at his clothes. They were form fitting; a khaki fatigue jacket over a black shirt, a new maroon chest holster with white insignias, a stiff looking, yet stretchy kind of khaki cargo pants, and fresh black boots.

"Thanks, it's new." Zack said.

"What brings you back here? I thought you only had to come here until Jewels passed you," he said, tilting his head to the side.

"Yeah, that was the mandatory period, yeah." Zack nodded, rubbing his neck. "I don't know. I guess I just sort of felt like coming back."

"Well I could set up an appointment for you! Or if you wanted to wait- oh speak of the devil." The kid trailed off as the door to Julia's office opened. Julia walked out with an older couple.

"See you next week, you love birds!" She said with a laugh, then turning to see Zack.

Her expression darkened rather notably when she laid eyes on Zack.

"Mr. Taylor, what are you doing here?"

"Dr. Crane, I was just-"

"Julia," she said. "I'm making an effort to respect your way of speaking, so I'd appreciate it if you could do the same."

Zack paused, then gave a little laugh.

"Actually I have a question about that."

"About what? My name?"

"Yes and no," Zack said, folding his arms and leaning against the wall. "Don't you think forcing people to call you by your first name sort of forces the whole 'being familiar with people' thing? It seems like it would cause the opposite effect."

"Oh?" Julia's chin moved like a boxer checking their teeth. "Well I certainly don't want you to feel uncomfortable. I mean, I've just spent years working at my craft and it's never bothered anyone else. By all means feel free to correct me," she said sarcastically.

"You sure say 'go get bent' in round about way." Zack rubbed his knuckles on his jaw.

Julia sighed. "Again, Mr. Taylor. Did you need something?"

You're being kind of a jerk man... Zack thought. He rubbed his neck and tried to reset his emotions.

"...I wanted to say thanks for passing me."

"Well, you're welcome. After all it's not like being a jerk is the same as being crazy." Julia folded her arms.

Zack smiled, thinking she was seeming a bit more human than before. *This is better than the overly nice therapist lady I guess.*

"And sorry for being an jerk. I had some stuff going on that I put on you unfairly. Sorry."

Julia's head flinched back a little bit. She tapped her arm with a finger. "Don't worry about it."

Zack rocked on his feet in silence for a moment.

"You mentioned before that you truly wanted to help people, or something along those lines. Did you mean that?" He asked.

Julia Looked like she was trying to figure out what his angle was. "Yeah, that about sums it up."

"So if I was to act like less of an jerk... You'd try to figure out how to help me?" He asked.

"What is it that you need help with?" Julia searched his eyes, and Zack shook his head.

"I don't NEED help with anything. I don't NEED. Help. And I don't NEED therapy, because I'm not crazy," Zack said. "But... I don't know, I guess it just seems like only fair to give you a chance since you gave me one. And you know, frickin..."

Zack trailed off trying to think of how to say what he wanted to say.

"I mean, if there is help to be had, that maybe I don't know about, then, that would be good."

Julia stood there for a moment tapping her fingers on her arm, then gave a little cough.

"I have a pretty busy schedule today, but I could get you in some time this week," she said, looking over to the kid. "Nathan, you want to set him up?"

"Thanks," Zack said, reaching into his pocket and pulling out a scrap of paper and handing it to Nathan. "They ended up getting us phones and stuff, so you can reach me at this number."

Nathan whistled again, taking the paper. "Fancy, fancy...."

"I'll see you later," Zack said, heading to the door.

"Mmm," Julia said as he walked past her. "The uniform really suits you by the way."

"Thanks, it's new."

* * *

Zack walked into the GSA building where he was staying with the other operatives. John was standing in the lobby with a new lady standing behind the reception desk. Zack's phone rang in his pocket, and John and the girl turned around.

"Oh there you are." John hung up his phone, which in turn stopped the buzzing in Zack's pocket. "Hey, turns out we got orientation in like five minutes."

"Yeah, I got the message. I thought we had it in, like, half an hour though?" Zack raised an eyebrow.

"Technically yes, but if everyone's here we can get this over with quicker," the girl said, then extended her hand. "Hello,

I'm Lily Hawkins. I'll be one of the GSA schedulers."

"Zack Taylor," he said, shaking her hand. "Are you doing this all by yourself?"

"Oh God no, I'm just doing the schedule and sometimes running the desk!" Lily said.

"Oh, okay." Zack nodded. She looked a little young and was rather squeaky-voiced like Nathan. Zack wondered if that was just how people from the city were. Zack and John headed into the big conference room, where a mass of people had already congregated. Rose waved him over where her and Daniel had found seats.

"Oh man, how hot was that receptionist?" John said as they sat down.

"Which one?" Daniel asked.

"The HOT one," John said, looking through his eyelashes.

"Ha, okay." Daniel nodded.

"Oh, so you know who he's talking about, huh?" Rose asked. "Point out this girl you think is so hot then."

"I didn't even say anything!" Daniel said, sticking his palms out.

"Yeah but you were thinking it," Rose said, folding her arms.

"Oh, my God," Daniel said, shaking his head.

"Alright, everyone is here, so let's go ahead and get started," a woman in a nice suit said, stepping up to a podium in the front of the room.

Speaker after speaker went on to explain the layouts of the palace, proper conduct with the employees, proper conduct outside of work, use of technology, and so on and so on. They took bathroom breaks twice before getting all the way through the garbage everyone needed to know.

"Alright, last thing I would like to mention before we let you go. We are keeping the traditional feel of the unit hierarchy that you all are comfortable with, so would the following people please stand up." The woman at the front read off several names, Daniel being one of them. "These are your captains. Should you have any kind of disputes, or need help solving a problem, they will be able to accommodate you. Are there any questions?"

A man in the front raised his hand.

"Yes?"

"Um, how come our captain isn't the same captain as back home?" The man asked nervously.

"Good question. Some of the captains have been reevaluated based on their scores throughout the evaluation process," the presenter said.

Another hand came up.

"Yes?"

"If that's the case, then why did the guys who scored first and second in the physicals not get a captain position?"

The room was quiet for a second. The receptionist pondered for a moment before smiling. "Mr. Coleman, you scored first in the physicals, do you know why you were not named a captain?"

She seemed to be looking at a black man sitting in his chair with three other black people. One of whom, a woman, was standing as a captain.

"I don't think they liked my accent." He laughed as he played with his chin. "I don't talk white enough."

"Mm. How about you, Mr. Taylor?"

Zack thought for a moment, swiveling in his chair. He figured it was probably because of that nonsense with Lydia but he didn't want to sell himself out.

"Because no matter how much of a raw, physical specimen I am, when it comes to leadership, this guy," Zack pointed his thumb at Daniel, "is the best S.W.O.R.D. has to offer. That, and I'm figuring that they gave the rest of you the handicap of one captain per group, wouldn't want you all to get jealous." He finished smugly.

His response was met with a few laughs and somewhere a light hearted 'Get bent!'.

"That's not what I heard," Coleman said. "I heard they wanted the 'bread riot butcher' on the down low."

The female GSA next to Coleman kicked him in the leg.

"Bread riot butcher?" Zack raised an eyebrow. "That's a new one."

"Wait, why is he called the 'Bread riot butcher'?" A younger GSA asked, looking around.

"He's not," John said rather loudly. "At least not by anyone other than a flipping turn coat. Sure you boys weren't in on that riot?"

"Hey, why don't you watch who you call a boy, cracker. We know whose side we on. Ain't like we out here killing our own," one of Coleman's unit's said. "Heard you boys can get away with killing your pops, though. That's some cold stuff, man."

"Figured y'all of all people would know the dangers of loose lips...." John rolled his eyes.

"The hell?"

Coleman and his friend rose out of their chairs, walking over, and Zack and John did the same until they were chest to chest ready to fight. It might have come to blows if not for the loud sounds of safeties clicking off around the room by all the non-S.W.O.R.D. personnel.

"You best watch what comes out of your mouths about me and mine, white boy. You forgetting who scored number one here," Coleman said, not breaking eye contact with Zack.

"Yeah? Maybe just keep to you and yours, and we won't have nothing to say," Zack said, not blinking either.

"Fine by me."

"Enough." The woman at the podium finally spoke over the group. "Sit down, please."

Daniel came over, putting a hand on Zack's chest to start pushing him and John back to the table, and one of Coleman's friends did the same. "Come on man, chill."

Zack stared down Coleman for another second before turning back to his seat. The meeting wrapped up without any more ruckus. Zack went straight to his room. He had enough of today.

He entered his apartment and laid back on the couch

feeling tense. He pulled out his cigarettes, but not having an ashtray decided that they were too much trouble. He instead decided to flip on the TV, which was blinking at him that he had messages. There were a few on the different procedures and guidelines, and also a schedule. Since he had a few hours of nothing to do he decided to check over everything to prepare for work. A few hours had passed before his phone rang.

"Hello?" Zack answered.

"Hey, Zack! It's Nathan, from Dr. Crane's office!" A squeaky, child-like voice shrieked in his ear. "I'm calling to set up an appointment for you to see Jewels, she got a few spots open this week. What times are good for you?"

"Mm... Hang on." Zack rubbed his eyes and flicked the buttons on the remote to find the message with his schedule. "Looks like I work noon to six all week this week."

"Oh prefect, she has an opening tomorrow morning at nine! How's that sound?"

"Sounds good, I'll see you then," Zack said, hanging up the phone. "Jesus Christ, kid, your voice...."

15. FIRST DAY JITTERS

"Good morning, Mr. Taylor," Julia said from the love seat in her waiting room. "You're a little early."

"Yeah, military personnel get super pissed if you're late so I'm always a little early everywhere," he said, walking over to her. "Am I your first client of the day?"

"Yep. Want to get started?" She motioned over to her office.

"Sure." He walked into the office and sat down as Julia grabbed some papers off her desk.

"So what was it that you wanted to talk about?" She asked, as she slowly strode over, flipping through papers.

Zack tilted his head a little. "You're not going to ask me questions this time?"

"You didn't respond very well to that before. And you came to me this time, so I figured you had something to say," she said, sitting down and meeting his gaze.

Zack noticed she wasn't as smiley as she was when they started these sessions.

I guess she's still kinda pissed about how I acted, he thought.

"Okay, that's fair... let me see...." Zack rubbed his lips, trying to think of a good place to start. "Yesterday, we ended up having a meeting or whatever about our jobs and... someone knew me by my reputation."

Julia's head bobbed back a little in surprise, or maybe confusion. "What do you mean by that?"

"I mean it was someone who knew about...." Zack suddenly felt nervous. "I mean, they knew what happened on one of my assignments."

"And that bothers you because...?" Julia asked.

"It's not THAT part that bothers me. It's- like-" Zack tried to compose himself. "It was an assignment that didn't go well...."

"Mmmm..." Julia nodded. "It might be better if you just walked me through this assignment first then. And when this happened."

"Alright. This was... four years ago now? Yeah I was fifteen at the time."

"Fifteen." Julia started to write in her notes. "So this was sometime around when you first became a S.W.O.R.D. operative?"

"Yeah, we might have been official for about six months. We had been on active duty at that point... two weeks."

"Two weeks of what exactly?" Julia asked. "Active duty doing what?"

"We had been sent in with a bunch of other soldiers to work as riot police basically," Zack said. "This was when all that crazy stuff was going down about grain shortages, you remember that?"

Julia put her pen against her lips for a minute, thinking. "I remember hearing something about a government annexing fields and bread being expensive a few years ago."

"Ha, yeah I guess that's all you guys would have heard up here." Zack shook his head. "Forget how the papers whitewashed it, the crap hit the fan down south."

"Wait, what do you mean the papers whitewashed it?" Julia said, putting a hand up.

Zack was the one to tilt his head this time. "Uhh... you know.... Anytime stuff really gets bad it gets played off as not being so bad?"

"What, you mean like the RCC network tries to play it off? Sure, they're biased, but Public Voice is usually pretty straight," Julia said.

"No, RCC is conservative and PV is liberal, but they're both full of it," Zack said.

"Well I don't know if I believe that. We live under

a constitutional monarchy not fascism, Zack." Julia adjusted in her seat. "We vote for politicians every five years. The government can't 'whitewash' the news, they're independents."

"I don't know what fascism means. All I know is I never saw the real story printed anywhere."

"Okay." Julia put her hands up, not wanting to argue. "Then tell me the 'real' story."

"The real story is the protesters ended up getting too riled up in Texas and we went live." Zack started to bounce his knee.

"What's that?" Julia asked, writing in her notes again.

"That's when we stop standing with shields using tear gas, and start using live ammunition." Julia looked up from her notes, Zack let his eyes drop. "It's what we do when it is decided from the top that things are getting too bad and losses are acceptable."

Julia was quiet for a minute. "So that's what happened? You got orders to go live?"

Zack sighed and rubbed his face. "So we're in Texas, and at this point we had been on the road for two weeks restoring order. It's my unit and a bunch of other S.W.O.R.D guys in the front with the riot shields. We were maybe twenty across in the middle of this big city that's like a hub for farming communities. And these guys are pissed. I didn't really know what was going on, something like the king had placed a ceiling on raw foods from farms that was set too low."

"So people were protesting that they weren't going to be able to pay bills?" Julia asked, writing notes.

"Yeah, basically," Zack said. "I didn't know how bad it was for real, but guessing by the way they reacted it was bad. People ended up throwing rocks at us, and two different guys came at us with pitchforks..."

"Seriously? That sounds intense...." Julia said, sounding concerned.

"Well, I mean for someone like you... I mean normal people, it's a bigger deal than it is for us," Zack said.

"How so?"

"Well normal people are... softer than we are. When the adrenaline is pumping through you and you're hot, GSAs go through a muscle tensioning. So if something hits you in a muscular part you usually won't get too hurt."

"Still, a pitchfork?" Julia looked at him incredulously.

"Well I mean, I've taken bullets before," Zack said. He pulled up his shirt to show where he had been shot protecting the princess. "See, look."

"WOAH!" Julia leaned back and put her hand up to block his stomach from her view.

"Wh- I'm just showing you where I got shot at, chill, Zack said, taken aback by her reaction.

"Well give me a warning before you start stripping, geez," Julia said, then tentatively looked at his back. Once she found the little yellowing scab, she leaned in a little bit. "That all there is to it? How long ago was this?"

"Eh, end of the physical tests so... pfft... two, three weeks ago?" Zack said before pulling his shirt back down.

"From a bullet?!? Jesus.... Anyway back to your story, sorry," Julia said, waving a hand.

"Right. The main thing you just need to realize is that we might be built a little bit harder, but it's not like we can't get hurt or killed," Zack said, rubbing his bruise. "Plus this was years ago, I mean most of us were just kids, we were still... raw, if that makes sense."

"Mmm. It must have been very tough on you...." Julia nodded.

"I'm not saying it was too much for us. There's nothing a S.W.O.R.D. GSA operative can't handle; that's what we're all about. It's just that there were first mission jitters still, you know?" Zack said, rubbing his face.

"Mr. Tay-... Zack," Julia said, stopping the pace. "What happened?"

Zack bounced his leg, taking a deep breath. He ran his fingers through his hair and looked around the room.

"I screwed up, maybe?" Zack said. "We would shove them

back with the shields every once in a while to keep them at bay. Anyway, Daniel goes to shove a guy off him, and a group of them catch his riot shield and he gets thrown off balance and they're on top of him in a second.... So I just reacted. I pulled out my gun and went loud before anyone gave an order."

Zack rubbed his hands together, waiting for a response, but Julia was quiet. "Can I smoke in here?" He asked.

Julia nodded.

"I had aimed high to keep Daniel out of LOF, which meant that the chance of me killing people was high.... One guy had his back to me, one second I can see the back of his head and then *poof* it's gone, like busting a water balloon.... Another guy jerked his head up and it looked like I had punched him in the nose. Nothing but blood and cartilage in the middle of his face.... Another guy, I caught him in the throat, he didn't go as quick...." Zack took a drag off his cigarette.

"What does LOF mean?"

"Line of Fire," Zack said, holding the smoke in his lungs.

"So what happened after that?" She asked.

"Well the mindset I guess, was that someone told us to go loud and nobody heard it; they just heard someone start shooting. So they all started shooting."

Julia's eyes widened.

"I was able to run up and grab Daniel with John and we started to pull him back. He's shooting into the crowd as we are dragging him. I look up and it's like...."

Zack put his hand up, almost trying to touch the scene in his mind. He shook his head and inhaled more smoke. "...Like there was a tube just rolling over the crowd, like.... Like there was one of those bulldozers with the rollers on the front that was just running them over. They started to run away and just line after line starts falling."

"Oh my God...." Julia said.

"Mmm... after all the chaos had settled, we had this big meeting-type thing. There was a video on what happened too. I thought I was gonna get reprimanded, but instead everything was okay. They had a vote and six of the seven commanders in charge of the mission said I acted on instinct to protect my fellow soldiers and the use of force was necessary. One of the commanders, an old guy, came really strong to my defense."

Zack took a second to put out his cigarette.

"He said 'it's absolute bull we would insinuate this was anything other than a massive success, our soldiers acted with autonomy and courage against a pack of ravenous thugs, and if you think anything other than that, you are a fricking coward,'" Zack said.

"Ravenous thugs?" Julia's jaw dropped.

"Yeah, and that's sort of the problem I'm dealing with now." Zack nodded. He got up to move around.

"The problem being...?" Julia asked.

"That some people seem to think I hate black people," Zack said, pacing through the room.

"What? You lost me again, why would they think you hate African-Americans?" Julia blinked and shook her head in confusion.

"Well the rioters were black."

"All of them?"

"Well, no, not literally all of them. But it was a mostly black area."

"Ah. Do you have any biases against African-Americans?" She asked. "I'm not going to judge you if you do. Oftentimes when we experience a traumatic event, we can demonize entire groups. It's more important that we acknowledge these biases and work to overcome them."

Zack sighed and sprawled out on the couch. "I mean, I don't think I do. I don't feel bad necessarily about shooting those people, I would have shot them no matter what color they were. I mean hell, they were going to kill Daniel, but it's not like I hate every black person I see. It just irks me when some people try to write it off like I just murdered innocent black people in the street. Screw that, they were gonna kill Daniel...."

"Well first off let me say I'm not justifying either side with this. But you might find it helpful to try to see it from their point of view as well. The government comes in and tells them they won't be getting their fair share, and when they get upset they bring in soldiers to keep them in line. And then a group of trained soldiers come in with big guns and shields and those who continue to fight for themselves without guns are put down like animals," Julia said.

"Okay, yeah, but you don't need a gun to kill somebody," Zack said.

"Yes, but it's much easier to kill with a gun than without one, isn't it?" Julia asked.

"No one would have gotten killed if they hadn't tried to fight," Zack said.

"True, but what happens if no one fought back at all? At what point do you stop sliding down the slope, Zack?" Julia said. "Some people would argue it would be better to be dead than in chains."

Zack sighed heavily. "That still doesn't justify them trying to kill my friend."

"No it doesn't. But most people will justify their actions by thinking they didn't have a choice. Did you have another option? Could you have saved Daniel another way?" Julia asked. "And you just told me how we didn't get the full story over here, so do you think it's true that all of those people were bad, because you were told they were bad? Don't you think that there is something wrong with that?"

Zack tongued the inside of his cheek. "Maybe.... But I still don't think I'm responsible."

"You don't have to. But does it feel like you weren't?" She asked.

"No... not really," Zack said, hanging his head. "So what do I do? Apologize? Daniel would never forgive me for that; most people I was there with wouldn't forgive me if I did that. We were all there, we were in it together."

"I can't tell you what you should do. But I think just acknowledging that people were hurting might be enough for today," Julia said, putting down her notes.

"Okay." Zack stood up.

"Can I say though, I'm really surprised. When you came in saying you wanted to meet with me some more I wasn't sure what to think. How come you didn't want to talk about this before?" Julia asked, standing up as well.

"I'm not sure. I guess before everyone was telling me to talk and I wasn't sure I could trust you," Zack said.

"And now?" Julia asked.

"Well, I still don't know, but I'm the one making the decision to talk," Zack said.

"Well, feel free to take it at your pace I guess." Julia smiled lightly. "But I hope you keep coming. I really only want to help, Mr. Taylor."

"Yeah, thanks, Julia...." He said, walking out the door. "...And Zack is fine."

"Okay. Zack it is." Julia started to smile a little wider.

* * *

Zack walked up the stairs of the palace toward the second checkpoint. He had to check in at the end of the drive some hundred yards back.

He took a second to stop and look back at the massive grounds, all of it still perfectly maintained. The sun was beating down on his head, it must be rough being on the landscaping crew in the summer.

The gentle breeze passing over a lush green lawn unscathed by the intense sun felt pleasant and calm. At first, he could hardly notice the small army of people working around the estate. Zack walked up to the doorman wearing the bright white gloves.

"Zack Taylor. Royal Guard," he said, keeping it short.

"Credentials?" The man asked with a smile. Zack presented his card that he had gotten with his apartment. The man turned and touched a control pad next to the door, which eventually made a heavy *CLICK* and the doorman opened it. “Princess Annabelle's room is on the third floor; it's a big pink door to the right of the stairs.”

“Got it.” Zack walked through the doorway to see a giant entryway with a massive staircase in the back. There were paintings and little end tables with flowers, candles, or trinkets. Zack suddenly felt extremely out of place. He hustled up the stairs to the third floor of the mansion and turned to his right to see a long hallway and about halfway down was a half open pink door. He walked in to see Princess Annabelle along with a GSA operative and a nanny.

Annabelle hid behind her nanny when she saw him, peeking around the nanny's skirt. Zack introduced himself and the other GSA operative took his leave.

The first hour or two the nanny, Ms. Jane, showed Zack around the estate, keeping Annabelle in tow. Zack couldn't help but be overwhelmed. The palace was somehow in the middle of the biggest city he had ever seen, but felt as if it were completely removed from the rest of the world. The giant brick walls that surrounded the outer edge that guards patrolled at all times seemed to block the noise of the city, other than an occasional rattle of a car.

“It's weirdly quiet here....” Zack said.

“The king wanted a place that he could remove himself from the bustle of the city,” Ms. Jane said. “It can be a little jarring when you first leave the city.”

Annabelle sat still looking at her light blue dress. She hadn't said a word the whole time.

“You know, the princess threw quite a fit this morning when she found out you weren't going to be here this morning. She's all quiet now that you're here though,” Ms. Jane said, looking at Annabelle who in turn scowled at her.

“I'm sorry princess,” Zack said softly. “This must be kind of jarring for you too.”

“Hm Nmm.” Annabelle hummed, shaking her head from

side to side.

"Well, I'll be coming around more often, is that okay?" Zack asked.

"Mmhmm." Annabelle nodded, her blonde curls bouncing.

"Okay. I hope you'll help me out if I get lost, okay? Your home is really big!" Zack said, raising his voice to a higher pitch for talking to a child.

"Okay...." She said, hiding her face, sweet as sugar again. "Is your house big?"

"My house?" Zack thought about his house back home, which he hadn't seen in a while. "Mmmm... not as big as here, but it's not a small house either. I've got two floors and a cellar you can get into from the outside."

"What about your yard?" She asked.

"My yard is pretty big too. I've got a garden too, but I grow corn instead of flowers," Zack said.

"Why?" She was looking up at him now.

"Well I need it to eat and feed the chickens. I've got a bunch of them in a coup too," Zack said.

"What's a coup?"

"It's like a house for chickens."

"Is the chicken's house nice?"

Zack laughed. "I think so, they keep laying eggs for me so they must like it."

"I don't think that's how it works..." Annabelle said, looking at her dress again.

"Oh no? Why not?" Zack asked.

"Because Dad told Mom the other day that 'just because we have someone in our house doesn't mean that I am happy about it!'" She said.

"Annabelle!" Ms. Jane whisper-yelled at her. "You know better than to go around repeating your father's words. I'm sorry, Mr. Taylor."

"It's quite alright," Zack said, still a little surprised. Though it was probably his fault for assuming that King David liked the idea of the GSA being here. Ms. Jane signaled that she had to go talk to someone for a second, and walked out of ear shot. After a moment Annabelle tugged at his arm.

"Are you happy to be here, Mr. Taylor...?" She asked quietly.

"Sure! Are you happy I'm here?" Zack asked.

"I don't know yet...." She said, swinging her feet on the bench.

"Well I guess that's fair." Zack let out a small laugh. They sat there looking out over the garden.

Man it'll be fall in a couple months, landscaping this has got to be a pain, Zack thought again.

"I'd really like it if everyone was happy."

Maybe it was the way she said it, but those words made Zack's stomach feel just a little uneasy. "Well are you happy little miss?"

"Right now, I'm not sad," she said, staring at her shoes.

"Well that's not quite the same thing as being happy," He said.

"Mom says 'It doesn't matter how you feel, it matters how you look.'"

"Mmmm. I guess that's true...."

That's real depressing, kid....

"Is your mom happy?" She looked up at him.

Zack bit his lip, unsure how to answer.

"I don't remember her being happy. She left when I was little, so I don't remember too well though," Zack said, trying to say as nicely as he could that he was abandoned.

"What about your dad?"

"He... wasn't around a lot either."

"So you were alone a lot?"

"Yeah." Zack wasn't sure how to explain it to a little girl.

"Was your dad nice?"

Zack hesitated. "No."

"Am I bothering you?"

"No?" Zack raised his eyebrow.

The little princess looked up at him, and searched his eyes. He didn't understand her expression, but it didn't make him happy.

"Everyone says I ask too many questions...."

"Well I don't think I have any answers." Zack said with a sigh. "But I'll try to answer if you'll ask."

"Okay...." She leaned her head on his arm.

* * *

"Alright! Day one is in the books! Cheers boys!" Daniel said, raising his glass of water.

"Cheers!" They raised their glasses in unison.

"Nah, see it just doesn't feel the same with iced tea." John shook his head.

"Well SOME of us don't want to go to work tomorrow with a hangover." Rose tilted her head like a know-it-all.

"We could have waited til the weekend," Zack pointed out.

Rose was all about going out to eat after work to celebrate the end of the first day.

"I wouldn't have been able to make it. I got a date," John said with a smug grin.

"Oh no kidding! You got a date with one of those receptionist girls? What's her name... Terry?" Daniel nodded.

"I thought it was Derek?" Zack added.

"Ha ha. Screw you guys." John rolled his eyes. "Her name is Lilly, and I pointed her out to you guys, she's the pretty one."

"Wow! Sorry we were so surprised, it's just that usually you hit on the prettiest one, then go down everyone that works there until someone takes pity on you," Rose joked.

"Oh Rosy... jealousy is such an ugly color on you.... I know it's hard but you HAVE to overcome these feelings for me. No matter how strong they are...." John said, placing his hand on her's.

"Oh Jesus, please hook up this receptionist and quit being

so thirsty...." Daniel said, rolling his entire head.

Rose glared at John.

"I don't know, she seems pretty cool. I might take this one kinda slow." John shrugged.

"Ooooh does this mean we get to meet this one?" Rose said, genuinely excited.

"We'll see how it goes...." John smiled and flicked his glass.

He looks happy.... Zack scraped his thumb against the edge of a straw.

"Hey, are you okay, Zack?" Rose asked, bringing him out of his own little world.

"Oh, man I'm sorry I didn't mean-" John started, but Zack cut him off.

"No, no! I'm fine, it's not that...." He said, setting down the straw.

"Well, what's up?" Daniel asked.

"I don't know it's just... What were your guys shifts like?"

John, Daniel, and Rose looked at each other.

"What do you mean?" Rose asked.

"I was sitting with the little princess, and she's asking me questions like crazy, you know, like a kid and all. But she was asking me if I was happy, if my mom and dad were happy, and saying stuff like she wasn't sad right now. I don't know, something about it was putting me on edge," Zack said, picking up his glass. Everyone was thinking quietly for a moment.

"I guess the queen started drinking at noon today." John opened his hand with a flip.

"Now that I think about it, the women who were working were all kind of acting funny around King David." Daniel played with his chin.

"Funny how?" Rose asked.

"I don't know, just funny. Like half of them were really cozy with him, and the other half were jumpy around him. It was weird...." Daniel shook his head.

"...I don't think that Armando guy is treating Princess Eliana very well...." Rose fidgeted.

"What makes you say that?" John asked.

"Girls notice when make-up is overused." Rose leaned her face on her hand.

"Crap, this isn't going to be good, is it?" Daniel said, rubbing his eyes.

"Hey guys! Back again, huh? No mom this time?" Olivia said, bringing a pizza to the table.

"Nope, looks like we're on our own this time." Zack gave her a tired smile.

16. CAN'T GET A RHYTHM

"Hey, hey!" Nathan squeaked from behind the glass window. "Well look what the cat drug in again this morning."

"'Sup, Nathan," Zack said, walking into Dr. Crane's office. He looked in the little dish by the window. "Oh sweet, did you finally get new candy?"

"Yeah, I got turned onto this adorable little candy store. It's the tops, but I hate how every gay store I walk into is fricking. Packed. With pink." Nathan flipped his hand around in a mini rant.

"Really? I thought you guys all love that fairy stuff," Zack said, snagging a hard candy.

"Wow. You seriously just said that...." Nathan leaned back with his mouth open.

Zack and Nathan made some small talk from time to time. It turned out Nathan was gay, and Julia's cousin. He lived in the city to get away from some family problems.

Zack had never met a gay person before, though. So occasionally Nathan had to help Zack 'acknowledge his ingrained bigotry' and 'undo his learned ignorance'. Nathan did clear some things up about gay people for him. He wasn't really any different than a normal city-boy.

"Not all gay people like froufrou over the top stuff like that. That is what we would call a 'generalization'. There are plenty of different life styles in the gay community, like... Bears." Nathan said.

"Wait... do like... bears act gay...? Or do you guys...?" Zack asked.

Nathan blinked silently at Zack for a second.

"I flipping can't with you today. Jewels? Taylor is out here." Nathan pressed on the intercom. "You know what? For the record, if anyone in this room is messing animals it would be you, country boy. Don't think we haven't heard the stories about you guys."

"What did we do?" Zack was confused now and still not entirely sure what Nathan was doing with animals.

"Hey, Zack!" Julia said, walking out of her office. "How's it going?"

"Not bad. Pretty sure Nathan here is sexually harassing me though. Something about bears and candy stores, I don't get all the lingo," Zack said, turning to Julia.

"Oh, you are such a little brat!" Nathan threw a box of tissues at Zack. "We were talking about that place I got the cupcakes from."

"Oh my God those were sooo good...." Julia said, closing her eyes. "Don't make too many gay friends, Zack; they'll ruin you."

"Oh yeah speaking of which, Zack, are you really as cut as Jewels was acting like?" Nathan asked.

"Cut?" Zack furrowed his brow and looked at Julia, who seemed a little embarrassed.

"Take off your shirt," Nathan said.

"Nathan, quit saying weird stuff; you're gonna get me in trouble!" Julia said.

Zack took off his jacket and started to take off his shirt.

"Don't actually do it, oh my God...." Julia covered her eyes and turned away.

"Holy cow!" Nathan gave a low whistle. "You know, I was expecting less hair and more ink...."

"Yeah, I want to get another one but I don't know what to get...." Zack said, turning around to show his back.

"God, you need to come clubbing with me just one night. I have some people I would love to rub you in their face." Nathan sighed.

"O-kay shows over, pack it up!" Julia grabbed his shirt and jacket and shoved him into her office. "Jesus did you run out of money and have to start striping to make ends meet? Nathan might just attack you, you know."

"Sorry, heh." Zack smirked, and put his shirt back on. He sat down on the couch.

"Anyway, how is work going? You've been in the palace for a month now, so are you getting used to it?" Julia sat down in the chair across the coffee table.

"Meh, I was starting to, but I guess I'm gonna be guarding the queen tonight six to midnight." Zack stretched out.

"I was gonna ask about that too. Why do you guys only work six hour days?" Julia said, picking up a mug of something.

"To keep us fresh and on our toes. We also have workout requirements of at least ten hours a week, but it's left up to us to decide when we do them," Zack said.

"Mmmm. That makes sense. You think you'll like watching the queen more, or are you gonna miss little Annabelle?" Julia smiled.

Zack had been getting along with the princess quite well so far.

"Yeah I hope they put me back with her soon. John said the queen isn't too bad, maybe a little stuffy but oh well." Zack shrugged his shoulders. "That's not what's been on my mind lately though...."

"What's been on your mind?"

"Well, my buddy Daniel asked me and John to come with him to buy an engagement ring...." Zack sighed, and slid deeper into the couch.

"Ah, you mentioned before that you were once engaged right? Though, if you still don't want to talk about it... no pressure." Julia put her hands up.

"I mean... well how long have I been coming here now?" Zack asked, stalling while he made up his mind.

"This is session... twenty-two," Julia said, looking through her notes. "Since you started coming here on your own anyway."

He hadn't really thought about it too much but more than a month had flown by already. Work had been going pretty good, Julia had been listening to his problems, many nights were spent right with John or with Rose and Daniel. On the rare chances he did have alone time, he had been giving reports to Salim and the group down at Wynn's. It was a little scary how easy it had become for him to stop thinking about the incident because he was constantly busy.

"Yeah, I was engaged to a girl named Sarah from back home." Zack nodded.

"How long were you guys together?"

"A little more than three years."

"What was she like?"

"She was... a good girl. She was studying to be a nurse under an apprenticeship, her mom was really serious about her getting an education. Ms. Evans had raised Sarah all alone," Zack said.

"But she was still pretty bubbly when you got to know her. She was never just there, you know? She was always on, laughing or crying; she just breathed personality."

He remembered her smile when they first went to the ice cream shoppe. And when she came to his house in tears because her neighbor's dog passed away.

"She was super smart but still a little girl about certain things. She was one of those people who would get super excited about something and would run out the door and forget her purse and keys and everything else!"

Julia giggled a little.

"And she had a sweet tooth BAD! I didn't know people could eat that much sugar without throwing up!"

Julia smiled with her eyebrows raised. She seemed to think Sarah was interesting.

"And we weren't just kids messing around, you know? It had been her promise to her mom that she would get a good job and not end up like she did working at a diner raising a kid all alone. So... we decided that we would hold off on the physical parts of the relationship until she finished school." Zack rubbed his neck and avoided Julia's eyes.

"Wow. So you guys never...?" Julia looked genuinely surprised.

"Uh... no. I never have... done those things actually...."

Oh God kill me now....

"That's... wow, I didn't see that coming." Julia was astonished. "I mean, not that there's anything wrong with that! It's just that I remember what teenage boys were like when I was a teenager and I just can't imagine...."

"You're kinda embarrassing me here Julia...." Zack fidgeted.

"No, no, no! It's fine it's just- I mean look at you! It's not like women wouldn't find you attractive! And plus you've been super comfortable with Nathan, so I thought if anything... you had sort of seen both sides of the field."

"What, like I might be gay?" Zack asked, looking up at her.

"Well not full out, but you seem like a man who isn't uncomfortable with his sexuality. I mean, not every girl who has had a wild steak is a lesbian!" Julia said.

"What?"

"People can be open to things without putting a label on it."

"Can we not talk about this anymore? Sorry...."

"No, I'm sorry. I mean it's up to you, no judgement here."

There was a good bit of silence as the air became a little uncomfortable in the room.

"So anyway, it sounds like everything was going great. What happened?"

And then there wasn't any air in the room at all.

* * *

Zack walked through the door to the palace and felt

tension rising in his neck. He was already a little drained from his talk with Julia so he hadn't noticed it at the gates, but everyone's faces were off. John walked down the stairs and seeing Zack, made a beeline for him.

"Hey."

"Hey, what's up? It feels tense in here...." Zack asked.

"Uh, yeah... see...." John looked around for a bit, then motioned Zack over to the front of the closet away from the maids and butlers scurrying around. Zack followed him.

"I guess... one of the girls who worked here threw herself off the balcony...."

"Frickin A' you serious?"

"Yeah... yeah... no joke." John nodded, biting his lip "It wasn't pretty."

"Well that explains that then."

"Hey man do you... want me to cover your shift? I mean it's all cleaned up but I didn't know if you feel... you know?" John shook his hands out, his eyes shifted from side to side.

"No, no I'm okay, really. Are you alright?"

"Uhh..." John sighed and rubbed his face. "I just need a beer. It's been a rough day."

John headed out, and Zack headed to work. The queen was in her study when he got there. A male servant told him that she didn't want to be disturbed, so they both waited outside the door instead.

Hours passed, all in silence, sitting next to a door.

Finally the servant knocked on the door, which was opened by someone else. They whispered for a moment then the door shut. A moment later the queen walked out and they headed to the dining room. They got to the table right as the older princess and the foreign prince were getting to the table with their escorts.

Ah dang it, what was his name?

"Queen Elisa, you are looking wonderful this evening," the prince said, giving her a bow.

Eh, dang it right on the tip of my tongue.

"Mm, thank you Armando." The queen nodded.

Armando! Zack nodded.

"Zack!" Zack turned to see the little princess running over to him with Rose in tow. Reflexively he knelt down when she extended her arms. "I thought you weren't coming today!?"

"No, I'm just protecting your momma today," Zack said, patting her back gently as she squeezed his neck. "Also, you should go hug your mom first! I'm just the help."

Annabelle let go and ran off to her mother, giving her knee a hug, when Zack noticed the queen giving him a bewildered look. Annabelle ran back to Zack.

"I played dollhouse with Ms. Rose today!" She said, swaying gently.

"Is that so? Did you win?" Zack asked.

"You can't win at dollhouse!"

"Haha, well you'll have to tell me about it some other time. The food's gonna get cold if you don't sit down. Run along now."

"Oookayyy...." Annabelle seemed to pout.

Zack stood and watched her walk back to Rose next to her chair.

"What was your name?" Zack tensed as he heard a louder, more authoritative woman's voice.

He turned back to see the queen staring at him.

"Zackary Taylor, your majesty," he said, bowing his head.

"Oh that's right. Mr. Taylor, you have a curious way of addressing my daughter...." She said, staring him down.

"Have I offended you?" Zack felt nervous.

"No, I suppose not. You just have an interesting way of speaking with her. I hope she doesn't pick up that accent of yours," she said, turning back to the table.

"I suppose the little miss is quite taken with him. If I'm not mistaken that's the one that saved her at those soldier exams we saw." Armando grinned.

"When?" The queen raised an eyebrow.

"When we went for the... what division are Bloods in?"

Eliana aimed the question at Zack.

"We are part of the GSA unit, your highness," Zack said.

"The GSA test, mother," Eliana said, turning her attention back to the queen. Queen Elisa turned back to Zack.

"Hmm. So it is. Forgive me for not recalling. If it's not someone trying to gun down my children in front of me, it's some whore throwing herself off my balcony," she said, pointing to the wine. One of the servants hurriedly poured her a glass.

"Mom...." Eliana made a face at her mother.

"Oh relax, they work here for a reason. They're not stupid enough to say anything," she said, drinking her wine. "Where is the king?"

"I can go find out, my queen," a servant said.

"Do that," she said coldly. "So, Mr. Taylor, what are the common people saying about today's events?"

"I wouldn't know ma'am. Common people don't usually talk to us unless they have too."

"Are you being cheeky with me?" The queen glared at him.

"I... don't know what that means.... Normal people tend to give us GSAs a wide berth though."

"Ahh... right I almost forgot how you people stick out." The queen nodded, realizing something. "I mean look at that girl. She has to be over 6 foot! It's ridiculous!"

Rose put her head down and made herself smaller. She looked hurt.

"Oh, I don't know, Elisa. I think bigger women are sexy." Armando laughed.

Rose got smaller. Eliana didn't react at all.

"Very well then, Mr. Taylor, what do the Bloods say about us?" She brought the wine to her lips again, not bothering to look at him. "Do they laugh at us?"

There's nothing funny about you.

Zack gently walked over to her, lowering himself to be at eye level with her. The queen flinched when she noticed him.

"If anyone laughed at you, I'd make it the last sound they ever made, my queen." Zack stared right into her eyes. At this distance he could notice the amount of makeup she had on.

"...Not so close...." She finally mumbled after a moment. Zack stepped back to his original place. He glanced up to see Armando's hand partially covering a grin, then stroke his goatee. The moment of silence was finally broken by a servant returning.

"My queen, the king is working on a difficult task at the moment and said to go ahead and eat without him," he said with a bow.

There was a moment of silence followed by a deep sigh from the queen. She stood up from the table.

"Excuse me. I've lost my appetite." She turned and started to walk back to her room.

"Mom!" Eliana stood up as well.

The queen stopped for a moment.

"You don't have to...."

"Come along, Mr. Taylor." Queen Elisa started walking again.

Zack followed behind her. She was silent all the way to the large oak door Zack had sat in front of all afternoon. When a servant opened up the door she finally turned back to him.

"Enter."

Zack hesitated just a second, then entered the room.

"We are not to be disturbed. By anyone."

The study was rather large. Bookcases, fireplace, couches, the whole shebang.

"There's a note over there on the desk. Read it," the queen said. She walked over to a table with some alcohol on it. Zack looked for a desk, there was one with a single piece of notebook paper on it.

"Should I read it out loud?" He asked, walking to the table.

"No."

Zack picked up the piece of paper, and turned on a lamp on the table.

I'll be safe come tomorrow
A luxury I've surely missed

I wonder if you'll feel any sorrow,
Or simply add another to your list.

I wonder if you'll stop and think,
Will my safety give you pause,
but I doubt you'll even blink,
You no doubt doubt your cause.

Tomorrow though the sun will rise,
And finally I'll be free,
Before I leave for my tomorrow,
Know your tomorrow comes for thee.

Do you even know me? See if you can write my name at the end of this note when you find me. When everyone is looking at you. When everyone is whispering just outside your ears. When everyone is laughing at your fake smiles because NONE of them believe your lies anymore. See then if you can remember me. I wish I could hurt you some other way. The way you hurt me. But I can't. I'm nothing. I'm no one. Worse than no one. Because you had to make me think for just a second that maybe I was someone.

Just so you could take it from me, just like you took it from every other girl here.

I hope you never sleep again.

"She hit it more head on than most." The queen took a drink.

"Most?" Zack shivered. This was that girl's....

What was her name?

"That's the... third? Third note I've seen after one of the girl's killed themselves in my house." Her eyes were glazed over. "There were two others I didn't get to read."

Zack was quiet. What was he supposed to say in this situation?

"What do you think?" She finally asked.

"About what?"

"About the grammar. What the hell do you think I'm

asking?" She said, tilting her head.

"...Are you sure it was meant for the king?"

Of course it is you bonehead.

"Ha!" She laughed and started to walk a little closer.

Zack set down the note. "You don't quite get it. You see being king comes with certain perks!"

"A-ah...." Zack's neck tensed.

"Yes...." She was in his personal space now. "Say, Mr. Taylor, I've seen it a couple of times now but, why do your eyes get so bloody?"

"Oh that? That's just something that happens to GSA operatives. It's a sign that we are in a zone, ready to go I guess." Zack shrugged.

"So it happens to all Bloods?"

"Yeah, pretty much. All the... Bloods I've ever met anyway." Zack remembered how Lydia had always hated that term.

"Do you know that you're doing it all the time?"

"No, not always. It can slip out of you." Zack shrugged again, then worded her question differently in his head. "Wait, I'm doing it a lot? I'm sorry, your highness."

"Don't apologize. Can you do it now? I'd like to see it at full force."

Zack looked into her eyes for a minute. He didn't understand the request but he got the notion that she saw him as some interesting pet. He closed his eyes, did his breathing exercises, and opened them again.

"Oh wow.... That's rather intense...." She smiled... differently. "You know I have to admit, while I'm not a huge fan of the Bloods. I think you're rather interesting, Mr. Taylor."

"I'm glad you approve of me, you highness," Zack said, at this point learning to ignore the casual hate.

"Elisa."

"I'm sorry?"

"Elisa," she said, pressing against his chest. "Whenever you and I are alone in this room, I want you to call me Elisa."

...What?

What?

WHAT?!?

"My queen, I could never-"

"My husband treats me so coldly anymore..." She started to feel up his torso. "Please?"

"Elisa?" Zack nervously added a question sound to her name.

"You're rather well built, Zack...." She cooed his name. "It's been so long since I've...*felt* a man."

"O-h...."

Oh please tell me this isn't happening....

"What about you, Zack?" Her hand was slowly sliding down his torso. "Mmm... if nothing else your quite well built. When's the last time you've *felt* someone?"

Zack tried not to panic. He tried not to, but he did. WHAT THE HELL IS HAPPENING RIGHT NOW?!?

"I never have...." Zack said in a small voice that even he could tell didn't fit him. Elisa stopped her hand and looked into his eyes for a moment.

"Ha!" She said, smiling and wincing at the same time. "Wait, you're joking right? I find it hard to believe."

"I was in a relationship for a long time with someone I loved, and she wanted to wait." Fear and arousal made it way too easy to tell the truth.

"Really?" Elisa laughed again. "Was, huh? What happened? She cheat on you? I promise I can do things a silly young girl couldn't even think of...."

Hoooooooooooooly cow....

"She passed away."

It was quiet. Motions stopped. She leaned against him, and he against the wall.

"How?"

"They hung her for treason," Zack said, his emotions all over the place. Angry, sad, scared, aroused, but mostly confused.

"...You must hate us." She looked up into his eyes. "If it

helps any, I hate us too...." Her lip started to tremble.

And then she started to cry.

It was a heavy, choking to death kind of weeping. She shook like she was terrified. Zack wasn't angry or scared anymore.

How could he be angry at someone so utterly pathetic?

He picked her up in a princess carry and laid her on the couch. She curled away so he wouldn't see her face.

"I'm- sorry. I've had- had a bit too much to drink." She spat out between the sobs.

"Just rest for now." Zack stroked the hair of the sobbing, snot dribbling queen until the sobs slowly faded away.

Zack walked out of the study to see his replacement was already sitting there, as was the servant who had been there before. He looked at Zack, seemingly wanting details. He put a hand on his shoulder to whisper to him.

"The queen has had a bit too much to drink. She's resting on the sofa now, you might want to get her a blanket. I don't know if she would want many people seeing her in this state, but I'll assume you know who she allows to help her?" Zack said.

The servant nodded and placed a hand on the door, instructing Zack's replacement to stay out. Zack left, feeling eyes glancing at him the whole way out.

Zack walked into his favorite bar, lighting up his third cigarette since leaving the palace. He sat at the bar taking a long drag, grabbing the ash tray a seat or so away.

"Well don't you look like wet hen this fine evening," Joshua said, walking over. "Hard liquor kind of night?"

"Yep. Make it a double." Zack blew smoke over his shoulder.

"What was it this time?" Joshua eyeballed the whiskey into the lemon juice and set it in front of Zack. He picked it up, took a few swigs, then stretched the pucker out of his mouth.

"A girl threw herself off the balcony and the queen tried to sleep with me," Zack said, looking up and dragging again.

Joshua looked into his eyes for a minute. "Your life is

hell...." Joshua poured himself a shot of the whiskey. They clanged glasses and drank again.

The next day, Zack was put back with Annabelle.

17. FIST FIGHTS

"Okay, we have this in both gold and platinum so it's really up to you..." Zack stopped listening to the saleswoman who would not shut the heck up. Daniel had invited both he and John to come with him ring shopping for Rose.

"You know, I think I'll take that in platinum, thank you." Daniel nodded. He might have been getting fatigued as well. The lady went to box it up. "Holy cow, I hate going shopping when people try to sell you things...."

"Ah cheer up buddy! This is PROBABLY the only time you're gonna have to do this!" John smacked his shoulder.

"Heh heh heh heh, screw you," Daniel mocked.

"Platinum was a good choice. She's gonna love it," Zack said.

"Yeah, all her rings will match this way right?" John nodded.

"Rose doesn't wear any other rings," Daniel said, seeming confused.

"Ah- ha... my mistake...." John shot Zack a look.

Zack pressed his tongue to his cheek.

"What?" Daniel raised an eyebrow at Zack.

Zack sighed. "Okay, you remember how when we first got the apartments we were getting used to all the technology stuff?"

"Here you go. Sign the top copy, bottom copy is yours." Daniel signed the paper and grabbed the little box they handed him. Then headed out the door.

"Uh huh."

"Well... The first message we got from you guys... might

have been a video message instead of an audio message...." Zack said.

Daniel stopped for a minute and then looked at John.

"...I WASN'T EXPECTING NIPPLE RINGS DUDE, WHAT THE HECK?!?" John finally burst.

"YOU BASTERDS!!!"

Daniel chased them through town for a little bit before they finally made it to the park. They settled on one punch each.

"What are you guys doing tonight?" Zack asked, lighting up a cigarette.

"Well I got the ring so I think I'm gonna ask," Daniel said, looking at the equipment.

"Did you make some reservation at a fancy place? Do it all big?" John asked.

"...Maybe I'll do it tomorrow."

"Well I have a date tonight at least." John nodded, walking on a balance beam.

"Oh wow, what is this date number five?" Zack teased.

"You guys doing all the crazy stuff yet?" Daniel joined in.

"For your information, Lily is a classy lady." John gave them the finger.

"Soooo no?" Daniel flared out his palms.

"You know, there's a lot to a woman besides what happens in the bedroom. Not that you would know Mr. Piercing-fetish."

"Okay first off, still kinda pissed you guys saw my girlfriend naked, so watch it. Secondly, she was the one who wanted them not me," Daniel said.

"Mmhmm. What about you, Zack?" John asked, hopping off the beam. He strode over to the pull up bars.

"I got a therapy session at 6."

"Whoa slow down there buddy. I know it's Friday but getting that crazy?" John started to do pull ups.

"Hey, does that stuff actually work?" Daniel leaned on the post that held up the bar.

"Well... I mean I guess it works if you want it to work, you know?" Zack dragged on his cigarette. "It's one of those things where you get out of it what you put into it."

"But it's been helping you?" Daniel asked.

"Yeah. Yeah I think so." Zack nodded. "I'm starting to cut down on smoking again too. I mean for a little while there I need, like, a pack just to keep from losing my mind."

"What are you at now?" John asked, hopping off the bar.

Zack walked up to it next, flicking away his cigarette.

"I'm at about a pack a week." Zack started doing pull ups. "I'm gonna probably quit for good in a month or so."

"That's good to hear man." Daniel nodded.

"Uh, you know... I could ask Lily if she had any single friends our age if you wanted me too," John said.

Zack hung on the bar swinging for a minute, letting his arms relax. He thought about Sarah for a moment.

"It's been almost four months now, huh?" He finally said.

"Hey, you know if you're not ready it's fine but... she'd want you to be happy, you know?" Daniel said.

It was weird to think about it. Before, he couldn't remember Sarah without hyperventilating. Now? He still loved her but it was different. He knew she was really gone. It still hurt some nights when he was alone in that apartment's bedroom, but it wasn't like it was. If anything he was feeling a little guilty that he was even thinking about moving on.

"I think I still need to work on me for a little bit yet...." Zack did a few more pull ups.

John and Daniel both nodded along.

* * *

Zack walked into Julia's office to see Julia rubbing her temples on the couch in the waiting room.

"Oh. Hey, Zack," she said tiredly.

"Hey, Julia. You okay?" Zack asked.

She didn't have any of her usual energy.

"She most certainly is NOT," Nathan said, carrying a glass

of water out from his reception area. "Zack, would you talk some sense into this girl."

"Oh my God... Nathan...." Julia whined.

"She hasn't had a day off in two weeks!"

"That's not true...."

"You shut your face, if you are working from home it is NOT a day off. And now you're getting stress headaches."

"You're not a doctor, you don't know...."

"Uh..." Zack tried to keep up with the conversation. "How much work do you have?"

"It's really not that much; Nathan's just being a drama queen." Julia rolled her eyes.

"Oh yeah? When was the last time you went out and did anything fun?" Nathan folded his arms.

"I do things!" Julia said.

"If by 'things' you mean go home, put on sweatpants, and watch tv."

"Oh go blank yourself." Julia started to get aggravated. "I am a professional, okay? I'm not gonna go out like you do and go to some big bubble party, and wake up next to someone I've never met before!"

"The hell is a bubble party?" Zack asked.

"It's wonderful, is what it is. You should come with me sometime. I have the perfect guy for you." Zack gave Nathan a look. "I mean a guy you would be friends with, or whatever."

"So you don't go out, Julia?" Zack changed the subject.

"She used to. Ever since she got this position working with S.W.O.R.D. she's been a shut in."

"My friends just usually get a little wild and all my colleagues are old farts," Julia said. "And they're all very judge-y!"

"Well what if we held a session in a place where I felt more comfortable discussing important topics?" Zack asked. "Like my favorite bar!"

"What?" Julia flopped her hands down and tilted her head.

"I thumbed through one of these pamphlets, and the cliffnotes say you have a duty to make your patients as comfortable as possible," Zack said.

"Oh yeah! That's right!" Nathan grabbed one of the pamphlets off the wall. "Right here: 'Setting a tone that is threatening or dismissive can cause patients to shut down emotionally. Providing a comfortable and safe atmosphere is imperative to patient health and well being.' Zack, are you feeling threatened in our office?" Nathan asked.

"Oh majorly. The walls are closing in around me." Zack nodded.

"Well there you go, Jewels, you need to go to a bar with Zack. It's work related."

Julia stared at them for a moment. "You two are so full of crap...."

"Now, now, you are being..." Zack looked at the pamphlet in Nathan's hands. "...dismissive at me, Dr. Crane."

"Dismissive AT you...." Julia shook her head trying to push away a smile with her tongue.

"Yep. Now quit your gripping. You're going out and that's final. I'll lock up, don't worry," Nathan said, picking her up and pushing her to the door.

"Ugh okay, okay!" Julia said, getting pushed out the door with Zack. She sighed a little, putting on her jacket. "So where are we going?"

"You ever heard of a little pub called Wynn's?" Zack smiled.

* * *

"Okay, wait wait wait..." Julia said, waving her hand. "You mean they let you in no problem? You were what, thirteen at the time?"

Sitting at the bar at Wynn's about three drinks in, Zack was recounting a particular story about the time he and John got thrown out of a strip club.

"Yeah, fourteen, thirteen, I mean we were tall. And we had the same uniforms as the rest of the military at the time so they just figured we were a couple of soldiers on leave," Zack said.

"Zack?" He suddenly heard a familiar voice behind him. He turned around to see John walking in behind him with a rather pretty brunette behind him.

"Oh well speak of the devil," Zack said.

"Hey...." John said, walking over. Out the corner of his eye he eyeballed Julia.

"This is Julia Crane, dear personal friend and master psychologist," Zack said. "We were just about to get into the massive amounts of molestation I had."

"Ah, well the bar is the place I'd like to discuss that." John raised his eyebrows and nodded. "John Henagar"

"Julia Crane," she said, shaking his hand. "We were just talking about you."

"Really? Only good things I hope."

"Eh. Something about you guys getting thrown out of a strip club?" Julia smiled.

The girl next to John folded her arms and raised her eyebrows with a smile at him.

"Ah... haha.... Yeah, no, that's ancient history. By the way the beautiful lady is Lily."

"Hello again, Ms. Lily, John never shuts up about you. I'm Zack." Zack hadn't really seen her since that night of orientation.

"Hi! Hello!" Lily said, to him and then Julia. "Yeah he tends to run his mouth."

"Hey, we were gonna have dinner, you guys wanna join us?" John pointed at the tables with his thumb.

"What do you think?" Zack asked Julia.

"Mmmm.... You know what? Sure! I'd like to get a little bit more of a profile on you anyway. I wonder if John has any interesting stories about you." She smiled devilishly.

"I was thinking the same thing." Lilly smiled the same way.

"...Okay you guys are making me nervous," John said

looking at them.

"Why? It's not like you have anything to hide, right?" Lily said, tilting her head at John.

"I'm... an open book...." John hesitated.

Two hours, and several more drinks later, things were going relatively smooth. Zack washed his hands in the bathroom. He wasn't even buzzed really, but if he started going at his normal pace he was sure one of the girls would get alcohol poisoning. Zack looked in the mirror for a second, then felt his chin. His stubble had grown a little long; he should have probably shaved again before coming out tonight.

Not that he needed to look nice or anything.

This wasn't a date or anything.

Right?

The thought put a little bit of a damper on his mood. It had been four months already. Should he move on? Was he moving on?

Just let it go man, Julia probably doesn't think this is anything more than friends hanging out at a bar.

Zack walked back out to notice a small entourage gathered by his booth. John was looking rather aggravated. Three men blocked the way back to Zack's seat.

"Excuse me," Zack said.

The guy who was leaning against the booth blocking the way to his seat turned around, eyeing Zack.

"Can I help you?" He asked, with furrowed brows.

"Yeah, you're sort of blocking the way to my seat."

The guy started to laugh."Yeah, don't worry about it bro, I just got to borrow it for a while. Talk to this fine young lady. Why don't you go find some spot at the bar?"

Zack tried not to laugh in this guy's face, he felt a little embarrassed for him. "You a couple cards short of a deck, huh?"

"...The hell that supposed to mean?" He said, getting in his face more.

"Oh dear..." Zack looked out of the corner of his eye for a second. "It's like a round about way of saying your dumb."

"Zack, let's just go." Julia started to get up.

"Uh uh," the guy said, putting a hand up at Julia. "No, Sasquatch over here just lost his chance."

"*Sasquatch*?" Zack repeated, now actually laughing. "I don't even know what that means."

"Zack, please, let's just...." Julia started to get up again.

This time the guy got in her face. "I SAID SIT-"

He didn't really get to finish. The moment he started to move at Julia, Zack had grabbed him by the waist and flung him diagonally into the wall next to the booths. The two other guys flinched.

"Hey, Joshua? I might break some stuff so don't freak out," Zack called over his shoulder, looking at the other two.

"'Kay. Try to stay off the widows; they take forever to get new ones," Joshua said from the bar.

The closest one to Zack pulled out a butterfly knife.

"AREN'T YOU GOING TO HELP HIM?!?" Lily suddenly yelled at John.

"Zack? You got this?" John asked, topping off his beer.

"Are you serious?" Zack tilted his head, and half closed his eyes at John. "There's THREE of them."

"Yeah, she's never seen us do this before." John rolled his eyes.

The closest one lunged at Zack's face with the knife. Zack grabbed it by the blade and snapped it so he was only left with a handle. He apple-sauced the man then grabbed his face and trip-threw him head first into the table of the booth behind them. His body spasmed once before going limp.

The next man jumped on Zack's back and attempted to choke him. Zack calmly walked over to another table, grabbed the man by the hair, and flipped him hard onto it. With the wind knocked out of him, Zack grabbed and held his mouth and nose. After a few moments of panic, the man went limp as well.

"Hey, Zack, the other guy is getting up," John said from the table.

Zack turned to see the man stumbling up to him.

As quick as the man could he pulled a gun on Zack.

Uh oh.

If Zack knew he had a gun he might have taken it a bit more seriously.

Zack grabbed the barrel in time to move the gun before the man fired, but a bullet still caught him by the collar bone. Zack felt a deeper sting then usual. John, seeing the gun, was on the man quickly, grabbing his throat from behind and slamming him into one of the brick pillars. Zack held onto the gun as John held the man off the ground by the throat.

“Did it catch you on the collar bone? That'll be a heck of a bruise,” John said, the dark blood painting his sclera almost black.

“No...” Zack felt his shoulder, confused at the feeling of an exit wound. He looked at the gun. “It went through me....”

“What?” John turned his focus on Zack. The gun was a five-seven, and taking the clip out revealed a rifle-style steel bullet. A highly illegal gun and round. Something that was suited for killing GSA ops.

“It's a steel point five-seven,” Zack said.

John's grip tightened as his face contorted.

“Where the hell did you get that?” John asked the man as Joshua put a rag over Zack's wound and pressed.

* * *

A woman in an ambulance looked at Zack's shoulder as a short, fat police officer and his female partner took notes from John, Zack, and the girls.

“So the first one to engage in violence would be you then, Mr. Taylor?” She asked.

“Nope. That was the guy with the gun,” Zack said, not looking at her.

“So the cameras inside will show the man you and your accomplice almost choked to death, attacking you, correct?”

"Accomplice?" Julia said, her head jerking back.

"Yep." John nodded.

"Get the hell out of my way!"

"Oh God...." John and Zack said in unison.

Lydia shoved a man into a car as several soldiers followed her.

"What happened?"

"Excuse me-"

"Shut the hell up!" Lydia practically screamed in the young woman's face. She turned to Zack and John again as a soldier walked over and grabbed the notes out of the female cop's hand. "Report."

"Some guys found us at the bar and started making trouble. We handled it but one of them had a steel point five-seven. Caught me in the shoulder."

"And where the hell were you?" She turned to John. "How. Many. Times. Have I told you, you have each other's backs. Every threat is a..."

"Real threat...." They answered in unison.

"Then act like it!" She shouted.

Everyone but the boys flinched.

"Um... ma'am we were just investigating-" The female police officer started again, a little bewildered. Zack stared at the ground; this woman was asking for it now.

"You were investigating?" Lydia turned to the woman again. "I'll tell you what happened very clearly. MY boys were minding their own business when they got jumped by three men, one of who was carrying an illegal firearm. And if you had run their IDs you would have noticed that these men are the personal bodyguards of the royal family. Meaning the men back there are national terrorists. With these absolute FACTS, what ARE you doing over here?"

The woman was quiet now. To be fair Lydia did have a pressure around her when she was pissed. The police officers ended up walking back to their car without another word. Several soldiers walked along with them, leaving behind only

Lydia.

"Are you okay?" Lydia's tone was softer as she walked up and checked Zack's shoulder.

"Yeah, I'll be fine. Won't even need to miss work," Zack said as Lydia examined him.

Lydia sighed.

"You almost gave me a nervous breakdown, you know that?" Lydia straightened back up. "Getting a call from John this late at night. 'Hey Lydia! Don't be pissed but me and Zack m*ight* have gotten attacked and Zack *MIGHT* have gotten shot with a five-seven steel-point. Can you come help us out before the cops come?' What the hell...." Lydia did her best John impression, then looked at the girls. "What were you all doing out here?"

"Right, this is Lily, she works at our apartment. We were on a date when we ran into Zack and Julia here," John said. "This is Lydia. She was our CO back home; she's mom away from mom."

"Hi, I'm Lily...." Lily gave a nervous little wave.

"A pleasure." Lydia nodded, then eyed Julia. "So, Dr. Crane, is Zack here checking out okay? Or... was this a personal meeting...?"

"Oh, well I- My job requires a bit of intimacy to help create a healing environment. I was hoping a less formal setting would make it easier to talk," Julia said.

Zack had forgotten that Lydia knew Julia from her work with S.W.O.R.D.'s GSA division.

"Mm. Well I wasn't sure Zack would be the kind for therapy. But thanks for whatever it is you're doing, I think it's helped." Lydia nodded.

"Why do you think he wouldn't be the kind of person for therapy?" Julia asked, seemingly unamused by Lydia's backhanded thanks.

Lydia pulled out her cigarettes, mulling over her response. An EMT walked up from the front of the truck.

"How are you feeling?" He asked Zack.

"Good. Are we all done?"

"Yeah you're cleared to go home. The military guys said that you would be checked out later by your own doctors."

"Got it." Zack stood up.

"Are you sure you don't need to go to the hospital?" Julia asked, swaying slightly.

Lydia made a face Zack couldn't quite interpret.

"Nah I'm fine. Not like it's the first time I've taken a bullet. Honestly, this hurts less than a 9 mil... it's kinda like a bee sting." Zack moved his shoulder around.

"I'm pretty sure bee stings hurt less than bullets!" Lily laughed in astonishment.

"You city girls ain't seen the bees we got back home." John laughed. "Couple beers and he'll be fine. Lydia, do you have time for a beer with us?"

"Well, I wouldn't want to intrude on your double date," Lydia said, exhaling some smoke.

Julia's eyes narrowed as she jutted out her chin like a boxer.

"Ahh, come on! Lily needs to meet my mom away from mom sooner or later." John grabbed Lydia in a side hug.

"Yeah, I would like to get to know you a little better too, Lydia," Julia said with a smile.

"It's a little quick to be on a first name basis, isn't it, Dr. Crane?" Lydia asked.

"Ahh... so that's where he gets it..." Julia smiled, but it didn't touch her eyes.

Maybe he was way off, but Zack thought they weren't quite getting along.

18. COFFEE?

Zack stood corrected.

"So, I show up to this strip club at three in the morning to find these two chowder-heads handcuffed together to a light pole and a mob of strippers cussing out the cops," Lydia half yelled in Wynn's.

Lily and Julia were both practically on the floor laughing.

"Wait, why were the strippers cussing out the cops?" Julia laughed, trying to catch her breath.

"Because we were the good guys!" John yelled. "Me and Zack are over here, doing our civic duty, standing up for the underprivileged, trying to make Lydia proud, and we got chewed out by the cops!"

"*Doing your civic duty*, haha!" Julia laughed so hard she started to shake.

Lily couldn't breathe at this point.

"Oh my God! Stop, Stop! I'll pee!" Lily swayed all over, drunk as a skunk.

"They were very nice ladies honestly...." Zack chuckled, remembering the event.

"Oh God... I have to go to the bathroom. I'll be back," Lily said, wobbling up.

"I'll go with you, haha! Don't fall!" Julia was also a bit drunk at this point, but she was keeping a pretty close pace to Lydia for a while there.

"They're pretty nice girls...." Lydia nodded once they were out of ear shot. "You've been dating Lily for a while now?" She asked John.

"For a little while now. She's nice." He smiled, feeling his hair.

"Should have known you'd fall for a city girl...." Zack shook his head, picking up his beer again.

"Yeah, yeah. You and Julia seem to get along well, you know." John said.

"She is also a nice girl." Zack nodded. "And a very talented therapist."

"Mmmm...." Lydia nodded back. Her and John shared a look.

"What?" Zack asked with a laugh.

"It's nothing. You guys might want to walk them home tonight just in case." Lydia changed the topic. "Oh, Zack, don't forget there is this cultural thing in the city if you walk a girl home. If she invites you into her place for coffee you have to accept."

"What? Why?" Zack said, confused.

"It's a chivalrous tradition in the city. If a guy walks a girl home and she offers him coffee he has to stay. It's offensive to refuse," Lydia said.

"Oh yeah! Someone told me about that last time we were here. You also can't ask about the coffee once inside. Something about patience...." John nodded along.

"That's a tradition here?" Zack asked, raising a brow. "Why coffee? I don't want to be up all night."

"It's just a custom you need to observe. Don't embarrass her, okay?" Lydia said.

"Alright. Alright." Zack raised his hands.

"I'mmmm a little drunk you guys...." Lily swayed back over to the table as Julia guided her. "You're not allowed at strip clubs! I'm so pissed!" She yelled at John.

"Wha-? It was a long time ago!"

"That's what you say to all the- All the girls! Bet!"

"Welp! I guess it's time to hit the road. I told the boys to take you guys home just in case. See you around." Lydia had her jacket on and was halfway to the door in a flash.

"BYE, LYDIA!!" Lily waved.

John held her up a little.

Julia laughed. "She's pretty wasted."

"Yeah, John will get her home safe," Zack said, holding open her jacket.

She slipped her arms through. "Thanks."

They said their goodbyes and headed out. Julia was a little drunk but she could still mostly walk on her own. She drifted a little bit too close to the road and Zack grabbed her elbow and pulled her back gently. She grabbed on to him a little to steady herself.

"Ha, sorry."

"It's fine, here." Zack put his hand in his jacket pocket and stuck out his elbow, putting her hand on his arm. "For balance."

"Well aren't you such a gentleman...." Julia smiled to herself. She slid her arm to interlock with Zack's.

"I try!" He said with a smile.

"You do." She giggled a bit again.

Zack wasn't stupid; he tried to play it off when John and Lydia brought it up, but there was definitely a mood between him and Julia tonight. Though it could just be the beer. It was hard to tell with her though.

"Your friends are nice," Julia said, breaking the silence.

"Yeah, I'm surprised you can keep up with Lydia! You're all sorts of impressive." Zack laughed.

"I may have the occasional drink! When I was younger...." She quickly clarified. "Hey, I'm sorry about the whole thing that happened with that guy...."

"It's not a big deal. Or your fault," Zack said, as they stopped at a corner.

"I live down this way," she said, as they turned down the corner. "I feel like it is though. I don't know why guys need to be like that! Does that work? Are there some girls who are just all about it, when a guy is a jerk like that?! You would think you would find out pretty quick that it doesn't work!"

"You girls sure have it rough." Zack reassured her by

patting her hand.

"We do! Wha- don't pat my hand like I'm some old woman!" Julia said.

"Sorry, sorry." He laughed.

"I'm right here...." Julia said, as she very slightly pulled him to a stop. They were in front of a little door built into the wall of a large building. Zack was looking for a house so he missed it.

"Oops sorry. Cute building," Zack said, swinging on his heel.

"Yeah...." Julia stood in front of her door. She squeezed his arm a little. "Well I guess this is goodnight...."

"Good night, Jewels," Zack said, with a smile. He wondered if John and Lydia were pulling his leg about the coffee thing. Julia walked to her door, but paused with her hand on the handle. She turned back just as Zack started turning to leave.

"Hey...."

Zack stopped.

"Do you... wanna come in for some coffee?"

Oh, there it is.

* * *

"Ahhh... it's good to be home!" Julia said, sitting next to Zack on the couch.

Zack laid his jacket on the coffee table as Julia threw hers onto a wooden chair. "Soooo... this is my apartment. What do you think?"

It's pretty small.... He thought as they sat on a little brown loveseat.

"It's cozy. I figured you for a house person though."

"Well eventually, but this is a cheap little place for now. And I never have to fix anything like I would for a house," she said, leaning back a little.

"Ah, well that's true. That would be a job for the future Mr.

Crane, right?" Zack laughed.

"Excuse me?" Julia flicked her head up, grinning. "What, like I can't fix my own house?"

"You're a city girl," Zack said.

"Woooooooowwww...." Julia sat slack jawed. "For your information country BOY, I am a strong, independent, city WOMAN, who does not need a man to fix her house for her. I simply enjoy the ease of apartment living where I DON'T have to fix it myself."

"Whatever you say Ms. City-Woman." Zack laughed.

"It's DOCTOR City-Woman," Julia said.

"'Oh I'm sorry ma'am, Ise just a country boy who don't know no better,'" Zack said, trying to sound as hick-ish as possible.

"I know you're trying to do a voice right there, but that is LITERALLY what you sound like half the time." Julia smirked.

"Screw. You." Zack laughed, throwing his head back.

"Is this your only tattoo by the way?" Julia asked, pointing to Zack's hand as he rubbed his face.

"Yeah, so far anyway. I'm not sure what to get next. I thought it would hurt more than it did," Zack said, looking at his knuckles.

"You should get a full sleeve! Tattoos are sexy!" Julia laughed, poking his shoulder.

"Oh yeah? Do you have any?" Zack asked.

He also began wondering about the coffee. Why was he not supposed to bring it up?

"I got one. You want to see?"

"Yeah! Where is your full sleeve?"

"Shut up!" Julia said, standing up and walking down the hall. "Close your eyes and I'll tell you when to open them!"

"What?" Zack laughed.

"Just do what I say! You want to see or not?!" Julia leaned her head out of her room.

Zack shut his eyes as he was told. It had to be somewhere private for her to do all that. Zack started to feel nervous.

"Okay... Open!"

Zack opened his eyes to see Julia facing away from him. Her blonde hair was in front of her to show off her now completely bare back. He looked down her toned, tan skin, to see a magnificently detailed pair of black wings. The feathers flared out as they reached down to her butt which was still covered by her skirt and pantyhose, which were... tighter than he thought they would be.

"Please say something...." Julia said, in a much smaller voice.

"That is amazing... holy cow...." Zack said, eyeing her back.

"Sexy?"

"Hell yeah it's sexy, dang.... How long did that take?" Julia turned a little to look at him, her hands covering her.

"Like twelve hours." She looked back at the hallway. "I don't want to go get my shirt...."

This has nothing to do with coffee, does it? Zack took off his shirt and stood about half way, he couldn't really straighten out, and pulled his shirt over Julia's head.

"Wha-?" Julia laughed as he pulled the shirt all the way down for her and sat back on the couch.

"Problem solved!" He said, quietly praying she wouldn't notice the problem he was currently having.

Julia pushed her arms through the sleeves and lifted her arms.

"Can I-?" She faced away from him reaching to one side and unzipping her skirt. She let it drop to the ground and raised her arms. The hem of his shirt was still able to cover everything on her.

"Yaaaayyy!! It's like a dress!" Julia cheered, quite pleased at the makeshift dress. She reached up and began to take off her pantyhose as well. Zack averted his eyes, feeling rather embarrassed to have a girl act so relaxed with him.

"Woah!"

Julia stumbled, and fell right onto his lap. He wrapped his arms around her on instinct and they sat there for a moment.

Zack tried not to freak out. Did she really fall? Was it on purpose? Did she invite him up here for... that?

He had never done anything remotely like this with Sarah. Julia was a fast paced city girl after all. Was this just normal? Is this what people in the city do? Were they going to start dating? Was it even okay with a drunk girl?

...Was he really over Sarah?

"Sorry I'm a little drunk...." Julia slurred, her voice soft and enticing. She shifted herself into Zack a little more. "Wow..."

"W-what?"

"Um, nothing."

Zack's hands were on her waist. He slid them around her a little bit, but wasn't sure where to put them exactly. Julia leaned forward to get her panty hose off, then melted back into his bare chest.

"Mmmm.... That's better," she said, her head leaning back on his shoulder.

Zack's hands rested on Julia's stomach, her hands moved over his. She turned her head towards his.

"...Does it hurt?" Her fingernails traced the bandage on his shoulder.

"I'm okay. Not the first time."

"You really dangerous, huh?"

Julia turned around. She gently pushed him back into the loveseat, straddling him. Her fingers gently moved over the bandage.

"Only when I have to be, I guess." Zack tried to steady his breathing. "Every princess need her knight in shining armor, right?"

"Oh I'm a princess, huh?" Julia giggled. "Does it take much practice to be that rotten?"

Rotten....

"I guess I'm just a natural." Zack tensely laughed.

One of Julia's hands gently moved to his neck, the other slid down his shoulder gently squeezing it.

"Well... if your the knight in shining armor...."

Julia leaned in gently touching her lips against Zack's, before her hand moved into his hair pulling his head back to kiss him deeply.

She kissed differently than Sarah had. Her lips were a little thinner, but her kiss was more aggressive. This wasn't gentle anymore, this was hungry, fiery. The kind of kiss that warms like hard liquor, and makes you loose control of yourself just as fast.

Their tongues and lips all melting into each other, Zack's hands ran up her rib cage. He had to squeeze her to try to keep his hands from shaking. Julia groaned in response.

"Your hands are huge." Julia reached down grabbing his wrists. "They'd be more comfortable here...."

Nerves were a funny thing. Zack's hands never shook when he held a gun, but holding Julia made him tremble. A knife in his face barely registered in his mind, but Julia's lips on his made his mind race. Being places he didn't want to be, doing things he didn't want to do, he barely thought about it.

But wanting something? Someone? That was terrifying.

Was this it? Moving on? Was that okay? Was it so wrong to want things? Instead of being angry, being happy again? Was this what he wanted?

Julia pulled back pressing her forehead to his, out of breath.

"I really like this shirt... I want to sleep in it." She said rubbing his stubble.

"I don't think I can go home half naked." Zack laughed.

"Then don't." Julia stared into his eyes. "You could be as naked as you want if you stayed here...."

...*Yeah*

He really did... it felt right, it felt like moving on.

"I'd love to."

"Carry me? My feet are sore." She giggled.

Zack moved his arms to support her and stood up with her in a princess carry. "OH! You actually picked me up!"

"Well yeah? You asked me to!" He laughed along with her

as they headed to her room.

"Aren't I heavy?"

Zack smiled at the typical loaded question.

"You're seriously light," he said, looking at her face. The dark rooms were only illuminated by the dim street lights.

Zack walked slowly, trying to feel along the edge of her bed. He laid her down gently on her bed as her hands wrapped around his head and neck as she pulled him down on top of her, kissing him. Her fingers grazed a now old scar on his head.

"What's this from...?" She said, breaking away.

But the past doesn't go away. Scars don't fade completely. Even when you move on, the places you've been determines your walk.

"When Sarah died... I went to a dark place for awhile." Zack said, unable to look at Julia. "Things... happened."

She didn't say anything. He didn't kiss her again. They stayed there holding each other for a moment, then she hugged him tight.

"Hey, um...." Julia mumbled into his neck softly. "Maybe... maybe we shouldn't do this right now...."

"Are you okay?" He asked.

"No, I- I'm just... you know I really kinda like you. And I always rush into.... And then it never works cause I set unrealistic expectations. And I mean it's your first time ever, and now I can't stop freaking out because I'm drunk and you might not enjoy it because it's supposed to be special. You probably think I'm-"

"Special" Zack started to sit up, Julia clung to him. "I think your someone special to me."

"I'm really sorry...." She mumbled into his shoulder, starting to cry.

"It's okay. It's okay...." He rocked her a little.

She eventually slid her arms down, curling up in his lap. "I'm really sorry...."

"Here...." Zack laid her down and tucked her in with the blanket. He slid down around her on her tiny bed. He slid his arm under her pillow as she nuzzled her face into his chest.

"You're really nice, Zack...." She slurred, sounding ready to fall asleep immediately.

Zack kissed her forehead. Then his phone started to vibrate in his pocket.

"Hello?" He said lightly, trying not to bother Julia.

"Meet at Wynn's tomorrow morning. Salim wants to talk to you." *Click.*

Damn it.

19. PICK UP THE PACE

Zack faded in and out of sleep most of the night. When the sun shined through the window he finally sat up on the edge of the bed. Julia must have woken up and made her way to the bathroom at some point. He vaguely remembered hearing the shower running, along with the sound of vomiting.

Zack held his head in his hands, the feeling of dehydration and a headache that sat in his eyes always made waking up after drinking suck. He rubbed his face and eyes, the morning light irritating him. Julia's bedroom got a ton of light in the morning. He looked up to see Julia's face dart into the room for just a second and back out.

"Hey, you're awake! That's good...." Julia said while hiding on the other side of the door.

"Ha. What?" Zack gave a little laugh.

"I don't know... um...." Julia groaned. "I forgot to grab clothes, and I feel like total trash right now, and I really just need to go to bed."

"Yeah, I know how that feels. Do you want me to go?" Zack nodded.

"I mean if you want to...."

"Well I doubt you want to hang out or whatever people do after they stay over drunk at people's houses.... Sorry I've never done this before." Zack felt like trash too. "I don't want you to think I'm a jerk!"

"No, no you're fine! I'm just kinda embarrassed and feel crappy, and don't really want you to see me right now. We can talk about everything later...."

"Okay."

Zack looked around to see if Julia left his shirt on the floor.

"...Are you mad at me?" Julia asked.

"What? Why would I be mad?" Zack got up.

"Cause I didn't... you know...."

"Jewels. I wouldn't get mad over that." Zack started walking toward the door.

"I know! I know! Sorry I'm just... wait don't look at me, I look gross!" Julia hurried into the bathroom and shut the door.

Zack walked up to the door and set his forehead against it.

"I LIKE you Julia." Zack tried to think of what to say through his hangover. "You mean a lot more to me than just... that stuff."

"I know... I just feel like crap and I'm embarrassed and... I need to stop talking. Let's talk when I'm not hungover, okay?"

"Okay." Zack paused. "Also, I think you have my shirt."

Zack heard rustling in the bathroom. Julia cracked the door open enough to hand it to him, then shut the door again.

* * *

"What's up?" Zack asked the room as he and Joshua descended the stairs. Salim, Olivia, and Micheal were already here.

"That's a bit more of a question for you today," Micheal said, looking over his coffee. "If you could try not to get a load of cops to investigate our bar in the future we would really appreciate it."

"Is that why you called him here?" Salim asked, looking over at Micheal. "I thought you were gonna talk about him getting close with Dr. Crane?"

"I was getting to that, Salim...." Micheal said, rubbing his tired eyes.

"First off. Sorry about the fight, but those guys started it. Second, what's wrong with Julia?" Zack said, raising his hand.

Everyone was quiet for a moment.

"We are a little worried about you getting into...." Olivia rocked on her heels, trying to find the right words.

"Micheal and Olivia are concerned that you receiving therapy, along with finding an emotional replacement for your companion that you lost, will cause a positive mental state that will prevent you from carrying out your assassinations that will ultimately lead to your death as a side effect," Salim said, very mechanically.

Zack took a second to figure out what he was saying.

"So... you're worried I'll wuss out on killing everyone because I might not want to die anymore? Because I've *replaced* Sarah?"

"Christ, Salim...." Olivia rubbed her eyes this time.

"Zack... you have to understand that we are in a position with you, that when the time comes, and we are ready for you to carry out your end, we won't be able to get you out," Micheal said.

"And when they catch you, you will be tortured and you'll have to sell out everyone and everything. That's not a knock on your toughness, it's just how things go," Olivia said.

"If we have everything set up perfectly, it will take at least a year to put it all in place and get the new government going," Micheal said.

"There's no way we could get you out alive." Olivia sighed.

"There's not a real easy way to say this... you might not want to get too attached to anyone," Micheal said.

"How much longer do we have till we are ready for me to kill everybody?" Zack asked.

Everybody turned to look at Micheal.

"We are somewhere between three to six months away yet," Micheal said, running his hand through his hair.

"Okay." Zack took out a cigarette and started back towards the stairs.

"What does 'okay' mean?" Olivia asked him before he could get there.

He stopped to light his cigarette, then leaned against the door frame halfway facing them.

"How many of you guys know what happens to GSA operatives?" Zack asked, putting a hand up. "I mean like how we die, if we don't get killed?"

Salim raised his hand quickly. Micheal and Olivia slowly raised theirs while looking away.

"We all get this disease: Adam's Polycythemic Leukemia. It's some kind of genetic thing, or it comes with GSA. If you have GSA you will have APL," Zack said.

He paused to take a drag on his cigarette.

"It hits you around forty. Something about cell regeneration. Your cells get all confused about how to reproduce. Your body starts thinking every cell you have is a blood cell. Bone cells, brain cells, tissue cells, they don't keep making those cells they start making blood cells. You literally start to... *Liquify*."

Another drag on the cigarette....

"When we were twelve, we had just started training in the GSA part of the military, they took us to a hospital to see what it was like. It was one of those 'Grow up, this is your lot' things. I saw a guy who didn't have his eyes anymore, they said they just melted out of his head. They told us they just popped like egg yolks one day; they couldn't hold themselves together anymore."

There was some wincing at that around the room. Zack itched at the stubble coming out of his jaw.

"Another guy just sort of drowned as his lungs liquified. A couple got dementia, some would just swell until something finally wasn't there anymore. It's a rough way to go. You got till about forty, that's it."

Zack took another drag on his cigarette and walked back to the table where Micheal was and looked him in the eye.

"I don't think I ever said it, but the only thing I've ever tried to be was happy. I never worried about trying to build things or change things, or doing something that mattered or whatever. I was never gonna see it way down the road; I had a timer on me the second I was born." Zack looked at Micheal, unsure of what he was thinking. "Sarah... our last fight, one of the last times I talked to her it was about that. About me not wanting to do anything worthwhile. She had big dreams, you know?"

Zack took one last hit of his cigarette.

"Is dying like this gonna be worthwhile? Is the world gonna be better?" Zack asked Micheal.

"...It is." Micheal said slowly.

"Then I'm ready to give up twenty years for that," Zack said. He dropped his cigarette on the concrete floor of the basement and stomped it out. "But I'll live these last months my way."

He left it at that and headed home.

* * *

Zack walked into his apartment, the door shutting loudly behind him. He picked up the new mail on his floor. There was a new itinerary for the week. He sat on the couch and started to open it when there was a loud knock on the door.

"Are you serious right now?" He sighed. He looked through the peephole to see Rose standing outside, hands on her hips.

"Yeah?" He said, opening the door.

She pushed past him into his apartment and went straight to the tv and started going through one of the menus.

"Yeah, no, make yourself at home."

"You know, John I can understand, but you are such an jerk for not telling me about this." She sounded agitated.

Zack stood there for a minute, unsure of what she was talking about, then he remembered.

The video.

"Also, you didn't delete it either? Are you serious?!"

"I thought it went away after I watched it?" Zack said, shutting the door.

"Suuuuure...." She said.

"Well sorry I didn't tell you anyway...." Zack opened his itinerary and sat down on the couch with her.

Rose sighed loudly, folding her arms and flopping back on the couch. "What time did you get home last night anyway?"

Crap.

"Eh... late," he said, looking at his mail.

"When did you leave this morning?"

"Uh... early."

"Zackary Taylor."

Zack didn't look at her. He felt his face getting a little hot. "Yes?"

"John told us what happened last night. And that you took that, quote, 'hot therapist' home last night."

"Yeah?"

"And we never heard you come home."

"What, did you stake out my door?"

"Did you spend the night at her house?"

Crap....

"It's... really not a big deal...."

"OH. MY. GOD!!" Rose slapped his arm.

"Oh my God...." Zack echoed.

"So wait did you guys...?" Rose raised her eyebrows and bobbed her head.

"No we didn't."

"But you spent the night...."

"Yeah, she was a little too drunk and we just thought it was better not to."

"Oh... so what happened this morning?" She turned fully to him on the couch.

"What do you mean? We didn't do anything, she was hungover." Zack raised an eyebrow at her.

"No, like what happened when you left?" She asked. "Like, was it awkward? Did she say anything?!"

"Uhh...." Zack tried to remember. "I mean, I don't think so...."

"So when you got up was she there? Did you wake up first?

Did you kiss goodbye?" Rose was so amped.

"She was still there. We woke up and she hurried to the bathroom and said she didn't want me to see her sick, so she would see me later," he said.

"Hmmm...." Rose did that thing where she moved her chin around.

"What?" Zack was kinda nervous now.

"Nothing. You think you'll try like actually asking her out on a date? Or just wait and see how it goes?"

"I don't know." Zack sighed. "I guess I'll talk to her about it next time."

"It'll all work out." Rose patted him on the shoulder. "I'm so excited! Hey, who did you get for tomorrow?"

"Annabelle." Zack always got Annabelle.

"Aww... switch with me!!" Rose whined.

"What? Why?" Zack asked. "Who'd you get?"

"Fricking Eliana." Rose sighed. "I just can't fricking deal with her anymore. She whines non stop to Josephine on the phone and she's coming back tomorrow. I just can't deal with that tomorrow."

"Whatever happened with that thing, you thought she was wearing too much makeup?" Zack asked.

"I haven't seen her with like bruises or anything. She has someone who puts the makeup on for her so maybe I made a bad connection," Rose said. "She will not let anything that Armando guy does go though. She thinks I can't hear her but I can and she acts like she is the most persecuted person in the world. I mean, I don't have to get married to some creeper, I get that, but good lord you are a LITERAL PRINCESS."

"Well, I mean there's other kinds of abuse besides physical abuse. We can hurt each other just as much with our words or actions to others."

"Oh my God, you almost sleep with your therapist once and you start psycho analyzing everything." Rose grinned.

"I- Screw you! I was gonna switch with you too but if you're gonna be a twat you can forget it." Zack tossed his itinerary on the coffee table.

"Don't call me a twat!" Rose smoked him in the head with a throw pillow. "You owe me anyway! You saw me naked!"

"Ughhhh...." Zack groaned. "Is it just whining about Armando?"

"Nope! Get ready for 'Mom doesn't even TRY to listen to me.' 'I am LITERALLY starving to death.' 'But how do I know if I got there Jojo?'" Rose did a few different mocking voices.

"Ewww...." Zack did a face at that last one. "Jojo?"

"Yeah that's Duchess Josephine's nickname or whatever," Rose said. "C'mon, pleasssse? Please please please???"

"Can you even switch?" Zack asked.

"John's girlfriend Lily can! And he owes me!" Rose said, still pissed off.

"'Ight, fine, you call John then." Zack shrugged. "What are you guys doing today?"

"Daniel's taking me on a date tonight! He said it's been a little while since we went on a nice date just the two of us. I think he's been a little lonely lately."

* * *

KNOCKKNOCKKNOCKKNOCKKNOCKKNOCKKNOCK-
Click. "*OHMYGODOHMYGOD-OHMYGODOHMYGOD!!!!!*"

Zack opened his very loud door to find Rose jumping up and down, shaking the ring on her hand violently back and forth. She was yelling a mile a minute.

"Rose, it is one in the God dang morning...."

20. SNAP DECISION

"Aren't you usually with my sister?" Princess Eliana said as she brushed her hair in front of the mirror.

"Yes ma'am." Zack nodded. "But they switched me this time. That's not a problem is it?"

"Ew, don't call me ma'am it makes me feel old," she said. "It's not, I just know you're Anna's favorite."

"Well, I'm not entirely sure how it works, but I think they have to rotate us somewhat." Zack shrugged.

"Mmmm."

This isn't all that bad. Rose made it seem like she whined constantly. Zack thought as he stood there waiting for her to finish getting ready.

"I just remember the FIT she threw last time you got put with my mom. I REALLY don't want to deal with that." She sighed and shook her head.

Alright if she talks like that the whole time this will be really annoying. He thought.

"I'm sure it won't be a problem."

"I mean I have ENOUGH to deal with without my little sister crying that I stole her boyfriend."

Ughhh.

"Is something bothering you, miss?" Zack asked.

Eliana sighed once again. "YOU wouldn't understand...."

Oh kill yourself, you crybaby. Zack decided to be quiet and let her finish getting ready.

"Hey."

"Yes, miss?"

"What are the limits on what I can tell you to do?"

That threw Zack for a loop. "As far as what, your highness?"

"Like... do you guys have to kill someone if we tell you to?"

"Well if we are going off of S.W.O.R.D.'s code of ethics, lethal force is usable when a threat is life threatening to ourselves or others in our company. That, or when unrestricted by a superior officer in good standing that is recognizable to the operative gives the order," Zack said.

"So that means I count, right? As the princess?" Eliana turned around to face him.

"I would say so. The only stipulation would be against other political or military personnel or if there becomes a conflict in orders. Like if we are supposed to escort you somewhere and there is an emphasis to not make a scene, I guess," Zack said.

Eliana stood up and walked over to the door.

"That doesn't bother you? Killing people?" She asked as Zack opened the door for her.

"Should it? I only kill when I have too." Zack shrugged.

"You still have to kill people," she said as they walked down the hall towards the stairs.

"Meh. I mean the first time kinda messes with you but after that, it's just work you know?"

"No I don't!" Eliana whirled her head around, looking at him as if he was completely insane. "You Bloods freak me out."

"Sorry, your highness." Zack bowed slightly.

You Royals are way freakier than we are little girl.

"Why did you ask about something like that?"

"No reason." Curt and quick.

They walked down the long staircase to where a flurry of people hastily prepared for the duchess's return with the new duke. Prince Armando was nearest to the door, his tie being adjusted by a giggling young maid. Zack wondered if Eliana noticed the flirtatious scene. If she did, she wasn't affected by it.

Closer to the bottom step was Queen Elisa, makeup flawless, face cold. John was a small distance away, he and Zack exchanged a short nod.

"Tighten up your belt, it's messing with your dress," the queen ordered after a quick glance at her daughter.

Eliana followed the instruction without stopping or a word to her mother. She kept walking over to a small couch by the door where she stopped and sat silently. Zack stood off to her right, choosing silence over forced small talk. Instead, he decided to keep surveying the room. Elisa had a few different attendants come up to receive instructions. He had noticed before, but it seemed that much of what happened inside the palace was under her supervision.

Glances at Armando always showed the same scene, total absorption into whatever girl was speaking to him. Slight touches, giggles, fawning. Zack didn't like Eliana much, but he felt bad for her all the same. She only sat though, quietly.

It was then that the room quieted and people bowed to the entrance to the king, Daniel walking just behind him. He walked to Elisa and they met each other with a smile warmer than Zack expected. It hadn't be that long ago that the queen had attempted to force herself on him.

How the hell do they do that? He thought.

"What?" Eliana broke into his thoughts.

"I'm sorry, your highness?"

"You were making a face."

Crap, was I?

"I was? I didn't mean to." Zack brushed it off.

"Mmmm." Eliana didn't seem to buy that. "You were with my mom the day that girl died, weren't you?"

"...Yes I was." Zack wasn't sure where she was going with that.

"Well don't think you're special just because she had one of her little 'get even' episodes on your watch. And I'd be more worried about keeping out of Dad's sight than how they act in front of everyone."

It took him a second to realize what she was saying. What happened to Zack had happened before.

This happened all the time here.

"I didn't sleep with your mother," Zack said, a heat hiding in his words.

Eliana turned to meet his eyes. They stared at each other in another silence that only held the two of them.

"My mother doesn't handle rejection well," Eliana said, turning away.

"No, not particularly," Zack said, turning as well.

"What happened?"

"She became very... sad at my reasoning for not wanting to."

"Which was?"

"Personal."

"You're not very good at talking to your superiors." Eliana seemed irritated.

"I'm not good at talking about personal or private matters. Especially matters that could hurt my superiors," Zack said. "Do you want to talk about how YOU'RE feeling?"

"I don't need to be analyzed, Blood. Thanks."

"They are pulling in now!" A voice called from the window. Everyone began to get in place.

"Where is Annabelle?" The queen asked.

"She's being fussy, they are still getting her dressed," a voice said from somewhere in the dissipating chaos.

Elisa sighed lightly.

Eliana felt her hair, making sure it was in place again as Armando walked up to stand beside her. His back was toward Zack but he ended up recognizing him anyway.

"Operative Taylor! Good to see you again! Not with Sonaja today?" Armando asked with a big white smile.

"What?" Armando threw a bunch of garbled up syllables in with his question.

"Hahaha! So-na-ja. It means little bell in Spanish, it's my nickname for her," Armando said.

"Oh. No, I'm on a different rotation today I guess."

"Ah I see." Armando turned his attention to the door.

"You're good friends with your cousin right?"

He must have directed that question at Eliana, but she didn't respond. Armando seemed to reach up slowly and grip her elbow. Eliana seemed to shift slightly.

"You're good friends with your cousin, right?" He repeated, but the tone was off.

"A-Hemm... yes, she's my best friend." Eliana made this weird sound in between a cough and yelp.

"Well that's good. It's good to have close friends." He released her.

Eliana turned her head to say something, but her words seemed to catch. She turned back to look at the door.

The heck is that about? Zack started getting that sick feeling in his stomach that he used to get around his step-dad.

"Presenting the Duchess and Duke of the American Kingdom!" A voice cried out. The door swung open to reveal a chubby, red-faced man escorting a young, spunky looking girl with highlights in her hair.

"I'm home!!!" The girl shouted as she waved so hard she began shaking the slightly flabby man she was holding onto.

There was a small commotion. Camera men swung around collecting footage for the news, which would be playing on repeat all day. People shouted questions for the new couple as a little press conference began on the spot. Cameras, questions, looking nice for the cameras, Zack had never really cared that much when the news came on and blocked out the only two channels they got back home.

Being so close these last few months really put things into perspective. They were all acting, scripted right down to their actions; perfect make up, perfect lighting, and only approved questions asked.

It went like that for maybe an hour, Annabelle and Rose sneaking in after maybe ten minutes, before it all started breaking up. Armando walked to introduce himself to the chubby man with the king. Eliana started to head toward Josephine, when Josephine broke into a run and jumped into her cousin's arms.

"Ellie!! I missed you so much!!!!" They both rocked back and forth in a big hug.

"Jojo!!" Eliana squealed back.

"Oh my God, Russia fricking sucks, there is NOTHING to do there." Josephine said.

"That kind of language is not becoming for a lady, Josephine," Queen Elisa said as she walked with John in tow.

"Aunt-E!" Josephine hugged the Queen rather tightly, causing Elisa to make that squished-groan sound. "Did you miss me? Did ya?!"

"It was certainly less exciting without you here...." Elisa sounded aggravated, but smiled nonetheless

"Awh... you gonna make me cry." Josephine held her cheeks and swung back and forth. Zack wondered if she was always this high energy and expressive.

"Hey, Zack?" Rose came up behind him, little Annabelle in tow. "She wants you."

"What's troubling you, princess?" Zack picked up little Annabelle and put her on his hip. He gently bounced her, and she wrapped her little arms around his neck.

"Hey Sissy! Why don't I get a hug first?" Josephine pouted as she tickled Annabelle's ribs.

"You want to give your cousin a hug?" Zack asked the little girl on his hip.

"Careful Jojo, she throws a fit if you pull her away from her little boyfriend." Eliana managed to put an eye roll into words somehow.

"I do not!!" Annabelle yelled at her sister.

"Well heck, I would too," Josephine said, looking Zack up and down. "Speaking of which, what is the deal with all these new, buff-tall-cute guys?"

"They're the Bloods dad added. I told you about this on the phone," Eliana said.

"Nah, nah, nah...." Josephine shook her head. "YOU told me about these annoying new bodyguards from the sticks. Not these seven foot hotties-with-bodies."

"Well thank you ma'am, you're too kind," John said with a voice Zack assumed was him attempting to turn on the country charm.

"No one was speaking to you boy, be quiet." Elisa stared daggers at him. "And Josephine, I'm sure your new husband would not appreciate you talking about other men in such a way."

"Yeah, well, he'll be flirting it up with the maids here in a week or so, so fair is fair. What was your name Mr. Annabelle's boyfriend?"

"Zackary Taylor, ma'am," Zack said as Annabelle hid her face in embarrassment.

"Awh man, he's even got a cute name...." Josephine seemed rather disheartened. "Some girls get all the luck, huh sissy?" She said, tickling Annabelle again, which made her smile.

"Both you girls need to quit filling her head with silly things like that." Elisa rubbed her temples slightly. "Josephine, you've been back maybe five minutes and I feel like all I've done is scold you."

"Ahh, come on Aunt-E! There will be plenty to scold tomorrow! Today is for girl chat!" Josephine began pushing Eliana down the hall.

"That's not reassuring!" Elisa called after them with an excitement to her voice Zack had not heard before.

"I wanna go too!" Annabelle wiggled, making Zack set her down. She ran after them as Zack and Rose walked after them a few steps back.

"Well she certainly brings some life to the place!" Rose laughed as her and Zack followed after the girls.

"Yeah. No kidding!" Zack couldn't help grinning as well. "I like her."

They followed after the girls who finally locked themselves away in Eliana's bedroom. Zack and Rose stood outside, letting them have their private time. Rose took the time to go off about her new engagement, wedding details, etc. It was kind of nice though, Rose was absolutely beaming, the happiest he'd ever seen her. He just let her gush as the minutes turned into over an hour.

"I have no idea who to pick to be my maid of honor." Rose sighed, goose stepping around slowly. "Daniel will probably have you and John up there, so I need at least two people."

"What about Lydia?" Zack was sitting on the ground at this point, spinning his keycard between his thumb and finger.

"You don't think that'd be weird?" Rose made a face. "She's like our mom."

"Your bachelorette party would be baller though," Zack said. "If you don't want her, we're gonna take her. I bet she buys Daniel a lap dance."

"Ew. She probably would." Rose laughed and nodded. "Hey, serious now though, if-"

"-THE HELL I WILL!!" The door slammed open as Josephine came out in a half walk, half run. Zack and Rose both jumped at the mini explosion, and were momentarily stunned.

"JO! WAIT!" Eliana came out behind her, as did little Annabelle. Eliana locked eyes with Rose then Zack. "STOP HER!"

Zack finally jumped up to his feet as Eliana and Annabelle began to chase after Josephine, and Zack and Rose followed quickly behind.

"What happened?!" Rose said loudly as they easily closed the gap to Eliana and Annabelle.

"Don't worry about what happened just go stop her!" Eliana shook her arms around in a panic.

Wha- stop her how? Like tackle her? Zack thought.

He looked to Rose, who seemed just as confused as he was. Bodyguards protected these people, stopping them from doing crazy stuff is someone else's job.

They picked up speed and caught up to the girl ahead on the warpath as she reached the top of the stairs.

"Miss-?" Rose tried to touch her arm and was slapped away violently.

"Don't fricking touch me...!" Josephine whispered

through gritted teeth.

Rose, eyes wide, shrugged her shoulders at Zack as they paused at the top of the stairs.

Well don't look at me! I don't know what the heck to do! Zack thought as he gave the same expression back to her.

"MOTHER-!"

Zack and Rose turned just in time to see Josephine airborne, streaking through the air towards the bottom of the stairs just as Prince Armando, King David, and the new duke reached the bottom. Armando had turned just in time to see what was coming straight for him when Josephine connected.

Zack's jaw dropped. Josephine had jumped from one of the steps and landed a rather impressive punch into Armando's teeth, finishing her insult. She couldn't quite stick the landing though, and they both ended up on the ground. It was then that Daniel ran over and, unknowingly mimicked the exact expression Zack and Rose had made just a moment ago, back up to them.

Spitting some words in Spanish, Armando got back to his feet before Josephine could, and kicked her in the stomach as she tried to stand. Daniel hastily got between them. Annabelle and Eliana ran past Zack and Rose, who began to follow them, finally overcoming their shock.

"Stop! Leave Jojo alone!!" Annabelle screamed as she outran her sister, closing the gap faster.

Zack knew how these situations played out. Once angry, a person like Armando would explode. It didn't matter who or what was around, if you're close, you're hit by the blast. Armando, his eyes wild, turned his rage toward Annabelle, his hand coming toward her.

A vein burst in Zack's eye, causing his vision to blur, the red tint in half of his sight disorienting him even more. His emotions got away from him, and he had held nothing back. Armando's hand never reached Annabelle.

Zack moved his hand away from Armando's face as he began shaking violently. Zack stood, his mind still trying to process what happened. Rose rushed past him, attempting to stabilize Armando but it was too late.

He wouldn't survive at this point no matter what happened.

Zack looked at the king, his bewilderment leaving him utterly helpless. The fat duke wasn't any better. Daniel looked like he was internally panicking. Josephine was clutching her stomach looking at Zack, Eliana was holding her part of the way up, her free hand covering her mouth. Annabelle had fallen down and quietly cried. John and the queen were nowhere to be seen.

It had hit the fan. It was either now or never. He could kill most of the royalty; nobody else would be able to react quick enough. But it would all be for nothing if he couldn't find the queen. And Salim and Micheal weren't set up yet, so he was definitely not supposed to go before they gave the word. Could they improvise?

Zack couldn't run away at this point either, and whatever punishment was coming for this would be hell. Maybe it was time to end it all here. He wouldn't have a chance after they grabbed him.

It was then that Annabelle found her feet again. She ran to Zack and he dropped down on instinct. Her arms clung to his shoulders with every ounce of strength that she had. Her sobs turned into screams.

“Shhh... princess.... It's all gonna be okay....” He slowly rubbed her back, trying to settle her down.

“NO IT'S NOT!” She screamed in between her hyperventilating sobs. “THEY'RE GONNA TAKE YOU AWAY!!!”

God dang it kiddo....

He hugged her back tight. Her little arms wouldn't let him do anything else.

21. FRIENDS IN LOW PLACES

KNOCK KNOCK

The door to Zack's cell opened slightly.

"Hey, you decent?" A voice asked.

"You guys only let me wear my pants, but yeah I guess so." Zack was naked except for his pants and underwear. No shirt or socks, ankles locked to a chain on the wall, handcuffs on his wrists.

"Go on in..." The voice moved a little.

Julia stepped through the door and it was shut and locked behind her. She held her elbow with her hand in a sort of self hug. White blouse, black skirt, blonde hair in the bun that she wore that made her hair look kinda spiky in the back, long bangs left down but kept in check behind her ear.

She was super pretty.

"Hey..." Zack said numbly.

"Hey...." She said.

"You look really pretty today," he said.

Julia looked at him funny for a second before slowly starting to laugh.

"What the hell? Why do you sound like a little school kid with a crush?" She laughed.

"You're even prettier when you smile." Zack grinned back at her.

"Oh my God, shut up." She shook her head and sat next to him on the bed. "God, why does this happen to me? I finally found a cute, hot, manly, guy with a good job and personality and, like, the second we're about to get together, *BOOM,* he's imprisoned for high treason...."

"You know, I really thought you were gonna comment on the lack of clothes and handcuffs. Like 'huh, this takes me back to my 21st birthday...'." Zack started laughing.

"Screw you! If anyone was going to be in handcuffs it would be me, and they would be cute fuzzy ones." Julia shoved him.

They sat there in silence for a minute.

"I couldn't think of what I was gonna say the whole way here," Julia said, hugging her knees.

"How did you hear about it anyway?" Zack asked.

"Well, I was the one who cleared you for service, so I got a bit of a chewing out," Julia said. "Terry was trying to undermine me with 'pattern of behavior' garbage."

"Who's Terry?"

"One of the senior therapists on the royal cabinet board or something. I don't know his real title but he's above me or whatever...."

"...'Pattern of behavior' huh?" Zack leaned his head back against the wall. "They mean when Lydia filed a report about my step-dad?"

"Yeah," Julia said. "Though there were some other people that defended you, if that helps. Not everyone thinks you did it."

"I did."

It was silent again.

"My step-dad was an angry person. He'd snap over anything. He'd tell you to do something but wouldn't explain how to do it. Then he'd start screaming and hit you."

Zack rubbed his palms on his knees, before pulling his knees to his chest.

"He had a drug problem too. I don't know if that caused it, but he'd do this thing... It was like he was talking to himself, or arguing with himself? I think maybe that's what it was. He imagined himself explaining stuff to you over and over and when he finally told you to do it for the first time and you didn't do it right, so you were doing it on purpose. Maybe he actually heard voices. Hell if I know."

Zack took a second to fiddle with his cuffs, he wished he had a cigarette.

"I started changing when I was twelve; they had us with Lydia when we were thirteen-fourteen. When I was fifteen, it finally hit me, you know? I'm fifteen, six foot three and already physically, you know, a man. And I'm scared to death of this waste of a human being half my size. God, I used to take fifteen minutes creeping down the stairs because I was so afraid to wake him up if he was asleep on the couch...."

Zack leaned back, bumping his head against the concrete wall is frustration.

"One day, he's there on the couch, passed out. There's this needle right next to him and I just put some air in it and...." Zack made a motion with his hand. "I went upstairs to my room and I barred my door, still terrified. I heard him making sounds at some point and I was so scared he was gonna wake up and just beat me to death.... But Lydia came to check on me the next morning and found him, he had a major stroke. I never told anyone."

Not even Sarah.

"I never felt bad about it."

Not for an instant.

"I'm sorry I didn't tell you. You probably wouldn't be in trouble right now if I had."

"I didn't think you actually did it...." Julia mumbled after a while.

"Why not?" Zack asked, looking at her.

"I went through something similar." Julia turned her head away so Zack couldn't look at her. "When my mom and dad got divorced."

Zack didn't know if he should say something. Maybe it was his turn to just let her talk.

"My dad had this girlfriend, she didn't want me around. She'd find any reason to blame me for everything. My mom at the time was so busy with work. I started doing bad things because, you know, I'm getting flipped out on anyway. I ran away from home for three weeks before my boyfriend and I got in a fight and he pushed me down the stairs. I messed up my ankle, and mom had to get me from the hospital."

Julia coughed and buried her face in her knees.

"Well, I ended up going to see a therapist and through our talks she was the one who helped me process everything that was going on in my head. I had tried to block it all out for so long I gave myself an anxiety disorder. I guess I was so messed up not having a place where somebody really cared about me, I just, stuck to anyone who showed even a little interest in me."

Julia picked at her pants not looking at Zack.

"It was weird. I wasn't mad really, not angry, I just wanted my parents to care. I wasn't even mad at the guy, I had this really bad mindset like it was my fault. Like I did something wrong, that's why dad left, why mom was busy, why he hit me."

"Like, you didn't want revenge; you just wanted to not hurt?"

"Yeah."

"I get that."

Maybe that's why Zack couldn't go through with it at the end. He didn't want to kill the royal family. He wanted Sarah to never have died in the first place.

"People shouldn't hurt kids." Julia reached out and held Zack's hand.

It made Zack remember something else.

"I think I'm okay with dying if I die because I was protecting a kid," Zack said.

"I wish you wouldn't die at all...."

She finally look up at Zack. With the restraints on him, he couldn't move enough to hug her. Her gently touched his forehead to hers.

In response she slowly reached up and rubbed his cheek, before kissing him gently.

"I'm sorry I hurt you."

"When?"

"When I got this close just to go away."

Julia reached around to hug him.

"Are you scared?"

"No." Zack shook his head. "Dying stopped freaking me out a long time ago. The scary thing was finding someone who made life seem... good."

Julia's back quivered.

"Stop being sweet. It's all your fault, being so... I didn't want to start crying again!"

* *KNOCK KNOCK* *

The door opened as a soldier stood halfway in the doorway.

"Time's up."

"Already? Can't we have like five more minutes?" Julia asked.

"Sorry." Two guards came in and quickly broke them apart.

"Wait! No!" Julia tried to reach for Zack again as she was pulled out of the cell. "I'm sorry!"

"It's okay!" He called after her.

She disappeared past the guard still standing by the door. Zack dropped his head into his hands, then laid back onto the bed and rubbed his eyes hard.

"It's okay...."

He tried to settle down, focusing on his breathing. Forget what he was thinking earlier, dying sucked.

"Your girlfriend, I presume?"

Zack looked over to see Queen Elisa just inside the door. She must have seen Julia leave. Zack sighed once again.

"Almost? I guess?" Zack ran his fingers through his hair. "She was actually the therapist you guys sent me to for evaluations. We kinda clicked."

"Leave us," the queen said to the guard.

He hurriedly shut the door.

"She's very beautiful."

"Yeah."

"I take it you two weren't intimate yet?"

"Nope... we were both...." Zack sighed thinking of a way to phrase it. "There is more there than that. Maybe it's better this way anyway. Maybe it'll hurt her less when I'm gone."

"Mm. I don't think you understand women very well, Mr. Taylor." The queen slowly paced around the cell, looking for something in the walls. "You are going to be sent to Mexico. David thinks that they might NOT start a war if they just take it out on you...."

"Well, I've never been to Mexico." Zack nodded.

"It's your own fault, you know."

"I know."

"Annabelle is really upset. Did you even think about what you're doing to her?"

"I know. I wasn't thinking."

"You think I wasn't upset? You think I didn't want to kill that monster?! The world isn't that simple *boy*! Sometimes you have to make sacrifices, and play nice with the people who make you sick!"

"So you knew?"

"Knew what?!"

"That he was hitting Eliana?"

Elisa quieted down at that. Zack stared right into her soul. She didn't shy away from his eyes, it would be a sign of weakness.

"Don't pretend to understand things boy...."

"There are some things I refuse to understand."

"You have NO idea what it's like. We don't get to make these choices, they are pushed upon us. Armando was a piece of human garbage like every other man with power. There was nothing I could have done."

Zack only looked at her in silence.

"Your actions put you in this cell, may put us in a war, and WILL put you in your grave. Perhaps you should think about the weight your actions carry, and how many lives you've just thrown away."

Elisa knocked on the door and it opened quickly.

"Get him dressed and ready to go," Elisa said. She paused. "My pain in the butt niece wanted me to pass along her thanks. You would have gotten along well with her mother."

"About Julia-" Zack stopped Elisa before she could leave. "She's getting some flak because she passed me. Is she gonna be okay?"

"It's a little late for thinking about that, don't you think?" Elisa didn't look back.

Zack didn't answer. He just stared up at the ceiling.

"...I'll see to it that she's okay."

She left as a group of soldiers came in with clothes and a black canvas bag.

* * *

How do these people stand it being this hot?!?

Zack was in a different cell now, he assumed. His head was still covered by the black canvas bag, so he wasn't totally sure. He had been blindly shuffled around into a car, then a plane, then a new car, and now here, wherever that was.

The plane had been an... experience.... After several hours half in and out of sleep, he was taken off and assaulted by the horrible, godforsaken heat.

Now he was sitting in... wherever, maybe in hell, it felt hot enough.

"Qué célula es?"

"Tercero a la izquierda."

Zack heard voices coming toward him. He assumed they were speaking Spanish, but they were speaking so quickly and smoothly he couldn't even tell the words apart. To him it was just a single word of gibberish from one person to the next.

A door opened close to him, and he felt two people entering his space.

"No le quitaron la bolsa?"

"Supongo que no...."

Hands reached toward his neck, but they didn't feel aggressive. They undid the draw strings, and the bag was lifted off his head.

It was mildly dim in the room, it looked like it was getting close to dusk, so his eyes didn't need to adjust much. Zack's eyes were drawn to the two men that were in the cell with him now. There were another four or five standing in the hall kind of gawking at him.

"So you're the American?" The closest man said to him, tossing the bag to the side.

"Yep."

The man was maybe in his mid to late 20s and wore a soldier's uniform. His skin was dark, a little wrinkly, but that was probably from all the sun he got. He had dark black hair, stubble, weirdly pretty eyes for a man. Zack guessed most women would find him attractive. Zack thought he seemed like a less slimy version of Armando.

I wonder if I'm being racist. I don't think I ever figured that out.

"You're a big son of a gun," the Mexican soldier said. He was maybe 5'10, 190 pounds, and his friends didn't seem much bigger.

"Yeah, I suppose."

They stood there in silence for a moment looking at each other.

"You smoke?" He asked.

"Yeah."

One of the other soldiers gave the one in front a folding chair. He handed Zack a cigarette and lit it, then did the same for himself as he sat down.

"You know," the man took a drag on his cigarette. "You seem weirdly calm for a man who was sent here to be brutally murdered."

"Yeah, I was thinking that too." Zack nodded along. "I

don't know.... I sort of knew I was gonna die after everything happened, and I was really panicky for like a couple hours but then.... I've just been thinking about my life, and I feel a little nervous but my mind keeps going to happy memories."

"Mm. Mm." The man nodded along. "Well I guess there's not much else you could do."

It was quiet again. Zack again questioned his mental state. He was sitting here smoking a cigarette in a foreign country, talking to a total stranger, being watched by a group of strangers who he assumed were his death squad. Yet he felt totally at ease.

Was this acceptance? He really hoped he wouldn't start crying like a baby before he died.

"So... what did he do that made you kill him?" The man asked, staring into Zack's eyes.

"Mmmm. He almost hit Annabelle...."

"Almost?"

"Yeah." Zack nodded. "I didn't let it happen."

"Good man."

"What?" Zack looked at the man, confused.

"Well between you and me there was a reason they sent him over to your country, I heard." The man tilted and nodded his head with a sigh.

"God dang, are you serious?" Zack tilted his head.

"Yeah." He nodded again, then smoked some more. "I, personally, was not a fan."

"Forget politics man...." Zack said. "I'm just a soldier. You tell me to protect a family and I frickin do. But how the hell do you protect a kid from that.... I think they all knew what he was. And they let it happen, for what? For power or something?"

"I know exactly what you're saying, Amigo." The man's english broke a little. "Soldiers do as they're told, trust what they're told, and what do we get in return, huh? We get sent to our deaths. They pass off trouble to someone else, then are surprised when he pisses off the wrong guy? They want to send us to our deaths because someone finally took out the trash."

"That's exactly right!" Zack leaned in, smoking his cigarette.

"How'd he die anyway?" The man asked. Zack exhaled and motioned with his hands.

"He was about to- well first off, he had stomach kicked the duchess because she found out he was hitting the princess, I think. So she slugged him straight in the face, so he knocked the hell out of her."

"No kidding!" The man was impressed.

"Yeah, yeah, she threw a beautiful punch too, it was impressive," Zack said. "Anyway, right afterwards everyone is stunned, you know? And he goes to swing back at Annabelle because she's running in trying to save her cousin. Before he can get there though, I slam into him from the stairs. I ended up bashing his head into the tile and slid with him a little bit and that was that."

"Did he die quick?" This guy stared into Zack's soul again. He must have really hated Armando.

"Nah... nah, I don't think so." Zack finished his cigarette. "I knew he was gonna die the second I realized what I did. I smashed his head *HARD*. He started having a seizure immediately. I would guess he died kinda slowly while they tried to save what was left of his soup brains...."

The man was quiet for a little bit. Everyone else stood in silence staring at Zack. The man took one last hit on his cigarette before dropping it down to the floor.

"My name is Julio by the way," he said, stepping on the glowing end of the cigarette.

"Zack, it's a pleasure." Zack extended both his hands, as they were cuffed, in a handshake motion.

Julio looked at the cuffs a moment, before reaching a palm up over his shoulder. The man behind him handed him a set of keys. Julio quickly unlocked the cuffs, then shook Zack's hand.

Zack thought this was a little odd, but his thoughts were interrupted by a dull banging from far away.

Was that gunfire?

No one else in the room seemed to react. Was it normal here? Maybe that was another prisoner getting killed or something?

"You know Zack, I envy you," Julio said.

"Yeah? Why's that?" Zack asked, rubbing his wrists

"You stood up for what was right. Didn't let politics stop you." Julio kept staring at him. Zack wondered if maybe it was a cultural thing.

Also that gunfire... *-that was gunfire, right?* It was too erratic to be anything else. It wasn't stopping.

"I wish I had had that strength earlier. I wish I had found him before they sent him off to America."

Julio leaned back into his chair, lost in thought. The other men avoided their eyes.

"I wish I could have been there to see him die."

...

Okay?

"Or better yet, I wish I did it myself. I had it all planned out." There was a heat to Julio's words now. "I would take him into the middle of the city. I'd kneel him down those salty sand of Me-he-co, and set him on fire, just so I could put him out and watch him squirm like the worm he was, in the salt and sand...."

Zack tried to process what Julio was sayin-

Okay, that's definitely gunfire... and it's coming closer....

"Then I would show them.... I'd say that this! This is what happens to the people who hurt us. This is what happens to the violadores, y ladrones y basura!"

Julio slipped back into Spanish as he started spitting. Zack couldn't help but look back and forth between the hallway and Julio.

"I don't really know what to say here, Julio...."

"Hahaha! That's okay, Zack. I just needed to get that off my chest." Julio laughed. He waited just a moment before nodding towards the hallway. "Anyway they're almost here...."

Zack looked to see if he could see anyone coming. The gunfire was closer, but he couldn't see anything through the small window on the door.

"I- well, WE have a proposition for you."

22. FUERA DE CONTROL

Zack focused on listening to where the bullets were coming from. There were several people shooting at him at this point so it was getting kind of hard to tell. One bullet rang out louder than the others. Zack quickly shot back without looking, moving his rifle barrel maybe an inch diagonally while holding the trigger to ensure a hit.

Julio who was taking cover against the pillar with him peaked out to see if he hit again. Zack had been in several gun fights, but he had always been in fights with his friends or other Bloods.

While he was grateful to Julio and his friends for freeing him on the condition that he help them with their revolution, and he would never say it to their faces... non-Bloods kinda sucked at fighting....

"Pinche gente blanca, how the hell do you keep doing that?" Julio asked.

Zack had probably shot around ten people so far without looking. "Mmm... you got to listen for the bullets." Zack bit his cheek back a little.

"The heck do you mean 'listen for the bullets'? Bullets are coming from fricking everywhere!" Julio said.

"You just got to wait for someone to mess up the firing rhythm and single someone out. You sort of know where they are if they aren't moving a lot so you just wait for them to pop out and shoot out of sync," Zack said.

Then again, it could be that non-Bloods and those untrained had trouble distinguishing the shots. Zack remembered Lydia being rather pissed that Zack and the others picked it up so fast when she was teaching them.

"I've been meaning to ask by the way, but what kind of drugs did they give you before they sent you over here?! We are getting shot at right now! I'm not saying you need to crap your pants but you could at least not look bored!" Julio's eyes were wide and he was breathing hard.

The main problem for Zack, however, was that the soldiers they were fighting were all neatly uniform in their weaponry. They all carried 9mm submachine guns with standard ammunition. While those guns packed a bit more punch than a standard handgun, they weren't even leaving exit wounds on the bodies of the soldiers he'd seen. Metal that soft and rounded coming that slowly wouldn't do much more than surface damage to Zack in most places, even though it would hurt.

Zack had been wondering why these soldiers who were supposed to be guarding the palace were so ill equipped. He hadn't seen one Blood this entire time, and security seemed kinda weak.

"Hey, aren't these guys kinda poorly equipped and trained?" Zack asked, trying not to offend.

"I don't know what kind of place your hellhole nation is mi hermano, but I was told this once about America." Julio slid out and took a few shots then returned. "Nobody liked America when the bombs fell way back when, because everybody had everything, living fat. So now, America doesn't have a lot of people, but does have a lot of things." Julio shot some more, this time Zack did as well. He hit somebody that was running in the leg. "Me-he-co on the other hand, everybody who had stuff were all in the big cities, but not everyone lived there. So we got a lotta people, but not a lot of fancy things."

"Okay, but why don't you guys have Bloods here?" Zack asked.

"Bloods?"

"People like me."

"We don't have many white people here."

"No, that's-"

A grenade rolled against Zack's foot. He picked it up and slung it at a soldier on the other side. It embedded itself in the soldier's face before exploding.

"Chingada Madre!" Julio turned away. "That's a bad way to go...."

"Eh, he probably didn't even feel it, it happened so fast." Zack leaned back on the column. The royal soldiers were falling back deeper into the palace. "Bloods are people that are big like me? Red eyes, fast and strong?"

"That just sounds like a tired, big man Amigo." Julio wasn't getting it. "By the way, not that it matters to me but, how many people have you killed?"

"What, like today?" Zack raised an eyebrow, secretly busting Julio's chops.

"You're kinda fricking scary, you know that?"

"I am- or I was, one of the elite bodyguards of the royal family. Cream of the crop, the top of the top, all that jazz. I've had a gun in my hand since I was twelve." Zack shrugged as he stepped out of cover, the soldiers were all out of range.

"Me too, but I ain't this fricking good with them." Julio did the same. He pointed at one of the several soldiers Zack picked off.

"That's S.W.O.R.D. training for you!" Zack grabbed some ammo from one of the downed men. He noticed other people coming in from the entrance who weren't wearing military fatigues.

"You know, I used to wonder why they made such a big deal about starting a war with you guys when we've got three times the men. I think I'm starting to get it a little." Julio started walking back to meet the men, Zack followed.

A woman was leading the pack; she hugged Julio when they got close and they started whispering. Zack stood out of ear shot, not like he knew what they'd be saying anyway.

"So... you're the one who killed Armando, huh?" She asked.

"That and half the people on the floor." Julio sighed. "Este tipo es una máquina de pelea...."

"Zack Taylor, nice to meet you miss...." Zack held out his hand.

"Sofia Flores Rios." She shook his hand. "My brother speaks highly of you."

Sofia was very short compared to Rose or Julia, maybe five foot two. She was kinda of... normal looking? Not pretty, but not ugly. She didn't wear any makeup and her hair was in a tight braid. Now that he looked though, she and the others were all wearing orange bandanas on their right arms.

"Zack, we need to get to the top floor before the military can scramble a helicopter to evacuate our king, queen, and two other leading members of our royal family. I'm told you have a lot of experience, and are very skilled when it comes to fighting. Is there any way to get to them quickly without sending our men to their deaths?" Sofia asked.

"Hmm... How far up do we have to go?" Zack asked.

"It's four floors, and they're all filled to the brim with soldiers." Julio sighed.

"Everyone fell back here when the fighting broke out," Julio said.

Zack headed to the entrance.

"Is there any way for us to get on the roof?"

"We'd have to climb the building on ropes; they'd pick us off before we got anywhere close."

"And I'm guessing you don't have the explosives to collapse the building?" Zack looked up at the fourth....

Julio there are five floors you idiot.

Zack looked at the FIFTH floor. It wasn't insanely tall actually. The ground floor must have been the only one that had high ceilings.

"We'd like to capture the royalty if possible," Sofia said.

"Nope." Julio said at the same time. Sofia shot him a look. He shrugged. "Saving royalty is on the list.... I wouldn't call it priority numero uno."

"But do you have something to scale the building with?" Zack stretched his shoulders.

Julio looked around a second. He walked over to a kid, maybe thirteen, who was on a four wheeler.

"This work?" Julio pointed to a winch cable.

"Is it long enough?" Zack came over to look, it was all Spanish though.

"Twenty meters?" Julio wondered.

"...Is that long enough?" The building was probably sixty feet.

"Yeah... should be." Julio didn't sound sure.

Zack unwound it from the four wheeler. It was stuck to the frame, but it had a release on the side. Making a lasso at the end, Zack flung it up and was able to catch it on a balcony just below the balcony on the top floor.

"Yeah, that'll work," Zack said to himself. He turned towards Sofia and Julio. "Okay, so when I get to the top, have a couple people shoot at the guys in there like we're making a push. Everyone else can stand out here and get ready to catch the royalty as I throw them down."

Julio and Sofia stared at him for a second.

"¿Estás bromeando con esta mierda?" Sofia said to Julio.

"Aférrate." Julio didn't look at her. "So... um... You're just gonna climb up there, alone, and just start tossing them down to us...."

"That's the gist of it, yeah." Zack nodded.

"Okay. You keep doing this thing where you don't seem to grasp that you have a really high chance of dying and I'm starting to feel really bad for you. So if you want to talk about it- Eh.... We will find you someone but-"

"Just- Flippin-" Zack rubbed his eyes. "Okay I'm just gonna grab them real quick. Listen to me or don't, but I told you what to do."

Zack's vision started to redden as he began to scale the building, sprinting up the brick wall while going hand over hand with the wire. Eventually he got to a point where the wire pulled him away from the wall. He swung back and forth, pushing off the building, he could easily grab the ledge to the fourth floor balcony. He scaled it, jumping to grab the next one.

Zack hung there for a moment. The blinds were dawn on the fourth floor, so he was safe for the moment. Eventually, he heard the gunfire below resume.

Zack pulled himself up, headed to the window...

And knocked.

A soldier pulled back the blinds and Zack quickly shot him in the forehead. He reached through the broken glass and tossed him onto the balcony floor. There were only a couple of soldiers in the room, a couple older generals, and four rich-looking people. The ones with guns started shooting immediately.

Zack dove into the middle of the room, shooting one soldier while in the air. He rolled once towards the door, kicking it closed before the soldier next to it was able to call for help. He could barely react before Zack put a bullet through his head, blood and brains painting the wall behind him.

Bullets, like a swarm of hornets, stung the back half of his torso. Zack grabbed the dead soldier, using his corpse as a shield to pick off the people that were shooting him.

This was his first chance to really get a feel for where everything was in the room. There were a couple of soldiers huddled over his targets, Zack had to bend at funny angles to kill the soldiers without shooting through them. Between the banging on the door behind him, and his exposed arm getting shot, making him flinch just a little, this was taking slightly longer than he was hoping.

As he shot the last soldier, Zack blocked the door with the body he was holding. He quickly picked up two more bodies and slung them at the door.

There were two men, two women. Zack grabbed the first by the waist as she screamed. Running to the balcony he chucked her over the side with some distance. One of the men ran at Zack with a knife, making him easy to throw using his own momentum. Turning back, one of the men was trying to open the door. Zack put a bullet in his leg and dragged him to the ledge, tossing him over as well.

Zack hurried back into the room to find the last woman shaking and crying. After double checking to see if she had a weapon, Zack picked her up and took a running jump off the balcony. Seeing a mosh pit of people below, Zack kicked the woman into the thicker part of the crowd. Curling up just in time, Zack hit the ground rolling, springing back to his feet, his blood pumping a mile a minute.

"WOO! STILL GOT IT!" Zack yelled, laughing to himself. It had been a while; he always forgot how much of a rush a good gun fight was.

There was a bit of chaos as the crowd restrained the royalty, but many people had their eyes on Zack. Julio and Sofia ran up to him eyes wide in disbelief.

"Dios mio!" Julio jumped seeing Zack's eyes. He stopped a few yards from Zack.

Sofia was braver. She came closer, reaching out to Zack's arm and pulled a bullet out of his skin.

"¿Que eres...?" She breathed as fear crept into her voice.

"¡El diablo!" A voice rang out from the crowd. "¡El es el diablo!"

"¡El Cucuy! ¡El Cucuy!" Some kids started to yell. They hid behind the older soldiers who looked just as scared.

Soon the crowd began to stir. Zack didn't know what they were saying, but he knew he was being feared at the moment. An uneasy feeling rose in his stomach.

Julio pushed past his sister, regaining his composure. He lifted Zack's arm that still had bullets in it and yelled to the crowd.

"¡El Cucuy vino a liberarnos de los verdaderos demonios! ¡Él pelea con nosotros! ¡Y él es una prueba de balas!"

And the previously terrified crowd burst into cheers.

23. POLITICAL FALLOUT

The worst part of a hangover was that nauseous feeling. When you throw up it's actually a little bit of a relief because that sick feeling sort of stops once it's out of you. But when you aren't throwing up yet, that slow build to it is the worst.

That and being too hot.

And moving your head, dang it, why does moving your head make the whole world spin?

Zack contemplated how horribly awful he felt as his eyes adjusted to the light. He felt so hot that he couldn't even move; he just had to sit there and FEEL how hot it was.

"Screw Mexico... it is too God dang hot...." Zack finally lifted himself up from the weird chair he was in and looked to see himself in a mirror shirtless. His right arm was covered in bandages.

...And his left arm was now tattooed in some way, along with some kind of crazy looking skull on his left pectoral.

"Whattttt the heck is that...?" Zack got up to look closer in the mirror. Then looked down at his body. On his forearm was 'El Cucuy' in a sleeve-like fashion, on his chest was a very colorful, flowery skull with 'Sarah' written rather beautifully across the forehead.

"Whhhaaaaatttt the heeeeeckkkk?"

It was actually beautiful, but why did he get a crazy, morbid thing like that!?

Zack looked around and became aware that he had fallen asleep in a tattoo parlor. He spotted Julio, who was asleep on the ground and went over and shook him awake.

"Hey! Hey! Wake up!" Zack said as Julio started to come to.

"Qu- Qué? Qué es?" Julio blinked rapidly as it took him a second to focus on Zack. "Uh- What is it?"

"What the heck is this about?!" Zack pointed to his chest. Julio rubbed his face groggily.

"That's a calaveras. Uh... you'd call it a sugar skull. We make them for Día de los Muertos, which is coming up. You saw a bunch of them when we passed the church, and when I explained what they mean you said you had to get one," Julio said.

"What DOES it mean?"

"It's like a... thing... honoring the dead."

"...And I saw and *BAM*, we go to a tattoo parlor?"

"Well, we were already on our way here to get that." Julio pointed at Zack's arm, then proceeded to walk over the end of the room. "Did you black out or something? What's the last thing you remember?"

"I remember you kept making me drink tequila, and it was disgusting...." Zack suddenly remembered several men making jokes like he couldn't handle liquor and then he chugged half a bottle because of his pride....

"...Anyway, what does this mean again?" Zack asked, looking at his arm.

"It's El Cucuy; it's a tale about this monster who takes away bad kids and eats them."

Of course it is.

"Drunk you thought it was *very* badass. At one point you screamed at Santiago with your crazy eyes and he fell on the ground and about pissed himself!" Julio cackled.

Zack noticed him looking through a phone of some kind.

Zack wondered if they had a lot of cell phones here. It could just be that this was the Mexican capital. Zack's hometown didn't have personal cell phone service, but some of the bigger cities did.

"Hey my sister has been blowing me up, I'm gonna go call her. There's water in the fridge." Julio walked outside.

Zack grabbed a water and guzzled it down. After a minute

the sick feeling got sharper. Zack found the toilet and waited for a second before vomiting up all the water he just drank.

"Ugh, kill me... I'm never drinking tequila again...." He mumbled into the bowl.

"Zack!"

"Here...." Zack mumbled louder into the bowl.

"Hey! -You alright?" Julio rushed over to the bathroom doorway.

"I will be."

"Good, cause we got to go!"

"Go where?!" Zack whined into the bowl.

"To see my sister because your king is on his fricking way. His plane landed this morning!" Julio seemed panicked.

"What?!" Zack leaned back into the wall. "Why would he do that?"

"I don't know, to start negotiating with our new republic! Trade and crap!"

"New republic? We captured your royal family, like, twelve hours ago! You guys set up a government in twelves hours?!"

"My sister is a pushy la perra! She made a speech and had them executed this morning on live TV, and THAT has been on repeat all day! So basically the whole world is under the impression that American and Mexican rebels overthrew the government and we have all our crap together!" Julio said.

"Wait, why would they think America had something to do with it? I'm the only American here!"

"Sofia mentioned you by name as leader of a unit. Which, screw you by the way, that was my unit! She basically credited you for the capture and overthrow of the government!"

"She did WHAT?!" Zack's eyes went wide. "Oh my God, I am so dead...."

So basically Zack was at fault for the whole world thinking his country overthrew another country.

"Well, she made you sound really cool! Anyway, we need to go try to smooth all this junk out, and we really need you there!"

"I get that you're so amped right now, but this is like the third time I've screwed everything up this week, so excuse me if I need a minute! God, I don't even know where my shirt is!"

"Where is your shirt!?"

"I DON'T REMEMBER GETTING TWO TATTOS LAST NIGHT! HOW THE HECK WOULD I REMEMBER WHERE MY SHIRT IS!?!"

"Maldito pedazo de mierda borracho!!" Julio ran out, then ran back in. "Here! Let's go!"

Julio handed him a black undershirt and hoisted him up off the floor. Zack put it on as they headed outside, where it was hotter and brighter. The shirt wasn't long enough, and the bottom of his stomach was on display.

"Oh yeah, no, flipping great...."

They hopped into the back of a Jeep that was there waiting for them apparently. Flying through the crowded streets, they came to some kind of library or something. They came out to find many Mexican soldiers outside, along with a few American soldiers.

"Dame tu abrigo," Julio said, to one of the Mexican soldiers. "Con rapidez, rapidez!"

The soldier quickly took off his coat and handed it Julio, who in turn gave it to Zack.

"Put that on."

Zack put on the coat, which was too small to even button as they climbed the steps. He was certain he looked completely ridiculous. They took the stairs up two flights, to where a meeting room was and they stopped before the door. Julio turned around to look at Zack. He was silent for a minute before sighing.

"We are so screwed. You need a haircut."

"Oh yeah, let me go fix that really quick," Zack said.

They opened the door as the conversation inside stopped. Julio walked in first as Sofia got up to hug him and start whispering.

Zack walked in behind him. On one side of the table there was Sofia, two people he didn't recognize, and two empty chairs. On the other side, King David sat in the middle of the wide meeting table. Looking Zack up and down he seemed to let out a small, whimsical laugh. Right next to him on his right hand side sat Lydia, oddly enough. The color drained out of her face in horror at his appearance. He wondered why she got such a close seat, but being hungover and stressed limits one's processing power. Three other chairs were filled by faintly familiar old men, scowling at him to different degrees.

Scattered in different positions were bodyguards for both sides, The S.W.O.R.D. operatives seemed to dwarf the Mexican soldiers, however. None of his other friends were there, but he did recognize Coleman standing closest to the king. When their eyes met, Coleman gave him a smirk.

Yes, I look ridiculous. I know.

"How nice of you to join us, Mr. Taylor," one of the old white guys said. "Tell us, how much do you plan on embarrassing us internationally?"

Zack had been mentally preparing for death for the last few days, his stress level was at a new all time high, he had been dealing with this God awful heat, and was very hungover.

He could NOT deal with *this* right now. Somedays you just give up and say forget everything.

"Sorry, who are you?" Zack asked.

"You can call me Mr. Davis. I am the one who has been responsible for securing our relationship with the Mexican Kingdom. My life's work which you have been trying your hardest to derail."

"'Ight I'm gonna call you Mr. Halfwit and here's why," Zack said.

Everyone's eyes seemed to bulge at him.

"So, you are the one who did all the negotiation junk with the royalty here, which has been just a massive screw up."

"I-!" Mr. Halfwit tried to speak up but Zack could yell louder.

"GONNA HAVE TO STOP YOU THERE, MR. HALFWIT! I've been ready to die for like, five days now, so don't think I'm not totally fine with the last thing I do being jumping this table, jamming my thumbs into your eyes, and splitting your face in half like a GOT DANG dinner roll!" Zack felt himself doing a crazy smile at the thought.

"Oh my God...." Lydia quietly mumbled to herself.

"Here's my evidence, you ready for this crap? Hey random Mexican soldier!" Zack turned to a Mexican soldier that stood behind him. The young man seemed to jump a little. "You remember Prince Armando? Was he a massive woman-beating, sex offending, piece of human garbage?"

"Si. Um... Yes," the man replied. For a fraction of a second, Zack was very glad this was one of the guys who could understand english. Zack turned back to the table.

"This guy is an average soldier and he fricking knows that! Yet that's the freaking guy YOU find to marry Princess Eliana!? Everyone here knew he was trash! EVERYONE! You sent her into the lion's den, for no reason!"

"A contract marriage was necessary for a North American alliance! A war with Mexico would have been far too costly!" Mr. Halfwit said.

"IT TOOK ME FIVE HOURS TOPS! ONE GUY! FIVE HOURS! That's how much it cost! And *BOOM*! New Government!" Zack pointed over to Sofia. "This is Sofia if you haven't already forgotten her name by the way. It took her about twelve hours to set up a new government, which, I don't know for sure, but seems incredibly difficult to do! So in conclusion, no more human trash in our palace, a wildly more competent and supportive neighboring nation. How much longer do YOU plan on having me clean up after your mistakes, Mr. Halfwit?"

Zack flopped into a chair on the Mexican side of the table and everyone was quiet for a second. Zack sighed loudly.

"Does anyone have a cigarette?" Zack asked, rubbing his face.

"Cigarrillos," Julio said from the chair next to him, his

hand over his shoulder.

A soldier put a pack in his hand, and he placed it on the table in front of Zack. He grabbed it and lit one up with the lighter inside. Slowly, everyone started to look toward King David for a response. He slowly removed his reading glasses and set them on the table.

"Well, that is the best argument I have heard all week," King David said, putting his tongue in his cheek. "Mr. Coleman, kill Mr. Halfwit."

Everyone besides Coleman seemed stunned. Coleman quickly walked over and snapped Mr. Halfwit's neck before he could say anything else. Zack blinked a few times, trying to process, but his hangover was killing him.

"I would like to talk to Mr. Taylor for a minute alone before we resume. Would you mind if we could have the room, President Sofia?" King David asked.

She nodded and everyone quickly exited the room. Zack sat there alone with his king. While he was certainly stressed enough to flip out even if they killed him, somehow being alone with his king felt far scarier.

"Pass me those, would you?" The king pointed at the cigarettes.

Zack grabbed the pack and placed it in front of the king. He grabbed one, lit up and took a long drag before he spoke again.

"You are quite famous back home, you know?" He said.

"I am?"

"Yeah... Your boys down in the GSA especially. They just about rioted, they wanted to march to South America to go overthrow the whole continent."

"Ha, yeah that sounds like us." Zack chuckled a little.

"And Annabelle has been the maddest she's ever been at me...." King David's weary smile could not cover up his melancholy.

"I'm sorry to have upset her.... I really didn't want to make her cry," Zack said.

"No, no... if I can be honest you did *exactly* what you

should have. You protected my girls, no matter the cost." King David met Zack's eyes. "I'm sorry. You should have been defended, but instead I let these... advisors... talk me into acting out of fear."

"Yeah, well... it's a soldier's job to lay down his life for his country. I'm sorry to have put you in a position like that, my king." Zack gave him a small bow from his chair.

"May I confide something to you, Zack?" King David sighed, obstructing his face with smoke slightly. "And, please, call me David."

"Of course sir. Or, David...."

This is really weird. Are kings supposed to act like this?

"I have not been very good as of late. As a king, or a father, or a husband."

David examined his cigarette for a moment.

"I used to be so sure of things, you know? Josephine's mother, my sister, Jessica she used to sort of keep me on track." David scratched the table with his nail, his eyes watching some other scene. "She's been gone almost seven years now. Jojo's been a real trooper, she's as wild Jessica was when we were young. She's adapted well but, I can't seem to find what I've lost."

Zack nodded along, but it didn't seem like this was a conversation he should be butting into.

"Do you have any religious beliefs, Zack?" David finally asked.

"I used to go to a Baptist church with my girlfriend and her mother. It was really important to them, so I would say yeah their beliefs eventually rubbed off on me. Why?" Zack couldn't help but notice the king's eyebrows rise slightly at 'Baptist'.

"Heh. You just seemed to have a moral compass. Though with your general behavior I didn't really expect Baptist...."

Yeah, I didn't quite get that part down.

"I asked because I believe that God puts people in our lives when we need them most. The test for all of us is recognizing when that happens, recognizing when someone is exactly what we need most in our lives."

"That sounds a bit like something else I've heard." Zack remembered some of the sessions he had with Julia in her office. "Like being able to set aside pride and admitting you need help. It's a lot harder than it should be."

"Yes, yes it is...." David nodded, inhaling and exhaling again. "So, put yourself in my shoes. And you come across a young man, who excels in almost every physical measure."

Zack guessed immediately that David was talking about him.

"...The first time you meet this man, he's the only person in the world in a position to save your daughter's life. And while you are surrounded by people who would like nothing more than to confuse or manipulate you with their words, he's plainspoken. Almost to a fault. He doesn't speak for fear of stepping on toes, he speaks to say the truth, or what must be said."

I'm gonna start blushing here boss.

Zack couldn't help feel a small smile creep onto his face. He tried to lick his cheek to hide it. It's so weird being praised by a king.

"He also respects the sanctity of marriage. Something YOU just can't seem to do...."

That's kinda heavy...

"He's a soldier that can single-handedly change the tide of a battle. A war hero. And not to mention your daughter absolutely loves him, as do many people. He seems to inspire a fierce loyalty wherever he goes...." David put his cigarette out on the table. "Tell me. What would you think about a person like that?"

Zack looked at David for a long while. His gentle smile almost hid the lines on his face. The years seemed to be kind to him, but if you looked close, you could see the stress a crown puts on your head.

"...I don't know sir.... I guess I'd think pretty highly of him." Zack put his cigarette out as well.

"That I do." David nodded along. "I don't think there is a

need to ask this anymore, but I will anyway. Zack, are you willing and able to do anything necessary for the good of our country?"

"Yes sir." Finally an easy question.

"I have a new task for you. Something I could only ask of you."

WRONG

"So I'm thinking we do a fade along the sides and back, just to make it look all together," Brea said as she combed and snipped along the back of his head. "This is gonna be tight."

"I trust your judgement." Zack mumbled as he almost fell asleep to the rhythmic massaging waves of his hair being cut.

Brea was far more gentle than any military barber. Rose had told him about this amazing hair stylist that worked just outside the city. The salon was kind of small and had a cozy feel. It must have been like the one Rose went to back home.

"Alright, anything else you want done today? Did I miss anywhere?" Brea asked, brushing his neck.

"Yeah, uh, there's this little line that some people get put into their hair? Can you do that?" Zack motioned to his head what he meant.

"You mean a hard part? Sure!" Brea took a little shaver and put the hard part into his hair. She then took off the plastic cover she had put over him. "How's that?"

Zack stood and looked at himself in the mirror. He was very impressed. He looked totally different.

He could barely recognize himself.

"This is without a doubt the greatest haircut I have ever gotten," Zack said in a rather quiet monotone.

"Awh... thanks! I just started recently so I'm still a little worried someone is gonna hate it." Brea put the shaver back in its place. "If you really love it, tell all your friends you got it from Brea Norris at Salon 305."

"Will do." Zack put a fifty on the counter. "Keep the change."

"Wha- it's only like, fifteen dollars!"

Zack walked out to where a car was waiting for him.

That was wrong too....

He got in and the chauffeur pulled away. He watched as the city began to fade into view. He felt a vibration in his coat pocket and pulled out his phone and answered it.

"Yeah?"

"What's your ETA?" Lydia asked. There was a lot of noise in the background.

"Ten minutes, if that."

"...Good. See you soon."

"See you soon," he said.

It was getting cold now. Zack wondered if the Hoosier boys were still looking after his house back home. He hadn't talked to anyone back home since he got back from Mexico. He should probably do that soon.

The car finally pulled to a stop in the back of a relatively massive church.

Wrong again. Completely wrong.

No sooner did he open the door, he was assaulted by a few different attendants for the royal family. They squawked away, explaining things Zack didn't care about. He nodded along somberly, trying not to act like a jerk as best he could. It wasn't their fault.

He was led to a room where he changed into a suit. Fitted black silk suit jacket, silk cream dress shirt, matching pants, black tie, cufflinks, shoes shined like mirrors. He took a look at himself in front of the full body mirror. Freshly shaved, new haircut, and a fitted silk suit.

Wrong. Wrong. Wrong.

* *KNOCK KNOCK**

"Come in," he said, turning away from the mirror.

"Hey." Lydia walked into the room, shutting the door behind her. "They're ready for you."

"Right." Zack walked over to the door. "You look nice in a dress by the way."

"Pff. Yeah right." Lydia rolled her eyes. She was wearing a floor length dress that was a dull pink. Or *champagne* as the designers called it. "You look handsome though. All you need is a smile."

"I'll fake one when we get out there."

Lydia gave him a bit of a sad smile. She gave him a tight hug, as he leaned on her for support. His body felt so heavy.

Zack walked out to a very large stage, in the center a pastor stood, his hands clasped in front of him. He gave Zack a gentle smile.

"You look nervous!" The robed man laughed at him.

"Yeah I suppose I am."

Screw you, old man.

"It's natural. Most men have their feet get a little cold." He gave Zack a smile. "Though becoming a prince? That doesn't happen to many people, but I'm sure you'll do wonderful. Everyone is so excited to see what you'll do, son."

...Oh God....

No.... No...! This is wrong! THIS IS ALL WRONG!!!

He should be back home! In that little Baptist church in Indiana! A small wedding with Sarah! No fancy stage! No robed pastor! No silk suit!

Music began playing loudly from a full orchestra, filling the chapel. It screeched like nails on the chalkboard of his mind. Zack's eyes turned to see the black ocean of faceless people, motionless as death. Daniel walked down the giant, blood-carpeted aisle with a woman he didn't know.

Or he should be with Julia, on a date in the park! She'd know some cute little hole in the wall they would go for lunch. She'd be able to fix him! He could fix her! Or maybe they'd find a way to just be broken together! She'd try to sell him the city, he'd try to sell her the country, but as long as they were together they could have a home!

John came out of the darkness next. He was escorting Josephine, who smiled bright, even giving the ocean a wave here and there.

Maybe he didn't hesitate that night after killing Armando. Maybe he hardened his heart enough. He was able to avenge Sarah. Micheal and Salim would have found a way to overthrow the government and kids with GSA didn't have to be soldiers anymore. And soldiers didn't kill the people they were supposed to protect! Maybe the GSA would be dissolved. Daniel and Rose could live happily ever after. Maybe he could see Sarah again in the next life if he couldn't move on! Was he moving on? Has he moved at all?

The four stood up on the stage in position. Slowly, the waves of black began to stand, a preamble to the coming tsunami.

He hadn't moved. He realized that now. Sarah was right. She died and even that wasn't enough to make him serious, was it? He was a soldier. He followed orders, followed others. It didn't matter how much they hurt him. He's traded every scrap of humanity, every shred of pride, for the simplicity of standing still. Immovable, with a cowardice made of concrete and steel. When had it happened? When had he sold his soul to become the devil's son?

I hate you... you shouldn't have been a wuss and pulled the trigger.

A soft violin couldn't calm the hornets of self-hate stinging every part of his mind. They burrowed their way through his throat and into his spine. They set every fiber of his body on fire with their toxins. He struggled not to pass out from the pain. He couldn't move anymore, it was too late.

The black horrifying sea was separated by a single white dress.

And the woman inside it was wrong.

ABOUT THE AUTHOR

Jonas White

Jonas White is a first time author of the novel Unavoidable Eminence. From Starke County Indiana, Jonas first began working on what would eventually become Unavoidable Eminence in the summer before he became an 8th grader in 2008. What began as a hobby slowly continued to build into the finished novel you see today, with the rough draft being completed in November of 2018 and final edits and publication in 2020, a 12 year process in total. During that time Jonas graduated from Indiana University South Bend with a degree in History, and married his beautiful wife Kacie.

www.ingramcontent.com/pod-product-compliance
Lightning Source LLC
Chambersburg PA
CBHW020547020726
47494CB00006B/1963

* 9 7 8 1 7 3 5 1 0 8 4 0 7 *